STABBING STEPHANIE

Emerging from the building, Jane realized the screams were coming from the left. She and Greenberg ran in that direction. Turning, they saw a figure huddled in front of a Dumpster. Approaching, Jane realized it was Norma, the cleaning lady. She was crying, nearly hysterical.

"Norma?" She put her arm around the old woman, who shook in her gray cloth raincoat. Her face was twisted in horror. "Norma, what's the matter?"

The old woman stuck her hands into her teased hair. Then she pointed at the Dumpster, and Jane now saw that the door in its front, a square metal trap that allowed easier access, stood open. Greenberg gently pushed Jane aside and looked inside. "Oh, God . . ." he groaned.

"What . . . ?" Jane said, searching his eyes. "What is it?"

"Don't look, Jane. It's—it's Stephanie."

She couldn't help herself. Before he could stop her, she peered into the hole. She scanned the contents of the Dumpster and then saw it—an arm, the palest white, poking from a dark mink sleeve. Stephanie lay facedown across several garbage bags. From the center of her back protruded the large hilt of what appeared to be a kitchen knife. . . .

Books by Evan Marshall

MISSING MARLENE

HANGING HANNAH

STABBING STEPHANIE

ICING IVY*

Published by Kensington Publishing Corp.

*coming soon

Stabbing Stephanie

EVAN MARSHALL

KENSINGTON BOOKS
Kensington Publishing Corp.
http://www.kensingtonbooks.com

KENSINGTON BOOKS are published by

Kensington Publishing Corp.
850 Third Avenue
New York, NY 10022

All Kensington Titles, Imprints and Distributed Lines
are available at special quantity discounts for bulk pur-
chases for sales promotions, premiums, fund-raising,
and educational or institutional use. Special book ex-
cerpts or customized printings can also be created to fit
specific needs. For details, write or phone the office of
the Kensington special sales manager: Kensington Publishing Corp., 850 Third Avenue, New York, NY 10022,
attn: Special Sales Department, Phone: 1-800-221-2647.

Kensington and the K logo Reg. U.S. Pat. & TM Off.

First Hardcover Printing: May 2001
First Paperback Printing: April 2002
10 9 8 7 6 5 4 3 2 1

Printed in the United States of America

To John Scognamiglio

Chapter One

"It's a fairy tale!" Jane leaned back in her chair and gazed at the poster on the travel agency wall, above Barbara Kaplan's head. At the top of the poster were the words DISCOVER NEPTUNE'S PALACE, and in smaller letters at the bottom, WHERE DREAMS AND REALITY ARE ONE.

Jane could easily believe it. In the foreground of the vivid color photograph, a deeply tanned man and woman in swimsuits lounged on chaises, tropical drinks in hand, and surveyed a complex of interconnected pools, fountains, and water slides. In the background rose the hotel itself, soaring twin coral-pink towers between mammoth outward-facing sea horses.

"Like two books between sea horse bookends," Jane marveled.

Barbara rolled her eyes. "Always the literary agent. Enough with the books already. *This* is why you need a vacation. So," she said, placing a brochure for Neptune's Palace in front of Jane and tapping it with a long pink-airbrushed fingernail, "is that your choice?"

Jane nibbled one of her own short fingernails and gazed down at four other brochures in her lap.

Barbara smiled knowingly. "You're leaning toward Decadence III, aren't you?"

"No, I'm not," Jane replied quickly, embarrassed. "A place like that"—with a shake of her head she removed the Decadence III brochure from her lap and put it on Barbara's desk—"just isn't my style."

Barbara made a sound like "Pfush!" and gave a languid wave of her hand. "Erik!" she called across the office. "Jane says Decadence isn't her style. Should I tell her what happened to that teacher we sent there?"

Erik looked up from his desk and wriggled his eyebrows suggestively.

"What?" Jane asked.

"Most conservative woman you could ever hope to meet," Barbara said. "Met a man, a film director from France—fifteen years younger than she, I might add—and . . ."

"And?"

Barbara's mouth twisted in a self-assured little smile, and one brow rose. "Never been heard from since."

"Was she murdered?"

Barbara barked out a laugh. "Jane, my darling, you've got murder on the brain. You *definitely* need to get away. No, she wasn't murdered! She fell in love with this wonderful man and got married. Moved to St. Tropez. And do you know what she said to Erik when he first suggested Decadence to her? That it just wasn't her 'cup of tea.' "

Jane found this story mildly interesting, but she still had no intention of going to Decadence III or any other of its editions. "I'm very happy for her, but it's still not for me. I've narrowed my choices down to Antigua,

Barbados, and Neptune's Palace on—what island was it?"

"Coral Island in the Bahamas." Barbara nodded. "You're going to choose that one."

Jane rose. "I'd better get back to the office."

Barbara glared at her with something akin to horror. "You're not going to reserve?"

"No," Jane said simply, "because I haven't decided yet." She slipped on her coat, shouldered her bag, and tucked the three brochures into its side pocket. Then she picked up her briefcase.

Barbara got up slightly from her chair. "Jane! My darling!" she cried, as if trying to be understood by a moron. "This is November seventh. You want to be away over *Thanksgiving*. That's November twenty-third. You want to leave on Saturday, the eighteenth, am I correct?"

"Yes."

"Every place is full! Even now if I can get you in anywhere it will be a miracle. Sweetie, you haven't got a minute to lose."

"It's true, Jane," Erik called across the room. "You don't want to sleep in the boiler room, do you?"

Jane shook her head. "I'll decide quickly, I promise."

Barbara gave a skeptical scowl. "You don't really want to go away. You like to fantasize, but you won't leave your office. You're not really going."

Jane just smiled. "I'll be back. Thanks for all your help."

I most definitely am going, she told herself as she left Up, Up and Away and stepped onto Center Street.

Next to the travel agency was Whipped Cream, and she considered stopping in for coffee and a chat with Ginny. Whipped Cream was Jane's favorite place to eat,

Ginny one of her best friends, so the temptation was great. But then she checked her watch and saw that it was nearly eleven. No, not a good idea. She had tons of work to do and hadn't even been to her office yet today, having spent a good hour and a half with Barbara Kaplan. Besides, if she went into Whipped Cream, she'd probably order a muffin—a definite no-no because today she was starting the Stillkin diet. Dr. Stillkin's book, *Melt to Svelte,* had been on the *New York Times* bestseller list for months. Jane figured if she couldn't be his literary agent, she would at least use his diet to lose eight excess pounds before her vacation. Anyway, she would see Ginny that night at their knitting club meeting.

She crossed Center Street and started across the village green, taking the path that ran past the big white Victorian bandstand on the right and pointed almost directly at Jane's office on Center Street, where it curved around to the other side.

The harshly bright autumn sun that had shone earlier that morning was gone. Now the sky was a brooding dark gray blending in places to black, and the air had grown noticeably colder. A strong wind had come up. It blew back Jane's hair, made her eyes water. She set down her bag and briefcase for a moment to button her coat.

A few brittle brown leaves remained on the ground, scuttling across the faded grass and dancing on the brick path before her. She gazed up at the towering oaks, which provided a nearly solid canopy of foliage in the summer. Now their branches were bare, and between them the foreboding clouds swirled. Closer to the bandstand stood three or four pin oaks, and she remembered Stanley explaining to her that these trees held their leaves through the winter—a useless fact, it had seemed to her, yet he'd been so serious as he'd shared it with her.

Dear Stanley. He had wanted to go on vacation with her, but she had gently told him no. This vacation, she had explained, was to be completely hers. It would be her first time away since Kenneth had died a little over three years earlier. Since then, on top of trying to adapt to widowhood, she had been there unfailingly for Nick at home and for the writers she represented at her literary agency. She needed some time just for herself, and thanks to several lucrative deals she'd made recently, she could afford it. And she *would* go, whatever Barbara Kaplan said. Jane just had to be sure, had to pick the perfect place.

She was nearing the bandstand, grand and white, with its ornate railing. She glanced inside, looked away, and looked sharply back. Someone was in there, someone sitting on the bench. She could just make out the person's shadowy form. It looked as if whoever it was was slouching, perhaps asleep. A man, she thought.

Who would be sitting out here in the cold? she wondered, eager to reach her office. Earlier that morning, when it had been sunny and warmer, she could have understood it, but now the wind had a nasty bite and the sky threatened to open up at any moment.

Shrugging off the question, she continued briskly toward the far side of the green. As she did, she saw out of the corner of her eye that the person in the bandstand had risen and was descending the steps. Curious, she glanced back and found herself staring.

It was a man, but not the kind of man she'd ever seen on the green before, or in Shady Hills, for that matter. He was tall and painfully thin, in baggy jeans cinched around his waist with a piece of rope. The tails of an oversize shirt—once white perhaps, now a threadbare gray—flapped above the jeans, and on his feet he wore dusty sandals that were too small for his long feet; dirty toes hung over the edges. Over all of this he wore a belt-less olive-colored trench coat that must once have belonged to an enormous man. It reached nearly to the ground and whipped and billowed around his spare frame in the rising wind like a Gothic cloak. One of its pockets was torn, and from the tear protruded the neck of a bottle.

She lifted her gaze to his face. It was not an unattractive face, broad and leonine, with a salt-and-pepper mustache and beard. Stiff spikes of gray hair sprang wildly from his broad forehead, reminding Jane of Nick's early drawings of the sun.

She realized she was staring. Embarrassed, she turned away. She heard his sandals flap on the path, following her.

"Excuse me."

She stopped. His voice had surprised her. It was not the kind of voice she would have expected, but a refined, urbane voice, carefully modulated, with a touch of an accent she couldn't identify.

She turned to him, smiling kindly.

"I do beg your pardon," he said, stopping as if sensing that it would make her uncomfortable if he came any closer.

"Yes?"

He smiled, as if grateful that she hadn't just walked away, as so many others must have done. She noticed that he had beautiful, even white teeth.

"I wonder," he said, "if you would happen to have a dollar to spare."

But of course, Jane thought, that was what he would ask her; what had she expected? Her gaze met his. She hadn't noticed his eyes. They were large, almond-shaped, and of a rich golden brown. As she gazed into them, they grew moist, no doubt from the sting of the wind.

He was waiting. His eyes pleaded. She felt a pang of pity for this poor man. Her gaze dropped involuntarily to the neck of the bottle protruding from his torn pocket; he followed her gaze, looked back at her, and bit on his lower lip.

"Of course." She set down her briefcase and rummaged in her bag for her purse. Before she knew what she was doing, she had pulled out a five-dollar bill and handed it to him.

"God bless you," he said, taking a half step forward, and she was hit by the strong odor of alcohol on his breath. "Thank you."

"You're welcome," she replied, turned, and continued along the path.

Nearing the edge of the green, she glanced at the front of her office. Daniel's handsome dark face peered out at her through the window beside a brass plaque that read JANE STUART LITERARY AGENCY. Pretending not to see him, she crossed Center Street and walked casually to the door. Then she burst in. He jumped away from the window.

"Snooping again?" she asked playfully.

Clearly embarrassed, he went to his desk at the front of the reception area and began leafing through a manuscript. "I saw you talking to that man. What was he saying to you?"

"Not much."

She dropped her bag and briefcase on the credenza,

hung up her coat, grabbed up her briefcase again, and sat down in Daniel's visitor's chair. She took out a contract she had reviewed for him the night before. An image of the man on the green flashed into her mind, and she shook her head sadly, remembering those moist light brown eyes. "Poor man."

"That's what Ginny says. She speaks to him. You know Ginny—wants to help everyone."

"True," Jane said, thinking about her friend. Lately, Ginny and Daniel had become quite serious about each other. They had become attracted to each other not long after Daniel's fiancée died five months earlier.

"You gave him some money," he said.

She shrugged. "How can you say no? Where do you think he came from?"

"New York. He and Ginny had quite a long chat the other day, after she left the shop for the day. Now they talk quite often. His name is Ivar—or is it Ivor? He told Ginny he used to panhandle in New York City. His spot was on Eighth Avenue, just north of Penn Station. He liked it there because he got a lot of commuters."

"How'd he end up out here? We're twenty-five miles from New York."

"One day he decided he'd had enough of the city, took train fare out of his day's earnings, and got on the next train to New Jersey. It happened to be one that stopped here. He liked what he saw and hopped out."

"When was this?"

"About three weeks ago."

"Really? I never noticed him before today."

"That's because he was hanging out near the library. But that was too quiet. He likes the green better because more people pass through; he gets more handouts."

She remembered the harsh wind billowing his voluminous coat. "Where does he sleep?"

"In the train station."

"The train station?"

"Yes. Old Kevin—you know him; he's the station cus-
todian—he's been leaving the waiting room open for
Ivor at night." He noticed the contract in Jane's hand.
"Did you have a chance to look that over?"

"Yes." She laid it on the desk and, turning it around,
opened it to a clause she'd marked with a paper clip.
"This option clause is for the birds. It's a matching option. We *never* agree to that."

He frowned. "Could you explain how the option
works—as it's worded now, I mean?"

"Sure. When you submit a proposal for Tanya's next
novel, the publisher has two months to consider it. If
they want to buy it, you and Millennium have a month
to come to terms. If you don't, you can take the material elsewhere, but if you then get an offer, you've got to
bring that offer back to Millennium, which can take the
book for the same advance."

He looked scandalized. "We won't agree to that!"

"You bet we won't. You won't agree to a ten-percent-
topping option, either." When he wrinkled his brows,
she explained, "With that one, if you get an offer elsewhere, you have to come back to Millennium, which
can take the book for an advance ten percent higher
than what's been offered."

"At least it's higher," Daniel reasoned.

"Forget it. We don t come back. If we can't come to
terms, we're done. Tell Arliss you'll give her a simple
first-look option. And tell her you want an answer in
thirty days, not sixty."

He jotted some notes. "Will do. Thanks, Jane. Anything else I should be aware of?"

"Whoa, yeah." She turned a few pages and tapped her finger on another clause she'd clipped, headed OUT OF PRINT. "You gotta watch these electronic rights. The way this thing's worded now, if the book is in print *in any form,* you can't get reversion of rights, and *in any form* includes electronic and print-on-demand."

He gave her a woeful look. "All this new stuff gives me a headache."

"Take an aspirin and learn it. It's important. Don't you see? The book could be sitting on a disk or on a computer somewhere, waiting to be printed out—and that would mean it's in print. Or it could be *available* to be manufactured, a copy at a time, by one of those infernal print-on-demand machines. That means the author would *never* get back the book, because it would always be in print!"

"So what should I ask for?"

"Change the definition of 'in print'." She gestured to the supply room, once Kenneth's office, where they now kept the contract and correspondence files. "Check the language I put in Goddess's contract with Corsair." A few months ago Jane had completed negotiations for the autobiography of her biggest client, Goddess, the international pop star. "Basically it says that to be considered in print, the book has to be earning a minimum amount of money, even if it's only available through electronic or print-on-demand. If it's not earning the minimum, it's not considered in print and the author can get back the rights."

He smiled appreciatively. "How do you know all this stuff?"

"I had a great teacher," she replied wistfully, and her gaze unfocused.

She saw Kenneth, lanky, sandy-haired, with light green eyes, looking up from his desk at Silver and Payne, where they'd first met, he the literary agent, she his assistant. She would ask him questions not unlike the ones Daniel asked her, and Kenneth gestured for her to pull a chair up next to his so he could go over a book contract with her. And he had, paragraph by paragraph.

She laughed to herself. Later he had admitted he'd chosen the Simon & Schuster contract because it was the longest of any publisher and would take the most time. She was glad he had. She could have sat there beside him, smelling his lemony aftershave, for a dozen contracts.

Ironically, it had been after a meeting with an editor at Simon & Schuster that Kenneth had stepped out of that publisher's building on the Avenue of the Americas to hail a cab and been hit by a truck driver concentrating on his sandwich as he swerved to the curb. They told her he'd died instantly.

"Jane?"

She jumped. "Oh. Sorry."

"You're thinking about Kenneth, aren't you?"

"Yeah." She gave him a little smile. "But it doesn't hurt as much now. I never thought I'd be able to say that."

Now it was Daniel's turn to look sad. She knew he was thinking about Laura, the fiancée he'd lost. But he had Ginny now, as Jane had Stanley.

"Subject change!" she declared. "How's the mail? Any big fat checks?"

He brightened. "Actually, yes. Bill Haddad's signing payment from St. Martin's."

"Oh, yum. Can you get that right into the bank? I know Bill needs the money badly, and the commission will come in mighty handy for me."

In truth, money hadn't been as much of a worry for Jane lately as it had been during the first two and a half years since Kenneth died. Several of the writers Jane represented had recently signed hefty contracts. Thanks to the commissions on those contracts, Jane would be in the Caribbean in a week and a half.

Remembering her visit to Up, Up and Away, she rose and grabbed her bag from the credenza. Glancing out the window above it, she saw the green, the branches of the oaks bending in the strong wind. She squinted, trying to see into the bandstand, but she couldn't tell if Ivor was inside.

She took her bag back to Daniel's desk and spread the brochures before him. "What do you think?"

"I think they all look like heaven. Does it really matter?"

"You sound like Barbara Kaplan. Yes, it matters. This vacation is very special to me, and it has to be just right."

"If it were me, I'd choose Neptune's Palace. It's *the* place. Everybody's talking about it. But can you possibly get in on such short notice?"

She shrugged. "Barbara's not making any guarantees." She laughed. "Erik—he works with Barbara—says I might have to sleep in the boiler room. But I think she could get me in. She's got connections there. She's just afraid I won't take any vacation at all."

"I have no fears about that! I know you're dying to get out of here."

She rose, gathering her brochures, and carried her bag and briefcase toward her office. "Nothing personal, but I am one burned-out literary agent. Oh—anything else interesting in the mail?"

"Publishers Weekly." Looking uncomfortable, he removed the magazine from the mail pile on his desk. "You might as well look at this now, get it over with."

"What?" She moved closer.

He opened the magazine to the back and spread it open to the hardcover best-seller list. He pointed to the title in position four and read, *"In the Name of the Mother.* Roger Haines. Brownstone, $25."

"Good heavens."

"That's about what I said."

She could only shake her head. She had once represented Roger Haines, had become more than just his agent. Ironically, what had caused their breakup was her urging him to rewrite that very book.

"I'm happy for Roger," she said.

"Liar."

"You're right. I'm not happy for him, and I'm not happy for his rat of an agent, Beryl Patrice, either."

"All natural feelings, under the circumstances. After all, you told Roger you couldn't sell the book unless he rewrote it—and Beryl has sold it, *and* it's a bestseller. Beryl tried to hire me—another strike against her. *And* Beryl wanted Kenneth."

"You really know how to make a girl feel good, don't you."

"Well, *you* got him!"

"True, true," she agreed thoughtfully, and let her gaze travel down the best-seller list. "Here—you missed this one. *Relevant Gods.* Carole Freund. Corsair, $27.95. How many weeks does this make? Twenty-three?"

"By my calculation," he said happily. "Congratulations yet again."

And this was a writer Jane still represented, a quiet, reasonable person who was almost finished with her second novel. "Thanks. I feel better now."

In her office, she threw her bag onto her desk, which was covered with its usual heap of work.

Daniel appeared and placed the mail on her desk. "There's something fun in here." He pulled out a manila envelope, opened it, slid out a color proof of a book jacket. The entire front of the jacket was a close-up of Goddess's pretty, young face, surrounded by her famous mass of light brown hair, on which sat a crooked crown, lavishly jeweled. She gazed provocatively into the camera, her lips pursed in a kiss. At the top of the jacket in bold letters was GODDESS, and in script at the bottom, MY LIFE ON TOP.

"Outrageous," Jane said, taking the proof from him, "like Goddess. I love it."

As Daniel departed, Jane stood the proof on her desk and regarded it. Simple but effective. The big-book look. And it had better *be* a big book, she reflected, since Corsair had paid Goddess an advance of $1.5 million for it.

She realized she hadn't checked in with Goddess in a few weeks to see how the book was coming along. More important, Jane needed to know how Goddess was getting along with the ghostwriter Jane had found for her—Carmela Gold, one of New York's slickest magazine journalists. Carmela was hip, innovative, and best of all, able to get along with just about anyone. Jane had felt that this last quality would prove invaluable in working with the sometimes-prickly Goddess.

Jane dialed Goddess at her town house on New York's

Upper East Side. Goddess's Broadway show, *Goddess of Love*, was still the hottest show in town. Goddess had told Jane that doing the show took so much out of her that when she wasn't at the theater, she enjoyed just hanging out at her town house. Jane had pointed out that this was fortuitous, since Carmela would need to spend a lot of time with Goddess, interviewing her for the book.

Lately Carmela had been meeting with Goddess at the star's home three or four mornings a week. Carmela would use the afternoons to type up her notes and work on the manuscript, which she was leaving with Goddess in portions as she completed them, so that Goddess could read and comment.

Today was Tuesday. Jane checked her watch: almost 11:30. Carmela would probably have left by now.

A maid answered and said she would call Goddess to the phone.

"Hi, babe, how's it hangin'?" Goddess said in her bored-sounding monotone.

Jane could hear her chomping on gum, something Goddess never seemed to be without. "It's hanging very nicely," Jane said, smiling. "How is yours hanging?"

"Never better. I was just reading some of Carmela's pages. Damn, I'm good."

"You mean Carmela is good."

"No, me. The book's coming out under *my* name, remember? *I'm* good."

Jane shook her head. She'd handled a number of ghosted celebrity books, and inevitably the celebrity started to believe he or she had actually written the book. But she'd never yet encountered a celebrity who believed this *during* the writing process. It didn't really matter. Carmela wasn't in this for fame; she was in it for fortune—and the amount of money she was getting paid to ghost this book was indeed large.

"You're happy with the pages, then?"

"Mm-hmm! I've lived quite a life, if I do say so myself."

"How did this morning's session with Carmela go?"

"She didn't come this morning," Goddess said nonchalantly.

"Oh? Why not?"

"Because I told her not to. I can't keep up this schedule, so many mornings a week. I told her two mornings a week, tops. With the show and all, I'm pooped. And Corsair ain't payin' me enough to bust my tail the way I have been."

Irritation rose in Jane, heating her face. While she was negotiating this deal with Corsair, she had pleaded with Goddess to let her hold out for a higher advance; but Goddess had wanted to close the deal and had instructed Jane to accept what had basically been Corsair's initial offer.

But Jane decided to point out none of this to Goddess. What good would it do? There were, however, other issues.

"Goddess, I've explained that Carmela needs as much time with you as possible. There's a very tight deadline on this book—Ham Kiels needs it by the end of the year."

"That's more than a month away." Goddess sounded bored.

"True, but Carmela needs time to *write* the book."

"She is writing it. She brings me pages every day. They're basically fine. Jane, baby," Goddess said, her tone growing more serious, "you need to chill out. You should hear yourself. Is anything worth getting so stressed over?"

Jane took a deep breath and let it out in a rush. "How did Carmela react when you told her to come only twice a week?"

"I don't know." Goddess's tone implied that what Carmela thought was of no consequence.

Jane would speak to Carmela. If she was happy with this, Jane was, too. "All right. Call me if you need me. I'll talk to you soon."

"Mm," Goddess murmured, and hung up.

Jane found her Rolodex at the back right corner of her desk, hiding behind the work pile, flipped it to Carmela's number in Greenwich Village, and punched it out. She got Carmela's machine, but when she started to leave a message, Carmela picked up.

"What's up, Jane?" Carmela snapped out in her deep voice.

"I was just speaking to Goddess. She told me she's going to be meeting with you less often."

"Yeah," Carmela said in a drawn-out whine, "I was going to call you about that. I don't know about this project, Jane. This woman is *very* difficult. Even when we were supposed to be meeting more often, she canceled half the meetings. When we meet, it's all I can do to keep her focused on what we're doing. And what's with the shoplifting?"

Jane knew of Goddess's penchant for pilfering. In fact, twice Goddess had swiped items for Jane—bottles of nail polish, though for what reason Jane had never divined.

"So she's a shoplifter," Jane said, as if she were admitting that someone was overweight or snored. "She takes things. It's a problem she's got—we've all got problems, right? But, Carmela," she said quickly in alarm, "you do know you can't put that in the book . . ."

"No, no," Carmela said impatiently, "I'm not putting it in the book. Right now I'm not sure there's going to *be* a book. I can't get enough out of her. And when I give her pages to look at, she comes back with comments like, 'I would never have worn a turtleneck.'"

"Look, Carmela, this book doesn't have to be *Remembrance of Things Past*. It can be short, and it can be fluffy. Most of all, it has to *be*. Ask her pointed questions, get the information you need, and stop showing her pages. She doesn't understand books anyway; I don't know what it is you expected to get from her. You're the ghost. So ghost! January first, I want a finished manuscript on Hamilton Kiels's desk."

"I don't like the way you're speaking to me, Jane. I'm not one of your little mystery writers. How would you like it if I withdrew from this project altogether? I don't need the money that bad. I could be doing bumper-to-bumper pieces for *McCall's*."

Jane felt a compelling urge to tell her to stuff it, but controlled herself and instead said, "I'm sorry, Carmela. I didn't mean to offend you. I'm just saying it's okay for you to take over this project. And I think you're expecting more from Goddess than she's capable of giving. I do think you should show her the manuscript, just as a matter of form, but when it's finished."

"Okay," Carmela said in tired resignation, added, "Bye," and hung up.

The second Jane put down the phone, her intercom buzzed. "Jane," came Daniel's velvety voice, "Bertha Stumpf's on line two. She wanted to hold for you. She's been waiting for about five minutes."

Jane rolled her eyes. The whiny Bertha, who wrote steamy, best-selling historical romances as Rhonda Redmond, was the last person Jane needed to speak to right now. "What's so important?"

"She says she's had it with her editor."

Bertha's editor at Bantam was Harriet Green, a marvelous young woman—bright, sensitive, conscientious, always professional.

"Why? What did Harriet do?"

"She's asking for more revisions on *Shady Lady.*"

"And?"

"And Bertha won't do any more. She says the manuscript is perfect the way it is."

Jane let out a groan of anguish. As she did, she glanced out the front window of her office and saw Ivor, the homeless man, step down from the bandstand and start along the path toward the far side of the green. She drew her gaze from him, told Daniel, "All right, I'll take it," and pressed line two.

"Jane . . ." Bertha sounded on the verge of tears. "Jane, I just won't put up with this anymore. This—this *child* who calls herself an editor has sent me a revision letter. *Another* revision letter. I'm telling you, Jane, I just won't do any more to this manuscript."

"Now, Bertha," Jane said reasonably, "you've been in this game a long time. You know this happens. Sometimes a book needs more than one revision."

"Not *my* books! I have never been so insulted. Don't try to placate me, Jane. I want you to get me a new editor, and I want you to do it *now*. Do you understand me?"

Jane's temperature was rising again. Her heart beat faster. "Yes," she said through gritted teeth, "I understand you just fine."

"So you'll do it?"

"I didn't say that."

"What? Jane, I've just told you to do it."

"I know that, Bertha, but I'm not convinced that changing editors would be in your best interest."

"Never mind what you think!" Bertha screamed.

Jane yanked the receiver away from her ear.

"I told you to do it. That's all you need to know. I'm not interested in what you think is in my best interest."

"I am your agent, Bertha Stumpf, and as such I am obliged to advise you in matters of your career. Harriet Green is one of the finest editors I know. Have you considered that she might be right?"

There was a very long silence on the line. Finally Bertha spoke. "I am not going to fire you, Jane. Not yet, anyway. I am going to give you time to think about this situation and what you just said." And with those final words she hung up.

Jane bounded up from her desk just as Daniel appeared in her door. "I'm out of here!" she sang, grabbing her bag. "Because if I don't leave this office immediately, I am going to have a heart attack. Worse, I might fire every single one of my clients."

Daniel stood watching her, clearly at a loss as to what to say.

"I'm going to ShopRite for my Stillkin diet foods," Jane said, sweeping past him and hurrying out to the reception area. "I can't guarantee I'll be back today."

"All right."

She went to the closet for her coat, and as she slid open the door the telephone rang. She groaned. Daniel picked it up. "Jane Stuart Literary Agency."

He was silent for a long time, listening. Jane frowned, curious. Finally he said, "One moment, please," and put the call on hold. "It's a woman named Stephanie Townsend."

Why was that name familiar? "Yes?"

"She wants to talk to you. She says she's a relative of yours."

A relative? Jane, an only child whose parents had both died years ago, had no relatives she was aware of—other than Nick, of course.

She smirked, shaking her head. "What some writers won't do to get through to an agent. Tell her we're not taking on any new clients at present."

"But that's not true."

"Daniel," she said, eyes bulging, "just get rid of her!"

"Okay, okay." He got back on the line. "I'm terribly sorry, but Mrs. Stuart is not accepting new clients at present." Then he listened carefully, frowning, as the person at the other end of the line talked—loudly, for Jane could hear her from where she stood.

"One moment," Daniel told her, and pressed hold again. "She says she's your cousin from Boston."

She stared at him, baffled. Her cousin from Boston? Stephanie Townsend? Jane had no cousin named Stephanie Townsend—or Stephanie anything, for that matter.

Then, all at once, she remembered. Stephanie was *Kenneth's* cousin. Kenneth's father, Michael, and Stephanie's mother, Mary, both gone now, had been brother and sister. The last time Jane had seen Stephanie was at Kenneth's funeral. Before that she had met her once, at her and Kenneth's wedding. Vaguely she recalled a rather unattractive dark-haired woman of about forty, with a spoiled, aloof air about her. Much more distinctly, Jane recalled not liking her.

Daniel was waiting, the phone in his hand. He raised his eyebrows inquiringly.

"All right. I'll take it here. What on earth could she want?" She took the phone, put on a phony smile. "Stephanie, hello!"

"Jane?" cried a whiny voice, high and nasal, not terribly unlike Bertha Stumpf's. "Cousin Jane? You're not going to believe this." She spoke as if she and Jane were intimate friends who chatted every day. "I'm moving there."

"Moving—where?"

"There, to your little village. Me—moving to Shady Hills! Isn't it priceless?"

Chapter Two

Jane was speechless, an unusual occurrence. She barely knew this woman who seemed to expect a gleeful reaction to her announcement.

"How have you been, Stephanie? It's been a long time."

"I know," Stephanie said sadly. "Since poor Kenneth. God, I loved that man."

"So . . . you say you're moving here? You're in Boston now, if I recall?"

"Yes. Well, Cambridge. But I'm moving to your sweet hamlet. Isn't that wild?"

"Yes, wild," Jane said, trying hard to keep sounding cheerful. "Why?"

"A marvelous new job," Stephanie drawled. "You remember I've been with Skidder & Phelps, the ad agency in Back Bay. Well, I've given them the heave-ho because I've found my dream job."

"And what is that?" Jane was growing impatient.

"Well. My best friend—Faithie, from Wellesley?" she

said, as if Jane should know this. "She and her husband own a publishing company, and they're moving their offices to Shady Hills! I'm going to work for them as an editor. So, not only am I coming to your adorable little village, but I'll be working with books, like you! You do still work with books, don't you?"

"Yes, I do—I'm still a literary agent."

"Oh, good."

"Stephanie," Jane said, curious, "who are these people, this . . . Faithie and her husband? What's the name of their company. "I'm not aware of any—"

"I'll save all the details for when I see you," Stephanie interrupted, and suddenly Jane was reminded of a conversation she and Stephanie had had at Jane's house after Kenneth's funeral. Stephanie had asked Jane to tell her all about Nick, but every time Jane tried to say something, Stephanie burst in to share her childhood memories of her and Kenneth. Jane had been unable to get a word in edgewise. Clearly, Stephanie was a person who liked to be in control of her conversations.

"But, Jane," she went on, "I wonder if I could ask a favor. Faithie and Gav want me to start right away—ASAP—so I'm coming right down there. I'm going to look for an apartment, but I'll need someplace to stay in the meantime. Could I stay with you? We're talking probably a few weeks."

Ugh. Jane, who cherished her privacy, hated this idea. She began to dream up some reason why that wouldn't be possible—her vacation plans?—when all at once an image of Kenneth appeared before her. There he was, tall, lanky Kenneth, with his pale green eyes and sand-colored hair, standing not four feet from Daniel, who was still watching her.

"Oh, come on, Jane," Kenneth said. He was smiling at her, but it was a gently reproachful smile. "Give the kid a break. It's only for a short time."

"Kid!" Jane burst out.

"What?" Stephanie said.

"Sorry. Nothing. Of course, Stephanie," Jane said graciously, and Kenneth was nodding now, "Nick and I—and Florence, she's our nanny and housekeeper—we'd love to have you. When, exactly, will you be coming down?"

"Tomorrow!"

Double ugh. "I see. And how will you be traveling?"

"By train." Stephanie did not sound at all happy about this. "I'm told I need to take Amtrak to Penn Station in New York, then a local train to Shady Hills. Is that right?"

"Yes," Jane said, feeling guilty but still not offering to pick up Stephanie in New York. "What time do you think you'll get here?"

"Around noon," Stephanie said vaguely.

"Okay. I'll tell you what. When you get here, call me at this number and I'll walk over and meet you. Then I'll take you out for a nice Welcome-to-Shady-Hills lunch."

"Fine." Stephanie sounded bored.

"Then I'll take you to the house to get settled. One thing, though, Stephanie. As it happens, I'm planning a vacation. I'm leaving on the eighteenth and will be away over Thanksgiving. You're still welcome to stay with us, of course; I just wanted you to know."

"Well, see you tomorrow, then," Stephanie said, as if she hadn't heard a word Jane just said, and hung up.

Jane stared at the phone. "What a strange woman."

"Company coming?" Daniel asked.

"Mm," Jane replied grumpily. "My *cousin* Stephanie. Kenneth's cousin, actually."

"I remember her," he said, his eyes widening. "Sharpish features, very black hair. Kind of . . . sour?"

"That's her. She's moving here, has some new job with a publishing company that's moving to town."

"A publishing company here in Shady Hills?"

"That's what she said. I can't have the details till tomorrow, though."

She found the thought of walking to the station, meeting Stephanie, and taking her to lunch—not to mention having her as a houseguest—utterly depressing. She glanced at the spot where the vision of Kenneth had been. He was gone. Now there was only the window, and through it Jane saw Ivor on Center Street at the far end of the green, strolling along in front of the tiny Tudor-style shops.

"Can't think about any of that now," she said with forced cheerfulness. "I've got shopping to do, and I've got to make that decision about my vacation or I'll be stuck here with her for the holiday." She gave him a troubled look. "How can I leave Nick and Florence alone with her?"

"I'm sure they'll get along just fine," he replied, like a parent to a child. Then he patted the travel brochures protruding from the side pocket of her bag and gave her a confidential wink. "Think fast."

"Don't you worry," she assured him, whipping out the brochures, and studying them as she made her way down the little hall that led to the suite's back door and out into the parking lot behind the building.

* * *

She parked twelve rows away from the supermarket, even though she'd seen an empty spot in the second row, near the store's entrance. One of the early chapters of Dr. Stillkin's *Melt to Svelte* stressed the importance of getting "incidental exercise"—making a point of executing little everyday tasks the hard way to add calorie-burning activity to one's day: taking the stairs instead of the elevator, walking down the hall to a colleague's office instead of phoning, parking as far away as possible from one's destination.

The morning's insistent wind had disappeared, but the air was colder nevertheless, and by the time she reached the store her face stung and her eyes ran. Entering the bright, cheerful warmth of the store, she grabbed a cart, whipped out the list she'd made of Stillkin foods she needed, and made straight for the cereal aisle. Dr. Stillkin recommended adding raw bran to virtually everything one ate, and Jane intended to stock up.

After placing six jars of bran in her cart, she checked her list and headed toward the back of the store. Next on the list were skinless chicken breasts. Dr. Stillkin allowed only chicken and veal on his diet, and since Jane didn't care much for veal, she would buy several packages of chicken breasts. She wouldn't need many, because Dr. Stillkin allowed only four ounces of either chicken or veal a day.

At the back of the store she made her way along the poultry case. Roasters . . . thighs . . . wings . . . breasts . . . legs . . .

Encountering turkey, she realized she'd gone too far. Simultaneously, her attention was drawn to a pair of legs—human legs—sticking straight up from the freezer case, their owner apparently digging deep enough to have virtually fallen in. These legs were disturbingly familiar. They were skinny, knobby-kneed, in lime-green polyester pedal pushers (originating from the *first* time the style had been popular), and navy-blue Keds sneakers.

All thoughts of chicken breasts were immediately jettisoned. Jane gripped the handle of her shopping cart, did a swift U-turn, and made for the soda aisle.

"Jane? Jane!"

She froze. Could she get away with making believe she hadn't heard? No, she knew she couldn't. Forcing a polite smile, she turned.

Puffy Chapin was making her way rapidly toward Jane, an immense frozen turkey under each arm.

"Hello, Puffy."

Puffy Chapin, whose real name was Patricia, was the matriarch of one of Shady Hills's oldest families. In her early seventies, she was small and wiry—*stringy* was always the word that came to Jane's mind—with wispy yellowish gray hair that had never in its life experienced a good haircut ("People like Puffy don't concern themselves with flashy things like stylish haircuts," Stanley had once told Jane), and leathery skin that Jane doubted had ever experienced sunscreen or more makeup than the occasional application of lipstick.

"How are you, Jane dear?" Puffy said, and they exchanged cheek kisses. Jane didn't really dislike Puffy. It was difficult not to find her endearing—it was just that she had so many vehement opinions on so many subjects that it was impossible to have a brief conversation with her.

"I'm well, thank you, Puffy. How have you been?"

Puffy opened her mouth to answer, then seemed to

become suddenly aware of the turkeys under her arms. "Oh, for goodness' sake," she sputtered. "Where is my head?" She bustled back to her cart and threw in the birds. Then she hurried back to Jane, wiping her hands on her pedal pushers.

"We're all marvelous, thank you," Puffy said in her characteristic Locust Valley lockjaw. Her face grew troubled. "But let me ask you, Jane, and please do be frank with me. What, I mean *what*, do you think of the things that are happening in our town?"

Jane started to respond, then realized she had no idea what Puffy was referring to. "Things?"

"Yes! It's shameful. On our beautiful village green . . . a—a bum!"

"Ah," Jane said. "Ivor."

"You what?" Puffy looked confused.

"Ivor. That's the man's name."

"You *know* him?" Puffy's eyes bugged out.

"No, I don't know him, but my friend Ginny does. She's spoken to him, in fact. Come to think of it, so did I, this morning when he asked me for money."

"Oh!" Puffy exclaimed, scandalized. "He approached you? Filthy beast. And what did you do?"

"I gave him some money," Jane replied simply.

Puffy gasped. "Jane, how could you! That's the worst thing you could have done. I've been after Reg Lewell," she said, referring to the mayor of Shady Hills, "to do something about getting rid of this . . . creature, and you're—subsidizing him!"

Jane rolled her eyes but had to smile. "Puffy, I'd hardly say I'm 'subsidizing' him. I gave him fi—some money."

"And you know what he'll do with that money, don't you." It was a statement rather than a question.

An image of the bottle neck protruding from Ivor's torn pocket flashed into Jane's mind. "What's that, Puffy?"

"Buy liquor, Jane, you know that. He's an alcoholic, a homeless alcoholic who has been *living* outdoors in our village. In the train station, because old Kevin has kept the building unlocked for him at night. It's unheard of. What next!"

"I don't see the harm in it, Puffy. Just because he's an alcoholic doesn't mean he's a bad person. He needs some help."

"Which you only too happily gave him."

"Some help with his problem, I mean," Jane said, growing impatient. If only she had the nerve to tell Puffy what everyone else in Shady Hills knew—that Puffy's own husband, Oren, was a raging alcoholic. "Why does he bother you so much?"

Puffy let out a burst of air in utter exasperation. "Because," she said, as if speaking to a cretin, "this sort of thing just doesn't happen in our town, that's why. Do you think they have bums in Mountain Lakes. Or Essex Fells? I assure you they don't." She regarded Jane thoughtfully. "I suppose it's easy for someone like you to be so liberal."

Someone like you. Jane knew that by this, Puffy meant *someone who isn't rich,* and resented the remark but decided not to take Puffy up on it.

"Really, Jane," Puffy scolded, "you owe it to our town to take this up with that police friend of yours. If you'll do that while I work on Reg, that awful creature will be gone in no time."

They were getting nowhere. "It's been nice seeing you, Puffy. Have a great Thanksgiving."

Puffy's face softened. "Thank you, Jane, and the same to you. We're having all the girls and their husbands, and all the grandchildren." She indicated her shopping cart. "That's why I'm buying two birds." She gave a small, self-deprecating laugh. "Loony me, when it comes to the rest of the groceries, I let Jasmine shop," she said, referring to her housekeeper. "But I *always* select the birds for Thanksgiving. One of my little traditions."

"Have a great one," Jane said, and started walking away, but Puffy pursued her.

"Jane, wait! I just don't feel we've resolved this issue satisfactorily."

Jane frowned. "What issue?"

"Of where our town is going. Of this liberal new element"—Puffy looked Jane up and down—"that's creeping in. For example, For Sale signs."

Jane stared at her in bafflement. "For Sale signs?"

"Yes. What do you think of that?"

"Of what?"

"You mean you don't know? Jane, *people are now putting For Sale signs on their lawns.*"

Jane scratched her head. "And?"

"And! We've never allowed For Sale signs on lawns in Shady Hills. Didn't you know that?"

"To be honest, I can't say I ever noticed or even thought about it."

"Well, think about it! How do you think a For Sale sign makes a house look?"

"Like it's for sale?"

Puffy just shook her head. "At the rate we're going, we'll be Paterson within a year."

"All right, Puffy, I promise that if I ever want to sell

my house, I'll put up a For Sale sign only if I'm absolutely desperate."

"Are you moving?" Puffy asked, alarmed.

"No, I said 'if.' See you soon." Jane pushed again at her cart.

"Speaking of moving," Puffy said, grabbing her own cart and walking along beside Jane, "I've had some nice news."

Jane stopped and turned, but she just couldn't smile anymore. In a minute she'd tell Puffy she had to get back to the office. "Nice news?" she repeated flatly.

"My niece and her husband are moving their offices to Shady Hills. Isn't that marvelous?"

"Yes, that's very nice."

"In fact, Jane, you'll want to know about this—professionally, I mean. My niece and her husband, they're publishers. Don't you, um, sell people's books to publishers?"

Jane nodded. Puffy had never quite gotten a grasp of what it was Jane did for a living.

"Well, there you are! A customer for you right in town."

"That *is* marvelous, Puffy. Gotta run." Jane pushed on her cart and began walking quickly away.

"Faith has had such a rough time," Puffy went on. "She really deserves some happiness."

Abruptly Jane stopped and turned to the older woman. "Her name is Faith?"

"Yes." Puffy looked bewildered. "Do you know her?"

"What's her husband's name?"

"Gavin."

Faithie and Gav.

Puffy said, "Things just weren't quite working out for their company in New York City. They were looking for new space, something less dear. So Oren and I offered them an empty suite in our building on Packer."

Puffy and her husband owned a modest two-story brick office building on Packer Road, not far from the village center.

"That psychiatrist we had in the building—you know that in the spring he and his wife divorced and he moved to Colorado. That left office space that Oren and I have had a dickens of a time finding a new occupant for. So when Faith told me she and Gavin were looking, I said to Oren, 'We *must* offer it to those dears—rent free, of course.' He completely agreed. In fact," Puffy said, wrinkling her brow in thought, "I believe they're moving in today!"

Jane had been listening intently, something she rarely did with Puffy. "Did your niece by any chance go to Wellesley?" Jane asked, knowing the answer.

"Oh, Jane!" Puffy puffed in exasperation. "Everyone knows Faith Carson went to Wellesley."

"Faith Carson!"

"Yes, of course. Who did you think I was talking about?"

Then that meant Stephanie's Faithie . . .

"Your niece is Faith Carson?"

"*Yes*, Jane. What on earth is the matter?"

"Nothing. Nothing. I . . . just didn't realize."

It would be just like Puffy not to make a big deal out of something like this.

Faith Carson's story was the stuff of fairy tales. It had been while she was at Wellesley that she had met and fallen in love with the crown prince of Ananda, a tiny country above India. They married and Faith became his princess. When the prince's father died, the prince became the king, Faith his queen. They had two children, a boy and a girl. Not long after, the king was assassinated, China took over Ananda, and Faith and her children fled the country.

These events were, of course, what Puffy had been referring to when she said Faith deserved some happiness. Jane had thought Faith found it, however: Not long after returning to the States, she married Gavin Hart, who had been her husband's assistant. Faith and Gavin had founded a publishing company—Faith capitalizing on being the granddaughter of Michael Carson, cofounder of the megapublisher Carson & Donner in New York.

It all came together now.

"You're looking very odd, Jane."

Jane snapped out of her thoughts. "I didn't know Faith Carson was your niece."

"Of course she is." Puffy looked irritated. "She's my sister Annette's daughter."

"As it happens, Puffy, I know more about this than you think. Kenneth's cousin Stephanie is apparently good friends with your Faith. In fact, Stephanie is coming down from Boston to work for her and her husband."

Puffy looked delighted. "She is? Why, that's marvelous. I remember Stephanie. She was at Wellesley with Faith, went to Faith and Ravi's wedding in Ananda—was her maid of honor, come to think of it. Oren and I also attended the wedding, of course. I believe Stephanie visited Faith at the palace several times. And I chatted with her after Kenneth's funeral . . .

"Anyway, what I was going to tell you is that I've decided at the last minute to give a little cocktail party for Faith and Gavin tomorrow night, and I do hope you can come. Of course, you're more than welcome to bring your policeman friend."

Jane couldn't imagine anything more unpleasant than a party at Puffy and Oren Chapin's, but after what she'd just told Puffy about her connection to Faith, how could she refuse?

"When is Stephanie coming?" Puffy asked.

"Tomorrow."

"Perfect! She'll come, too, then." Puffy checked her watch. "Goodness, I've got to go. I promised Oren I'd bring him back some fried chicken for his lunch. Have you tried the fried chicken they make here, Jane? It's quite good."

"No, I haven't tried that yet. Actually, I'm on this new diet—"

"I'm sorry, Jane, I know you love to chat, but I've really got to run." She glanced into Jane's cart at the six jars of raw bran and frowned. "How very odd . . ." She glanced up at Jane. "You'd better hurry up or you'll never get your shopping done. See you tomorrow night. Around seven." And she scurried away.

Jane blew out her breath and consulted her Stillkin list. She never had gotten those chicken breasts. She hurried over to them, grabbed a package, and threw it into her cart. The next two items were kale and pomegranates. She hurried toward Produce.

A sack of groceries under each arm, Jane climbed the stairs from the garage and entered the house by the back hall. Florence was in the kitchen, bending to place a sheet of chocolate chip cookies in the oven.

"Missus! What brings you home in the middle of the

day?" Florence wore jeans and a white sweatshirt that flattered her pretty figure. She brushed something from her cheek and left a streak of flour on her flawless brown skin.

"Wanted to drop off my diet food." Jane dumped the bags on the counter.

"Diet!" Florence said with disdain. "Missus, if you'll forgive me saying so, you look quite beautiful just as you are. I don't know why on earth you've gotten these strange ideas into your head just because of some foolish book."

"Thank you, Florence," Jane said, removing the items from the bags, "but I'm a good eight pounds heavier than I like to be, and I've got new swimsuits and a tankini to wear on my vacation."

"Ah!" Florence exclaimed with a wave of her hand. "In Trinidad we pay no attention to such nonsense. You are what you are. It's what's *inside* that counts."

"I agree, Florence, and I'm doing this for me. *I* want to be thinner for my vacation. I'll feel better."

"Okay, okay." Florence set the timer on the stove to eight minutes. "If it will make you happier." She surveyed the odd variety of items Jane had placed on the counter and shot Jane a look. "But you could have let me go shopping for you. I could have done this."

"Thanks, but I wanted to see what they had." Jane laughed. "In one respect, it would have been better if you'd gone. I wouldn't have run into Puffy Chapin, and I wouldn't have to go to her awful party tomorrow night."

"Mrs. Chapin is having a party?"

Jane told her about Faith Carson.

"Moving *here*?" Florence cried, awestruck. "An everyday American girl becomes a princess and then a queen. So romantic . . . and then so sad. And you say she's coming here, to Shady Hills? You're sure?"

"She's moving her office here."

"And she is Mrs. Chapin's niece?"

"That's right."

"Unbelievable. Like Grace Kelly, or Hope Cooke, or that Queen Noor."

"Mm," Jane said. "Lisa Halaby. I guess it is a romantic story. But with a tragic ending—the king being assassinated, I mean. I hope she's found happiness with Gavin Hart."

"Yes . . ." Florence carried her baking utensils to the sink and began rinsing them off and placing them in the dishwasher. "I've done a lot of reading about Faith Carson. She's very beautiful."

"*Was* very beautiful. It was twenty-one years ago that she married the prince of Ananda. Who knows what she looks like now."

"I'm sure she's still beautiful," Florence said, smiling to herself.

"We'll get to find out firsthand, I'm sure," Jane said, and told Florence about Faith Carson's friend and Kenneth's cousin, Stephanie Townsend, arriving the next day.

"But I know all about Stephanie Townsend! She was Faith's maid of honor. She'll be staying here? With us?"

At that moment Winky, Jane and Nick's tortoiseshell cat, padded silkily into the room and jumped up onto the counter with a spirited rumble that said, "I'm here!"

"Ah, Miss Winky," Florence said, stroking her mottled head. "Exciting days are ahead for us. The best friend of a queen will be in our home, so you had better be on your best cat behavior. We might even get to meet the queen herself!"

"At the very least, I'll give you a full report tomorrow night," Jane said. "Watching Faith will be a good thing to do while I'm avoiding talking with Puffy. If I have to hear one more word about For Sale signs and homeless people on the green, I swear I'll burst."

Florence, now cradling Winky in her arms, turned sharply to Jane. "You know about that man down in the village, missus?"

"Sure," Jane said matter-of-factly. "His name is Ivor. He came out from New York. I can't understand all the fuss about him."

"Well, missus, a beggar here in Shady Hills . . ."

"So what! He's actually quite polite—"

"You *spoke* to him?"

"Yes, of course I spoke to him. I gave him five dollars."

"Five dollars! Not a good idea, missus, not a good idea. My mother, she always said to me, 'Don't give your money to beggars, Florence, because either they'll spend what you give them on drink, or in truth they're richer than you are!' " She gave Jane a sly look. "There is actually a rumor that this man, who you now tell me is called Ivor, was once very wealthy but fell on hard times."

"That may be," Jane said easily. "It doesn't really matter—though he did speak in a very educated sort of way." As for what Florence's mother had always told her, Jane saw no need to mention the bottle neck poking out from Ivor's coat pocket, or the strong odor of alcohol on his breath. The poor man.

"I'm outta here," she said, heading back to the door to the garage. "Give my love to Nick when you get him at school." She breathed deeply. "Mm, those cookies smell good."

Florence smiled a big smile. "They're Toll House. I'm making a second batch for your knitting club meeting tonight. You can enjoy them then."

"Florence, thank you so much—I'd completely forgotten there's a meeting tonight, not to mention that it's my turn to bring the refreshments. You're a lifesaver. But unfortunately Toll House cookies are not on Dr. Stillkin's diet food list."

"Oh, diets!" Florence muttered, opened the oven door a crack, and peeked in. "They *do* look good, don't they, Winky? And I think they're just about done. You and I, we'll have ourselves some of these cookies. We'll get big and fat together and have so much fun, just us girls!" Then, squeezing Winky's fluffy orange-and-brown mottled body until the cat's eyes bulged, she threw back her head and let out one of her wonderful fruity laughs.

Grinning and shaking her head, Jane went back out to her car.

Now Ivor was sitting on the ground against the thick trunk of the one of oaks on the green—one of the pin oaks, Jane realized. He was eating something. Jane squinted. Was it a slice of pizza? It could be—Giorgio's, the village's only Italian restaurant, was nearby on Center Street.

Why was she so interested in him? Was it the intelligent humanity she'd seen in those whiskey-brown eyes? Whiskey-brown . . . An unfortunate way to describe those eyes.

Turning from the window to sit before a pile of manuscripts she'd placed on her desk, Jane smiled at what Florence had said about Ivor, that he was rumored to be a once-wealthy man fallen on hard times. Whoever or whatever Ivor was, Jane decided, was Ivor's business. As far as Jane was concerned, as long as Ivor was doing no one any harm, he had a right to be wherever he wanted—regardless of what Puffy thought.

Jane took the first manuscript from the pile. These were manuscripts she had asked to see in response to writers' query letters. Most of such manuscripts turned out to be rejects; many writers, she'd learned over the years, had a gift for writing provocative query letters about less-than-provocative books. But once in a while Jane found a gem that made the search worthwhile, so she continued to selectively ask to see manuscripts. Reading them was a job on which she consistently fell behind.

The first manuscript was entitled *The Blue Palindrome*. Its author was a man named Nathaniel Barre. Nice name. Interesting title, too. *Palindrome* . . . Jane knew what that was: something that read the same way forward or backward. *Able was I ere I saw Elba. Madam, I'm Adam.* What was that awful joke Jane had once heard about the dyslexic woman whose husband's name was Otto?

She looked down at the manuscript, ready to read, then felt restless, anxious somehow, and let her gaze wander. She'd call Stanley, she decided. As she lifted the receiver, her intercom buzzed.

"Barbara Kaplan from Up, Up and Away on line one," came Daniel's voice.

"You're in luck," Barbara said triumphantly. "We had a client reserved for Neptune's Palace who had to cancel. She was going for Thanksgiving, same days you wanted, and she was staying in the Trident Tower—remember I told you that's the newer one, the nicer one.

It's a miracle. Just give me the go-ahead and I'll grab it for you, work it out with the hotel."

"That is a miracle," Jane said. "Why did she cancel?"

Barbara made a cluck of impatience. "What difference does it make?" she cried shrilly. "A death in the family—who cares! The point is, this is a real reservation—one we made for her almost a year ago, I might add—and I'm offering it to you. Now you can do this right."

In the background, Jane heard Erik chime in, "And not have to stay in the boiler room!"

"Yeah, that's right!" Barbara said. "So what do you say? Do you want it? Tell me now or I'll have to give it to someone else."

Jane hesitated, not so much because she was unsure how to proceed but because she was, she realized, afraid of Barbara. "I'll . . . have to let it go."

"You'll WHAT!"

"Barbara, I'm just not ready to make a decision. I've just learned I have company coming tomorrow."

"So? What does that have to do with it?"

"Things will be hectic. I'll just have to let Neptune's Palace go."

"You're not going on vacation," Barbara said flatly. "I just know you're not. You're wasting your time and mine."

Not this conversation again. "I appreciate your thinking of me, Barbara. I promise I'll call you as soon as I've made up my mind."

"Made up your mind! How do you know that whatever you decide on will be available?" Barbara was screaming again.

"If it isn't," Jane said evenly, "I'll choose someplace else."

There was a brief silence. "All right," Barbara said in tired resignation, and hung up without saying good-bye.

Shaking her head, Jane dialed the police station and asked for Stanley Greenberg. Buzzi, the desk sergeant, told her Greenberg was out but that he'd give him the message. A moment after she hung up, Daniel buzzed and said Greenberg was on the line, calling from his car.

"So which enchanted isle have you decided on?" he asked when she picked up.

"Not you, too!"

"What?"

"Never mind. How are you?"

"Fine. Busy today."

"Busy? Yes, Shady Hills is a regular hotbed of crime. What happened, did some little old lady drive through a store window?"

"Don't laugh," he said seriously. "That really happened once."

"I know, you've told me. Sorry, I was only teasing. What's going on?"

"We've had some break-ins. One on Oakmont, two on Christopher, way up."

Jane sat up, alarmed. "Rhoda's on Oakmont, and Doris is on Christopher," she said, referring to two members of her knitting club.

"It wasn't either of their houses. Totally different part of Oakmont. But the one up on Christopher, that was actually a few doors down from Doris."

"Who do you think is doing this?"

"Some kids," he said easily. "Probably looking for drug money."

"In Shady Hills?"

Now it was his turn to laugh. "Yes, in Shady Hills. We are part of the real world."

She shook her head, then remembered he couldn't see her. "Nah, I bet it was kids from—I don't know, Paterson or something. What did they take?"

"Small stuff. Jewelry, some cash. We're pretty sure of who's doing it. There's a kid we've had a lot of trouble with before. And believe it or not, Jane, he lives right in the heart of idyllic Shady Hills."

Jane was afraid for Doris, who was elderly and lived alone, as well as for Rhoda, now alone with the children after her divorce from David. Then it occurred to Jane that Florence was also alone in the house most of the time. Maybe Jane should have an alarm put in. She'd give it some thought, ask Stanley for his advice.

"Now that we've discussed my day," he said, "how's yours been going?"

"Okay," she said, feeling uneasy though unsure why. Instinctively she glanced out her front window. It had begun to rain, a light mist she could see only against the darkness of the evergreens at the far end of the green. Ivor was nowhere in sight. "Stanley," she said thoughtfully, "do you know about this homeless man, Ivor, who's been hanging around on the green?"

"Not you, too," he said with a groan. "Yes." He was clearly trying to be patient. "He's completely harmless. Came out from New York on the train a few weeks ago."

"Mm, sleeping in the train station."

"How do you know that?"

"Ginny told Daniel. She speaks to Ivor."

"Regularly?"

"Probably. You know Ginny, she'll make friends with

anyone. And she does work right here on the green. She told Daniel the poor man's quite gentle. I thought so, too."

"You've talked to him, too?"

"Once," she said hesitatingly. "He . . . asked me for some money. He seemed very nice, spoke in a refined sort of way."

"And that surprised you?"

"Well, yes. Why are you using that amused tone?"

"Because you're a snob, my girl. You don't think vagrants can be educated people, any more than you think burglars can live here in Shady Hills."

"I am not a snob. It's just that you don't expect it."

"I understand." Greenberg's tone was serious now. "It's human nature. We have preconceived notions about people, or kinds of people. But the reality is that many homeless people were once like you and me. They've fallen on hard times and can't get back to where they were."

Jane thought once more about the bottle in Ivor's pocket, about his strong breath.

"Others, of course," he went on, "have mental or emotional problems."

"I see," she said thoughtfully. "What else do you know about him? About his background, I mean. Is he a former millionaire, for example?"

"What!" He roared with laughter. "You have a vivid imagination—too vivid. Due, I suspect, to reading too many of the books you sell."

She frowned. "Of course I read the books I sell. How do you expect me to sell a book I haven't—"

"I'm kidding! To answer your question seriously— no, I know nothing of Ivor's background, have no idea if he was once a millionaire. And frankly, Ivor's background is not our concern."

"No need to get huffy. I'm just curious about people, you know that."

"I'm glad. Especially that you were once curious about me."

She smiled. "Still am."

"Good. Don't forget I'm taking you to dinner and a movie Saturday night. You can further satisfy your curiosity then. Oops, better go. I just got to the gas station and Chaz is waving at me, and I don't think he's trying to say hello."

"Oh! Okay, bye, then, I'll talk to you," she said, and hung up quickly.

It was exciting having a police detective for a boyfriend. Lately Jane had been making a point of not prying too deeply into his work, though. The previous spring, he had been investigating the murder of a young woman found hanging in the woods behind Hydrangea House, the only inn in Shady Hills. In the end, it had been Jane who solved the mystery, thanks in part to her being privy to information Greenberg had about the case. He told her later he'd been reprimanded for allowing her to "insinuate" herself in police business to the degree she had. The last thing Jane wanted was to get Stanley in trouble, so she resolved to respect his professional boundaries. Suddenly a thought occurred to her: Had she crossed those boundaries inappropriately just now, when she'd asked him about Ivor? Nah.

Besides, she and Stanley were comfortable enough with each other that he would tell her if she crossed the line. That's what she liked about him—his complete honesty. Since they'd begun seriously dating six months ago, she had come to value this quality in him, along with his kindness, gentleness, and down-to-earth intelligence. He was someone she simply enjoyed being with, so that their quiet Friday or Saturday nights—going to the movies or a play, an occasional opera or ballet, before dinner—were enough for her.

With a little smile, she returned her attention to Nathaniel Barre's *The Blue Palindrome*, turned over the title page, and began to read.

Almost immediately, Jane could tell this was something special. The writing was crisp and spare, launching immediately into a story of a young American in Venice who had recently broken up with his fiancée and was inconsolably lonely. Even contemplating suicide, he wandered the ancient streets in search of solace, though without any idea where it could possibly come from. He earned his living teaching English at a small university, but he began to miss his classes. Letters from the university started to pile up at his door . . .

The intercom buzzed. "Abigail Schwartz on line one."

Abigail could only be calling about Elaine Lawler, a client of Jane's who wrote Regency romances. Jane liked Abigail, who was of the old school of editors. Accordingly, Abigail preferred to carry out virtually every piece of business relating to a book through its author's agent. Elaine could be difficult, so Jane got a lot of calls from Abigail.

"Jane, you've got to help me," Abigail said, sounding exasperated. "I love Elaine, you know that, but she's driving me nuts."

"What did she do?"

"It's about the cover of *Naughty Miss Norton.*"

The cover. Elaine was what Jane called a cover nut. She obsessed over every detail of her books' covers, from the painting, to the size, style, and position of the type used for the title and her name, to the back cover copy.

Jane had seen a copy of the cover of this book and thought it lovely. "What about it?"

"Do you have it in front of you?" Abigail asked.

Jane could just make out what she thought was a corner of the cover poking out from her work mountain. Wincing, ever so carefully, she slid it out, successfully removing it without shifting the materials above it. "Okay, got it."

"See the woman's left boob?"

Jane blinked. "Her *boob?*" In the cover painting, the heroine, the naughty Miss Norton, lay on a chaise in a deeply décolleté gown, gazing up into the eyes of the hero. Jane squinted at Miss Norton's left breast. "What about it?"

"See that darkish pink spot on the boob?"

"Abigail," Jane said, able to bear it no longer, "do you think you could refer to it as a breast? I don't think I've used the word *boob* since high school."

"Oh, excuse me," Abigail said fussily. "Her *breast*. Do you see the shadow?" she said, raising her voice.

"Yes, I think so. What about it?"

"Elaine is convinced it's her nipple."

"Her nipple! You wouldn't let her nipple show."

"Exactly! What does she think, that we're idiots? The distributors would take a total pass on this book if we did that. I want you to tell her it's a shadow, Jane, not a nipple. And I want you to tell her to leave me the hell alone." Abigail sounded as if she were about to cry. "You know, Jane, there comes a time when the life-is-too-short alarm goes off, you know what I mean? I love Elaine and we've worked together a long time, but these *are* just little Regency romances, and—"

"Say no more, Abigail, I completely understand. I'll speak to Elaine. You just leave it to me."

"Thank you," Abigail said on a grateful exhalation, and hung up.

Frowning in disbelief, Jane dialed Elaine in Idaho. She began to explain what Abigail had said, but Elaine would have none of it.

"Bullshit! That is a nipple, Jane. You have nipples, I have nipples. I think I *know* what a nipple looks like. Tell me that doesn't look like a nipple to you."

"It's a shadow!"

"A shadow," Elaine scoffed derisively. "Jane, how much do you know about Bernardino?" she asked, referring to the painting's artist.

"How much do I know? Nothing! What is there to know?"

"A lot. Jane, Bernardino is a prankster; I know this from my writer friends. He tries to slip things past the publishers' art directors—things that shouldn't be on book covers."

"Like what?"

"Like on Bertha Stumpf's cover for *Shadow of Roses*, he had the hero rubbing the heroine's nipple. I'm telling you, he's fixated on nipples. It must be some kind of Oedipus thing."

"Elaine," Jane said patiently, "as you well know, I represent Bertha. I saw that cover, have looked at that book countless times. And I can tell you the hero's hands are nowhere *near* the heroine's nipples."

"Exactly! That's because the art director caught it and made Bernardino fix the painting. Which is why the hero's arms aren't even in sight. They were painted out."

"Abigail insists it's a shadow."

"Jane. Jane. *Helloooo,*" Elaine said, as if trying to get through to someone who is mentally deficient. "It doesn't matter *what* Abigail says. She can say it's a scoop of ice cream, and she can even believe that, but if the distributors, the booksellers—readers!—think it's a nipple, *they won't buy the book!*"

"All right, Elaine, all right," Jane said, placatingly. "You're right. I will call Abigail back and see what I can do."

"Tell her to make him fix it! How dare he fool around with my book?" Elaine cried, and hung up.

Jane put down the phone. She wanted to scream. Vagrants . . . FOR SALE signs . . . burglaries . . . cousins . . . nipples!

"Nipples!" she cried out in frustration.

Daniel's calm face appeared in her doorway. "Nipples?"

Jane jumped up from her chair. "I can't stand it anymore. I'm outta here. I'm going to Whipped Cream to see Ginny—I just realized I never ate lunch—and then I'm going home. If anybody calls, I'm gone for the day. And please don't call me with any messages."

She put *The Blue Palindrome* into her briefcase, which she then grabbed up along with her bag. She stomped out to the closet in the reception room and yanked her coat off its hanger.

"Does Whipped Cream have the right food for your diet?" Daniel asked gently.

She gave him a withering look. He actually took a step backward.

"I hope they don't," she said, her voice softly menacing. "In fact, I don't want any Stillkin food. I want a great big greasy cheeseburger with lots of fries and onion rings, and for dessert I want a hot fudge brownie sundae."

"All right," he said solemnly.

"Nipples," she muttered, slammed out of the office, and headed across the green.

Chapter Three

Jane looked up from her menu. Ginny's pixieish face had grown concerned, a trembling little smile on her lips.

"You're sure that's what you want?"

"Mm-hm." Jane nodded pleasantly. "Bacon cheddar cheeseburger, fries, onion rings, Coke. Not *Diet* Coke. I'll talk to you about dessert afterward."

Ginny seemed afraid to speak, but finally managed, "Aren't you . . . on that new diet?"

Jane gave her a stony look. "*This* is my diet," she said, her voice deadly.

"You got it!" Ginny said with false brightness, spun around, and headed for the kitchen.

"Hello, Jane," came the gruff voice of Charlie, one of Whipped Cream's owners.

She peered over the counter and could barely see the top of his toupeed head. She made a little frown of curiosity. It was unusual for the gruff Charlie to speak to her, or anyone, let alone initiate a conversation by saying hello.

"Hello, Charlie," she said warmly. "How are you?"

"Great, Jane. Um, Jane . . ."

Suddenly the top of another head appeared next to Charlie's—that of George, Charlie's partner in life as well as in business.

"You sure you want this?" George asked. His arm shot up and in his hand was Ginny's order slip. Jane could just make out the word *bacon.*

Jane let out heavy sigh of exasperation. "Yes, I want it," she said testily. "Why?"

"Well," Charlie said (they often took turns in conversations, speaking together as one), "we thought you were on this new diet—you know, so you'd be skinny for your vacation."

Stunned, Jane glanced around and spotted Ginny, smiling meekly at the end of the counter.

Working to control herself, Jane said, "Thanks, friends, but I know what I want to have for lunch. Is there a problem?"

"No. No," they all shot back in unison.

"Good," Jane said, and opening her briefcase, took out *The Blue Palindrome* and continued reading.

A moment later she was aware of Ginny standing at the table and looked up.

"Sorry, hon. We don't mean to mind your business."

Jane had to laugh. "This whole *town* minds my business!" She returned her attention to the manuscript.

Ginny fell into the chair opposite Jane's and waited, silent. Finally Jane met her gaze and smiled. She couldn't stay annoyed at Ginny, one of her dearest friends. And recently Ginny had been seeing Daniel, which in Jane's eyes brought Ginny even closer into the circle.

"Boy, something's eating you," Ginny said. "I don't think I've ever seen you like this."

"Like what?"

"So . . . bitchy!"

They both burst out laughing.

"You're right," Jane said, "I am being bitchy. I'm burnt out. I need that vacation. In fact, after lunch I'm going next door to tell Barbara where to make my reservation."

"Great! Which place have you chosen?"

"Neptune's Palace."

"Oh!" Ginny cast up her eyes. "That glorious place. Someday I'm going there."

"Ginny!" Charlie hollered, and a plate appeared on top of the counter. Ginny got it and placed it before Jane. Three strips of bacon glistening with fat poked out from under gobs of orange melted cheese and lolled over the sides of the bun. A heap of fries and golden brown onion rings took up the rest of the plate. It all smelled heavenly. When Jane looked up, Ginny was looking at the plate, literally biting her lip.

"Good. Keep it that way," Jane said, picking up the burger, unable to repress a smile. She took a big, crunching bite and moaned in ecstasy.

"Boy, you *do* need a vacation," Ginny said, looking at her with concern.

"You have no idea. Just found out I've got company coming tomorrow." When Ginny frowned, Jane explained, "My cousin Stephanie. Kenneth's cousin, actually. I'd forgotten she even existed."

"Why's she coming?"

"She's moving here. Got herself a job with a publishing company that's moving into Shady Hills. Hear about that?"

"Ooh!" Ginny grew suddenly animated, her dark curls quivering. "It's that Faith Carson, right? Can you believe that? *Faith Carson,* right here in our town. To just go off and marry a prince," she mused dreamily, "and then become *queen.* What a story."

Jane shrugged. "Anyway, Stephanie will be working for Faith and her husband. She'll be staying with me until she finds a place to live." She explained that Stephanie had until recently lived in Boston, working for an advertising agency.

"I'll look forward to meeting your cousin *and* Faith Carson," Ginny said. "Of course you're going to Puffy's party."

Jane nodded. "I suppose she's inviting the whole town."

"Practically, from what I hear."

At that moment there was a movement through the café's window and they glanced up to see Ivor peering in. Ginny looked surprised but gave him a little smile. Then she turned back to Jane.

"He'd better not try to come in here. Charlie and George would have kittens." She paused thoughtfully. "Maybe I've been too nice to the poor man. He seems to have latched onto me."

"Daniel says you speak to him every day."

"Sure I do," Ginny said, a little defensively. "He's a person, like you and me. Why not?"

"I completely agree! It's people like Puffy who think he's got no right to be here and should be removed."

Ginny shrugged. "I feel bad for the man. What's going to become of him?"

At a loss, Jane shook her head. She looked down at her plate and did a double take. Her burger was gone. So were the fries, and all the onion rings but one. "What happened to my food?"

"You ate it! Wolfed it down. And I haven't even brought you your Coke!" she suddenly remembered.

"Might as well make it coffee."

Ginny hurried off for it. Jane looked at her plate. So much for her resolve to lose those eight pounds, to follow the miraculous Stillkin diet to the letter. Could it only have been that morning she'd stocked up on Stillkin foods? She felt disgusted with herself.

Ginny reappeared and set down a steaming mug of coffee along with a small pitcher of milk and a container of sugar and Equal packets. "Why the sour look?"

"I'm hating myself. At this rate, I'll be eight pounds *heavier* by the time I leave for my vacation."

"Ah!" Ginny waved her hand in dismissal. "You look fabulous. Stop being so silly."

"I'm not being silly. Half the slacks in my closet cut me in half. My bra is biting into me like piano wire." She shifted uncomfortably.

"Ouch. That is a problem. Well, Scarlett, tomorrow *is* another day!"

"True," Jane said, brightening. Then she remembered Stephanie, and her shoulders slumped.

Jane had never been much interested in Faith Carson and her storybook past, but after all the talk of her today she had to admit she was the slightest bit curious. After all, Stephanie, Kenneth's cousin, was one of Faith's best friends.

Heading home on Packer Road, Jane slowed her car when she reached Puffy and Oren Chapin's office building, a rectangular two-story red brick structure. A grimy midsize moving van sat at the curb directly in front of the building. Passing alongside the truck, Jane saw that the tailgate was down. She checked her side mirror, made sure no one was behind her, and slowed even more, practically coming to a stop when she reached the end of the truck. Would she catch a glimpse of Faith herself?

Two young men in T-shirts and jeans sat on the tailgate, munching on enormous hero sandwiches. These reminded her of her lunch, and with another pang of guilt she sped up and turned left on Grange Road, which took her on a winding route up into the hills for which the village was named. On Lilac Way, her street, she drove slowly uphill beneath a latticework of bare branches, then turned into her driveway. Taking her briefcase and bag from the passenger seat, she got out and made her way up the path to the front door of the deep brown chalet-style house.

Florence opened the door just as Jane reached it.

"Missus, I didn't know you were coming back so early."

"Had to get away from the office," Jane said, striding past her. "I'll work here, get some reading done." She hung up her coat in the foyer closet.

"I was preparing a little surprise for you," Florence said.

"Oh?"

"Yes. I felt bad about making those Toll House cookies and tempting you, so I'm making you a Stillkin shake!"

An image of the bacon cheddar cheeseburger with fries and onion rings flashed into Jane's head, and with it came yet another rush of self-disgust. Then she remembered what Ginny had said. But why wait till tomorrow? Why not start over right now? She'd bought all those special foods. And dear Florence was making her something special for her diet.

"Florence, that's awfully sweet of you. How did you know how to make it?"

"There was a recipe for it in the *New York Times*. You'd mentioned that you were thinking of trying the diet, so I cut out the recipe. Would you like it now? Did you have dessert after your lunch?"

"Why, no, I didn't," Jane said, realizing she'd forgotten to order the hot fudge brownie sundae. So she hadn't been as outrageous as she'd meant to be. "But I am kind of full. Could I have it a little later?"

"Of course! Just say when." Smiling, Florence hurried off to the kitchen.

At that moment Winky hurried in from the family room and greeted Jane with a high mew. Jane scooped up the cat and stroked her fur. "And how were those cookies?" she asked with a laugh. "Maybe you'll need to go on the Stillkin diet, too!"

Jane carried Winky into her study off the living room and resumed reading Nathaniel Barre's manuscript with Winky on her lap.

With each page, Jane felt a rising sense of excitement. This man was good, exceptionally good. This book was not simply of publishable quality. This writer was quite possibly a rare talent, an artist of unusual insight. At this point in the story, the young man had just been fired from his position at the university. Now he had nothing and no one. Jane found herself wiping a tear from her eye. She found as she read that she literally could not stop reading. From years of experience, Jane knew this was a true find.

"Missus—"

Jane jumped. Winky let out an irritated squeak.

"Sorry," Florence said. "I didn't mean to disturb you. But I have a question. I'm making barbecued pork for dinner, a recipe from my mother in Trinidad. Can you eat that on your Stillkin? I have a feeling not."

" 'Fraid not, though it sounds fabulous. Don't worry about me. I have the foods I bought today. I'll be fine."

"Okey-doke," Florence said, but looked doubtful as she walked away.

Jane returned to her reading. The young man had returned to the mysterious old alchemist's shop, and as he explored it, magical events began to occur. His cat spontaneously levitated while standing on the ancient worktable. A page in an open book turned. Yet the author related these occurrences in a completely matter-of-fact way, the young man barely reacting at all, which made Jane wonder what the author hadn't yet revealed about him. It was all quite strange, yet totally engrossing.

A few pages later, Winky stood up on Jane's lap and began kneading her upper arm.

"Winky, stop it. You know I hate it when you do that. Ouch!" With an exclamation of impatience she shooed the cat off her lap. Now that her attention had been drawn away from the manuscript, she realized, to her amazement, that she was hungry and would like her Stillkin shake now. She placed the manuscript on her desk and wandered into the kitchen.

Florence looked up from onions she was chopping. "Ready for your shake?" she said, as if reading Jane's mind.

Jane nodded eagerly.

Florence, bless her, had all the ingredients neatly lined up in front of the blender. Deftly she poured in skim milk, yogurt, a banana, a dash of cinnamon, and a full cup of the bran Jane had bought that morning. She blended all these ingredients for a good half minute, then put ice cubes into a tall glass and poured the shake over them.

"Here you go!"

Jane took the glass. "Would you like a taste?"

"Yes, as a matter of fact I would," Florence said, and took a healthy sip. She grimaced. "It's . . . different," she said in a strangled voice, and quickly handed it back.

Warily Jane eyed the pale yellow mixture. She mustn't hurt Florence's feelings. She smiled and took a big gulp. It tasted like . . . a barnyard. Wanting to spit it out, Jane forced a huge close-mouthed smile. "Mmm!"

"It's awful," Florence said. "I won't be offended if you dump it out, missus."

"Not on your life. This is just what I need. Thank you for your thoughtfulness, Florence. With your help I'll get rid of those eight pounds and be stunning in my tankini."

"That's the spirit." Florence checked the clock on the wall beside the fridge. It was 2:30. "Ooh—better get my little man at school." Hurriedly she removed her apron and headed for the door to the garage. "Be right back."

Jane wandered back to her study, Winky close at her heels, and they resumed positions, Winky a curled-up fluffball in Jane's lap as she rapidly turned the pages of *The Blue Palindrome.* From time to time she remembered to sip at the Stillkin shake. It truly was awful. She considered flushing it down the powder room toilet but rejected that idea. Dr. Stillkin had said in his book that this particular combination of ingredients stimulated the metabolism to burn fat at an amazing rate. That sounded good to Jane. She pictured herself, breathtaking in her tankini one day, another day in the new teal one-piece she'd bought because the saleslady had said it went perfectly with Jane's auburn hair.

She returned to the manuscript, to Venice . . .

"Hey, Mom."

Nick burst into the room, still wearing his backpack. It bulged hugely, as if about to explode. He came up to her and she grabbed him tight around his slim waist, pulling him to her and planting a big kiss on his cheek. "We've got to do something about that backpack. What do you say we get you one on wheels, like Aaron has?"

"No, Mom, I told you—that looks like a suitcase. It's stupid."

"Well, what do you suggest? I don't think a fifth-grader should be forced to carry such a heavy load. You'll dislocate your shoulders. I'm going to have to speak to Mrs. DeSalvo about this."

"You'd better not, Mom," Nick said threateningly, and grabbed Winky from Jane's lap. Suddenly his eyes grew wide. "Hey, Mom, did you hear about the bum who's really a billionaire in disguise?"

She slid him a baffled look. "Come again?"

"It's true. There's this dirty old man who hangs out on the green. He's all smelly and yucky and gross. But it's all just a cover. He's really a billionaire! Everyone's talking about him."

Poor Ivor. Now he was the subject of the town's never-ending flow of gossip and speculation.

"Nicholas, I know about the man you're referring to. I've spoken to him. He's just a man . . . a man who's fallen on hard times. It's really not nice to speculate about him like that—and it's certainly not nice to call him a bum and those other words you used."

Nick rolled his eyes. Florence appeared behind him in the doorway. "Nicholas, your snack is on the table."

Nick left the room with Winky in his arms. "You can share with me," Jane heard him say to the cat.

Florence's eyes were bright. "I couldn't help overhearing what he was saying. About the man down in the village, I mean."

Jane waited, eyebrows raised.

"My friend Noni," Florence said, referring to one of several of her friends who were fellow Shady Hills nannies, "she called me just before you came home. I forgot to tell you what she said. Noni, she says the man is a drug lord."

"A billionaire drug lord?" Jane asked innocently.

Florence opened her mouth to respond, but before she could, Jane went on, "Florence, I appreciate the report, but I don't want to speculate about this poor man, and I *must* finish this wonderful manuscript."

Florence looked troubled and her eyes darted to the stack of pages on Jane's lap. Reluctantly she withdrew, closing the door behind her.

Laughing to herself, Jane sank contentedly into her chair and returned to Venice.

Chapter Four

That evening, in the living room of Hydrangea House, the six members of the Defarge Club had just seated themselves to begin the activity for which the club had been formed—knitting. The room felt wonderfully cozy, Jane reflected, admiring the fire Louise and Ernie, the inn's owners, had made in the great stone fireplace in the wall facing Jane.

Jane loved these club meetings, where she could really let down her hair. That was something she needed badly these days—that and her vacation.

Louise had placed the platter of Florence's Toll House cookies on the coffee table in the center of the group, and now removed the aluminum foil covering.

Should I? Jane thought, recalling her visit to ShopRite this morning for her Stillkin foods. *Oh, screw it!* And she reached for a cookie.

"Are you sure you want to do that, Jane?"

Jane froze, her arm suspended in midair. Across the coffee table, little old Doris Conway peered at Jane over her knitting, her eyebrows raised.

"What do you mean?" Jane asked innocently, sounding to her own ears uncannily like Scarlett O'Hara.

"Aren't you dieting?" Doris asked flatly, and cast her gaze up and down Jane's seated figure.

Jane felt herself blush. Quite deliberately, she resumed her reach to the cookie plate and took not one but two.

Doris shrugged. "Suit yourself. Or should I say 'Swimsuit yourself'?" And she broke into her characteristic low chuckle.

Jane slumped her shoulders in exasperation. "Is my diet on a billboard or something? Why is everyone in the world making my weight their business?"

"It's my fault." Ginny, seated next to Jane on the sofa, winced guiltily. "I guess I mentioned it to a few people—but as a *good* thing. You know, how you're so excited about your vacation that you're trying to slim down to look great in your bathing suit."

"Jane . . ." Penny Powell said in her whispery voice. She sat in an armchair at the end of the grouping, the yellow-and-green-striped scarf she was knitting trailing down onto the Oriental carpet. "Where are you going on your vacation? Have you decided?"

"No. I wanted Neptune's Palace, but apparently I waited too long."

"Neptune's Palace!" exclaimed Rhoda Kagan, directly opposite Ginny on the second sofa. "I went there with David, damn him, for our fifteenth anniversary. That place is pure heaven!"

"Thanks," Jane said.

Rhoda shrugged and resumed her knitting. "Sorry. You can always go another time."

Penny said, eyes downcast, "Alan and I are thinking of going there."

Everyone looked at Penny, silent. It was no secret that Penny's husband, Alan, was domineering and chauvinistic, and that the only way Penny had succeeded in maintaining harmony in their marriage had been to consistently acquiesce to his wishes.

Finally Doris spoke up. "Whose idea is that?"

"Alan's," Penny replied.

More silence. Penny raised her head and looked around the group. "I know what you're all thinking. 'Why would they go on a vacation together when their marriage is so bad?'"

They all quickly refuted this.

"No, no, it's okay," Penny said. "But I'm happy to report that things are better for Alan and me now. I've"— she let out a nervous giggle—"been standing up to him lately . . . telling him what *I* want."

"Penny," Jane breathed. "That's marvelous."

Penny smiled shyly, tugging back one of the necklength curtains of brown hair she usually hid behind. "Tonight at dinner he announced he was going bowling in Boonton with his friends. I reminded him that I have my knitting club meetings every Tuesday night. He said that was too bad, because he was going out, and I needed to stay home to watch Rebecca."

"What did you say?" Louise asked, her birdlike face pursed intensely.

Penny smiled serenely. "I said that if he wanted to run the risk of leaving Rebecca alone, that was his choice, because I was going to this meeting whether he liked it or not. And I told him to mark his calendar so this would never happen again."

"Whoa!" Rhoda cried. "You go, girl!"

Penny nodded modestly, as if in response to applause.

"Speaking of marriages falling apart," Doris piped up, turning to Louise, "what's up with you and Ernie?"

Louise turned shocked eyes on her; so did the rest of the women. In the spring, Louise had discovered Ernie was cheating on her—and not with just one woman, but several. Louise had been tense and subdued ever since, though she and Ernie were still together, still running Hydrangea House.

"I appreciate your subtlety, Doris," Louise said with uncharacteristic sarcasm, and the others snickered. "Actually, things are much better now between Ernie and me. We've been seeing a wonderful marriage counselor, a woman in Livingston, and she's helped us enormously."

Everyone looked pleased at this announcement. "Glad to hear it," Doris said firmly, and resumed her knitting. Jane noticed that Doris was knitting faster than ever. She was on some new wonder drug for her arthritis, an expensive medication she had to give herself by injection once a month. Apparently it was working; in general, Doris was more agile lately, and in excellent spirits. As if reading her thoughts, she looked up at Jane. "How's Daniel, Jane?"

Jane knew that Doris was referring to Daniel's having lost Laura, his fiancée, in the spring, and to his seeing Ginny for several months now.

"I'll answer that one myself," Ginny said, smiling at Doris. "Daniel *and I* are fine, thanks very much."

Doris looked taken aback, as if that wasn't at all what she'd meant. "Glad to hear it!" she blustered. Then, as if in retaliation, she narrowed her eyes at Ginny and said, "And how's your friend on the green, Ginny?"

"My friend?" Ginny said, pretending not to understand, though Jane knew she did.

"The bum!" Doris said. "I've seen you chatting him up. Last Friday I was coming out of the dry cleaners and the two of you were blabbing away like old friends."

Jane looked at Ginny, who had blushed deeply. "He's just a sad old man, Doris. I feel sorry for him. He doesn't have anybody. I say hello when I pass him. Is there something wrong with that?"

"No!" Doris said, all innocence again.

Penny looked up, placing both her knitting needles in one hand and pushing the hair on the right side of her face behind her ear. "Know what my neighbor Mr. Mattarazzo says? That that bum is an FBI agent in disguise, that he's on an assignment to bust a drug ring—right here in Shady Hills!"

"Oh, for heaven's sake," Rhoda muttered, not looking up from her work.

"Can we please stop calling him a bum?" Ginny looked at Penny. "That theory is ridiculous. I think people in this town should stop gossiping and tend to their own business."

At this point Rhoda looked up, placing her knitting firmly in her lap. "I'll tell you what *is* my business," she said, a mean look coming over her face. "I don't pay outrageous property taxes to live in this *supposedly* exclusive village, so that I can see some dirty old drunk stumbling around the green every day. He should be removed! Jane, ask your friend Stanley to get rid of him."

"That's not like you," Ginny said, looking hurt for Ivor.

Rhoda shrugged and resumed her knitting.

Doris said, "Who cares about some smelly old hobo!" She wiggled her eyebrows. "Today I saw someone really worth talking about."

"Who?" they all asked.

Doris looked up. "Faith Carson! I was driving along Packer, near that brick office building, when who should step out of a car but the queen herself! In jeans and a sweatshirt, no less! I was so excited I nearly hit a tree."

Now the women were atwitter. Jane told them about Kenneth's cousin Stephanie coming to Shady Hills the next day to work for Faith and her husband, and about meeting Puffy Chapin, Faith's aunt, at ShopRite.

"Puffy's having a party to welcome them," Ginny said. "Everyone's invited."

"Wow . . ." Penny said, now pushing the hair at both sides of her face behind her ears, her eyes dreamy. "So romantic."

"Like a fairy tale," Ginny said. "Like . . . Grace Kelly."

"And look how *she* ended up," Doris put in.

"That was a car accident, Doris," Ginny said.

"That's right," Louise said. "What's important is that she'd found her true love."

"So did Faith Carson," Rhoda said. "She married that prince of—what was the name of his country? Sounded like a banana."

"Ananda," Jane said.

"That's right. Handsome man. But that ended tragically, too. He died. Skiing accident? Everyone seems to be skiing into trees lately."

"Assassinated," Doris said.

Rhoda nodded. "Right. And China took over the little country. Faith and her kids had to get the hell out of there."

Ginny said, "Yes, a boy and a girl."

"Grown up now," Louise reflected. "Can you imagine? Faith Carson coming here. And running a publishing house."

"I never liked her," Doris said, and again the ladies just stared at her. Doris went on, without looking up, "Gold-digging slut. She saw her chance to get rich, play queen of the castle. Got what she deserved, if you ask me."

"I don't think anyone did ask you," Jane said good-naturedly. "Anyway, she was already rich, Doris. Her grandfather was one of the founders of Carson & Donner, the publishing house."

"I know what it is, Jane."

Jane said, "You're such a cynic, Doris. And if that's what you think of her, why were you so excited to see her today?"

"She's still a celebrity!" Doris said.

"If you want to know what *I* think," Rhoda said, "I say you're all right. Yes, she saw an opportunity—and let's face it, girls, who among us wouldn't have taken it, too? But she was also deeply in love."

Doris made a sound of disgust.

Jane, knitting madly away—she was by far the fastest knitter of the club—frowned thoughtfully. "Until today, I'd never given Faith Carson's story much thought. I really have no opinion about the woman either way, and I wouldn't have thought twice about her if Kenneth's cousin weren't coming to work for her."

"Where will she live?" Penny asked.

"She'll be looking for an apartment. Until then she'll be staying with me."

Louise said, "I wonder why they're coming *here?* I mean, Shady Hills isn't exactly the center of things."

"Apparently their company isn't doing as well as it might," Jane said. "They can't afford New York City rent anymore. Puffy offered them an empty suite in the building she and Oren own. Today was moving day, in fact. I'm sure that's why you saw her in jeans and a sweatshirt, Doris. I saw the moving van."

Penny said, "I wasn't aware anyone had moved out of that building."

"Penny," Louise said, "you can hardly expect to know the comings and goings of every business in Shady Hills."

"But we can try!" Rhoda said with a laugh.

"Try nothing!" Doris burst out. "I'd wager that among the six of us, we know *everything* that goes on in this town. And as it happens, I do know who left that building: a psychiatrist. He'd been in a suite on the second floor for over ten years."

"Of course!" Ginny said. "It was Dr. Kruger. Tim Kruger. He was a regular customer at Whipped Cream. We chatted all the time. He was a psychiatrist. Adults and children. A woman who was a customer of ours at Whipped Cream used to bring her toddler to Tim for play therapy."

"I remember him," Rhoda said, nodding. "He and his wife lived on Oakmont, near me." Her face grew puzzled. "Whatever happened to them?"

Ginny leaned forward. "I'm surprised you don't know, Rhoda. His wife ran off with a *plumber*, some guy from Wayne, and poor Tim decided to start a new life in Colorado."

Doris began to laugh. "A plumber, eh? Bet he unclogged *her* pipes."

Jane rolled her eyes. "You know, Doris, for a woman who was a schoolteacher, supposedly a mature woman who set an example for our youth, you have an especially adolescent sense of humor."

"Where do you think I got it!" Doris exclaimed, and they all laughed at the irrepressible old woman. "Jane, I imagine you'll be especially interested in Faith and her husband's business, since you're a literary agent. Maybe you could peddle some of your books there—or don't they publish the kind of trash you handle?" she asked with a guffaw.

Jane took mild offense at this remark. "As it happens, they don't publish what I sell. I believe they publish mostly coffee-table books—not what I handle. But trash is in the eye of the beholder, Doris. Yes, I handle *genre fiction,* but it gives a lot of pleasure to a lot of people, and that counts for a lot.

"You're forgetting," Jane went on, "that I handle all kinds of books, not just genre books, or 'trash,' as you call it. I don't think anyone would call Carole Freund's *Relevant Gods*—which, I might add, has been on bestseller lists for nearly six months—trash."

"Excuse me, Mrs. Big Shot," Doris said, and met Jane's gaze. "What about the autobiography of Goddess, that cultural icon? I suppose that will be great literature?"

"No!" Rhoda chimed in. "But the commission will sure pay off a lot of Jane's mortgage!"

"Amen to that!" Jane said, and everyone laughed.

Ginny said, "I believe Faith Carson does publish books about famous people. You know, memoirs, autobiographies, biographies. People she's connected to . . . people she knows from society."

"Right," Louise said, "the way Jacqueline Onassis did when she was an editor at Doubleday."

Doris made that disgusted noise again. "Mm, she published such society figures as Michael Jackson. You remember his classic, *Moonwalk?* I *read* that book," she announced, as if bragging that she'd dug a twelve-foot ditch. "What a piece of dreck." She began purling wildly.

"Jacqueline Onassis," she said with contempt. "Another one. No better than a common whore, marrying that ugly old Onassis—"

"Jane," Louise broke in, and when Jane looked at her, her expression was one of horror. "You're the best knitter here. Could you help me turn the heel of this sock? I've been trying for the last half hour, and I just can't seem to get the hang of it."

"Of course, Louise," Jane said, giving her a knowing smile, and as Jane took Louise's knitting from her, they both slid a glance at Doris, who appeared to have withdrawn into her work, at least for the moment.

"Hello, missus." Florence, in white robe and slippers, carrying a hardcover book, descended the stairs to the foyer as Jane entered the house. "You've had a phone call. Your cousin Stephanie."

Jane winced. "Please don't call her that. She's my late husband's cousin, not mine."

"Oh. Sorry, missus. Why don't you like her?"

Jane glanced sharply at her. "Who says I don't like her? I barely know her."

Florence shrugged. "You've met her twice, you said. At your wedding, and at Mr. Stuart's funeral. But it's very clear you don't care for her, if you don't mind my saying so."

Jane hung up her coat. "I don't suppose I did like her—at least not from those two meetings. But you know how things are. Once she's here I'm sure I'll get to know her better, think she's positively marvelous, and wonder how I could ever have thought such things about her."

Florence looked dubious. "Maybe, missus. Anyway,

she called to remind you that she'll be arriving late to-morrow morning. She'll call your office from the train station, as you and she worked out." Her face grew dreamy and she showed Jane the book in her hand. On its jacket was a close-up photograph of a lovely, creamy-skinned young woman with unusually large violet eyes, long pale lashes, and a mass of lustrous light brown hair brushed back from her strong forehead. *Queen of Heaven,* the title read, and at the bottom: *Faith Carson.*

"Where did you get that?" Jane asked.

"At the library this afternoon. I felt I should brush up on details."

Jane had to laugh. "Florence, it's Stephanie Towns-end who'll be staying here, not Faith Carson."

"I know that, missus. But your cousin—oops, I mean Stephanie *is* one of Faith Carson's best friends, and Faith Carson will be working right here in the village. Why, I might bump into her at the 7-Eleven!"

"Somehow I doubt it. How's the book?" Jane led the way through the family room into the kitchen, where she filled the kettle and put it on the stove. "Tea?"

"Yes, thank you, missus." Florence and Jane sat down at the kitchen table. "The book is fascinating," Florence said. "You really should read it. I'll give it to you as soon as I finish."

"Thanks." Jane gave a small polite smile.

"The title comes from the fact that many travelers to Ananda—that's the country Faith and the king ruled—said it was the closest place on earth to heaven. High in the Himalayas, a palace among the clouds . . ."

Oh brother, Jane thought. "You're really into this," she observed. "What else does it say?"

"I haven't read much yet; I've only just started it. Right now she's still at Wellesley College and she's met the prince, who is studying at the same time at Harvard. She thinks she's in love with him. And look at this," Florence said, opening the book to a photo insert in the middle. "Here's a picture from the wedding. So beautiful!"

She spun the book around and pushed it across the table to Jane. The photo was of Faith in her wedding gown with a voluminous train, and beside her stood Stephanie Townsend herself, smiling brightly. This Stephanie was young and fresh, far different from the thin, tired-looking Stephanie Jane remembered from Kenneth's funeral. But then, Jane reflected, Faith and Ravi's wedding had taken place eighteen years earlier.

Winky leapt onto the table and promptly sat down on the book.

"Winky! Shoo, shoo!" Florence gently pushed her away, then closed the book. Winky stepped down onto Florence's lap and curled up.

Jane shook her head in wonderment. "I must say I'm impressed at your thoroughness, reading up on our guest. Fill me in on what it says about her, will you? In case I don't get to read it right away."

"Of *course,* missus." Florence raised her slim shoulders and giggled. "This is going to be such great fun!"

Jane nodded, at that moment actually beginning to believe this.

But by morning, this feeling had completely abandoned her. Nick, however, seemed to have caught the excitement bug from Florence.

"Come on, Mom, she's my *cousin!*" he pleaded in the car on the way to school. "It would be rude if I didn't meet her at the station with you."

"Nice try," Jane said, turning the car into the drive in

front of Hillmont School, "but I'm not even meeting her train. She's going to call me at the office when she gets in."

"Meanie," Nick grumbled, getting out of the car and heaving his backpack onto his back.

"We'll have a special dinner to welcome her tonight," Jane told him. She had already discussed this idea with an enthusiastic Florence. "Good-bye, darling. Have a wonderful day. I love you."

Nick just slammed the car door, turned, and started toward the school building. With a shrug, Jane pulled away from the curb and headed for the village center.

When she walked into the office, she found Daniel looking troubled.

"What's up?" she asked him.

"When I got here this morning there was a police car out in front of the office." He gestured toward the front door. "I realized it was Greenberg and that he was talking to Ivor, asking him to move on."

Jane frowned. "Really?"

"Yes. I spoke with Greenberg. He told me Ivor spent the night in front of our door, on the sidewalk."

Surprise and sadness overcame her. "We have got to help him. It was freezing cold last night. I wonder why he didn't sleep in the train station as usual."

"Maybe he'd had too much to drink and passed out here," Daniel ventured.

"Maybe." But she remembered the callous things Rhoda had said about Ivor at the Defarge Club meeting the previous night and it crossed her mind that someone might have told Kevin, the train station's custodian, to lock the waiting room to keep Ivor out. Who could be that cruel?

"No one should have to sleep outside in the winter. There's got to be someplace he can go for a bed and hot meals."

Daniel chewed his lower lip. "Shady Hills has never had much need for homeless shelters or soup kitchens. Perhaps I could help him . . ."

In the spring, Daniel's father, Cecil Willoughby, the founding owner of *Onyx*, the world's leading magazine for African-Americans, had died, leaving Daniel quite wealthy. One would never have guessed this from Daniel's appearance or behavior, which had not changed in the slightest since his change of fortune. In fact, this was the first time Jane could remember hearing him refer even obliquely to his newfound wealth.

"That's not what he needs," she said. "He needs to be helped back onto his own two feet, given work and a sense of self-esteem, so that he can take care of himself again. And," she added sadly, "he needs help for his alcoholism."

"How do we know he doesn't need psychiatric treatment as well? I believe transients often do."

"That may be. For now, though, I'm going to work on the basics—shelter, soup kitchen, that kind of thing. There must be towns around here that have these."

She spent the first hour of her day at her desk studying a contract she'd just received from Silhouette for three romances by Pam Gainor. She jotted some notes, then set the contract aside to be gone over again later; she always looked over contracts at least twice, so she wouldn't miss anything.

She took the manuscript of *The Blue Palindrome* from her briefcase and set it on her desk. She was about three-quarters of the way through. By now she was certain she would offer to represent this man, whoever he was. He was a remarkable talent. She would finish quickly so as not to waste any more time. She didn't want to lose this one.

A few minutes after eleven, Daniel buzzed her. "Stephanie on one."

"Ugh." She forced her mouth into a big smile and picked up the phone. "Stephanie! Are you here?"

"Yes!" came Stephanie's nasal voice. "Can you believe it? Me—right here in your little burg. Isn't it priceless?"

Chapter Five

At one corner of the village green, Center Street veered off on a curving route to the Shady Hills train station. Walking along this road, her hands shoved deep into her coat pockets against the cold, Jane crossed the station's parking lot and approached the station building, thinking of Ivor.

There was no one around. Frowning a little in puzzlement, Jane climbed the five steps to the platform and went inside the building. There, on one of the shiny dark high-backed benches of the waiting room, sat Stephanie, staring straight ahead, her back rigid, her hands placed decorously in her lap. Hearing the door, she turned her head, saw Jane, and gave the slightest hint of a smile. Then she rose, at the same time taking up the handle of a large black suitcase.

"Jane, *darling*," she said dramatically, and trotted toward Jane on high heels.

Jane put out her arms for the hug she figured Stephanie expected, but Stephanie just put her cheek forward, so Jane did likewise.

Stephanie looked far better suited to Boston or New York City than to Shady Hills. She wore a full-length black mink coat that Jane could tell was of the highest quality. Expensive black shoes, black cashmere gloves. She wasn't a bad-looking woman, Jane reflected. Nice clear skin, her features bold if perhaps rodentlike. She wore her hair, a harsh black, in a stiff old-fashioned pageboy. Jane knew Stephanie to be only four years older than Jane's thirty-nine, still a young woman, yet there was a dated quality about her, as if her fashion sense had died in the early seventies, or as if she'd never bothered with fashion at all, opting for the "classic" look instead.

"Welcome to Shady Hills," Jane said. "You're looking well, Stephanie."

"You, too," Stephanie said in her nasal drawl. "Love your hair! Was it this color at Ken's funeral?"

Ken. No one—not even a special, privileged relative—had ever been allowed to call Kenneth Ken. Jane decided to ignore this, and hoped that by her own continued use of *Kenneth* she could convey the message that this was how her late husband had preferred to be addressed.

"Yup, same old hair," Jane said. "Here, let me take your bag." She bent and searched for a retractable handle.

"What are you looking for?"

"A handle? Wheels?"

Stephanie looked at her in bafflement, then pointed to a small handle at the top of the case. "Handle!"

"Right," Jane said with a polite laugh, picked up the bag, and let out a loud grunt. It could have been full of rocks.

"Heavy?" Stephanie asked, strolling along after Jane.

"A bit." Jane wondered if she should get the car, then rejected this idea. Her office wasn't that far away.

"All of my worldly possessions, as it were," Stephanie said melodramatically.

Jane stopped and look at her. "All your things are in this suitcase?"

"Mm-hm," Stephanie said with a happy nod. "Live light, as my Uncle Mike always said. He was Ken's father—my mother's brother—but you know that."

"Yes. What about your furniture, your . . . stuff?"

"Stuff? I've always lived in furnished rooms, so I've never had furniture to lug around. As for clothes, I go in for a few good classic pieces. And I loathe knick-knacks and such. So everything I own in the world, you hold in your hand!"

Jane hadn't remembered this dramatic streak in Stephanie, but then, she'd only met her twice, briefly, under hectic circumstances. Feeling her face redden with exertion, her hand, wrist, and back aching, she led the way along Center Street, turned left onto the sidewalk that led to her office, and stopped at the agency's front door. "Here we are."

Stephanie regarded the plaque beside the door. "I love it." Then her face grew sad. "This was where you worked with Ken?"

"Yes." Jane pushed open the door. "Come in; I'll introduce you to Daniel."

Daniel, who had obviously heard them coming, suddenly opened the door and bent to help Jane with Stephanie's bag. Then, smiling warmly, he greeted Stephanie and put out his hand. She hesitated for the merest fraction of a second before taking it.

"Stephanie Townsend," Jane said, "I would like you to meet my dear friend—and my treasured assistant—Daniel Willoughby."

"How do you do," Stephanie said with a tiny smile, then withdrew her hand and looked around. "This really is quite sweet," she said, putting the drawl on *sweet*.

"Would you like the grand tour?" Jane said jokingly.

"No, some other time perhaps." Stephanie stood at the window that looked out on the green, peering out. Jane shot Daniel a suffering look. He responded with a wide-eyed stare of alarm.

"All righty, then," Jane said. "Why don't we go for some lunch? I'll just grab some work—I'm not sure if I'll be back today," she told Daniel. She headed into her office, put *The Blue Palindrome* into her briefcase along with some contracts and book proposals, and carried the briefcase and her bag out to the reception area. "All right, ready?"

Stephanie gave a small restrained smile.

"We'll go out the back way," Jane said. "My car is parked there."

"Allow me," Daniel said, lifting Stephanie's suitcase with a grunt, and followed the two women out to the parking lot. Jane opened her trunk and he placed the suitcase inside.

"Pleasure to meet you, Stephanie," he said.

Again she gave him a tiny smile, but made no response. She and Jane got in the car as Daniel went back inside.

"He's a marvel," Jane said, starting the engine and backing out of her parking space. "A dear young man."

"And a Negro," Stephanie observed brightly.

Jane's head snapped sideways and she stared at

Stephanie. "I don't believe I've heard that word in thirty years."

Stephanie simply stared back, as if waiting for Jane to make a point. "He is quite handsome," she said at last.

Jane slammed on the brakes. Remembering to smile, she said, as calmly as she could, "Listen, Stephanie, we'd better get one thing straight right now. When it comes to people, I don't see in color. Daniel is my friend. Period. Heaven knows I have my faults, but racism isn't one of them. If you are a racist—and it seems you are—keep it to yourself . . . or you will quickly be without a relative in Shady Hills."

Stephanie just gaped at her. "I—I—"

"And I've got another surprise for you," Jane went on. "Daniel happens to be the richest person I know. How do you like that? He has more money than you and I put together—maybe even more money than your friend Faith Carson."

"But how?"

Jane gave her head a little shake. "Doesn't matter. The point is that if Daniel wanted to, he could look right down that handsome nose at you, because you haven't got his money and never will. But Daniel won't do that, because that's not the kind of person he is, which is why I love him so dearly. So!" she said, steering the car onto Packer and past the municipal parking lot toward the railroad crossing. "Are we clear on that issue?"

"Quite," Stephanie said coolly, her gaze fixed out the window at the trees.

"Good. Then we can start again." She turned and gave Stephanie her biggest, warmest smile. "Let's go home and have some lunch." Suddenly she had a thought.

"Oh—I'd better tell you. Florence, my son's nanny and our housekeeper . . . she's Trinidadian. Another person I love dearly. She's the one who's busy making our lunch, by the way."

Stephanie nodded, her expression cold, and drummed cashmered fingers softly on the console between their seats.

Feeling a headache coming on, Jane crossed the tracks.

This wasn't going to be easy.

"Pretty town," Stephanie said, her first words since Jane had confronted her.

"Yes, it is," Jane said pleasantly. Her head pounded more fiercely than ever; even turning her head slightly caused her pain. She turned off Grange onto Lilac Way and started up the hill toward her house. "This is my street."

"Ah," Stephanie said, taking in the spacious homes nestled among the trees—a majestic Tudor, a sprawling Colonial, a comfortable porch-wrapped Victorian. She turned to Jane. "I'm sorry for what I said. You must think me an awful person."

Surprised, Jane looked at her. These were the last words she'd expected. "I appreciate your apology and, no, I don't think you're an awful person." She patted Stephanie's gloved hand. "Let's start again."

"Deal," Stephanie said, and more animated now, continued, "It's nice to be visiting you under happier circumstances than last time."

Jane felt a shadow pass over her at the memory of Kenneth's funeral. But she knew Stephanie hadn't meant to sadden her. "True," Jane said, and wiped a tear from her eye.

"If you don't mind my asking, are you . . . seeing someone?"

"Yes," Jane replied brightly, "I am, as a matter of fact. A wonderful man named Stanley Greenberg. He's a police detective, right here in Shady Hills."

"I love it," Stephanie said, as if Jane had selected Stanley's occupation for him.

Jane turned into her driveway. "And this is my house. Do you remember it?" She and Kenneth had held their wedding reception in the side yard, under a massive white tent. Eight years later, Jane had invited mourners back to the house for refreshments after Kenneth's funeral.

"I certainly do remember it." Stephanie gazed out the windshield at the house against its backdrop of blue-green pines. "Such a pretty place."

Jane agreed. She loved this house, would never leave it. It had been hers and Kenneth's.

They got out and Jane heaved Stephanie's suitcase from the trunk. Stephanie carried Jane's bag and briefcase, and they started up the short path to the front door.

"Thank you for being so welcoming, Jane. I really appreciate it."

"Don't be silly," Jane said, turning toward her as she started up the steps. "You're family." She unlocked the front door and led the way into the foyer. Delicious savory smells filled the house.

"Mm, someone's cooking," Stephanie said.

"Yes, Florence, as I told you." Jane helped Stephanie out of her mink. She stroked the dark lustrous fur. "If you don't mind my saying so, this is some coat." Carefully she placed it on a padded hanger and hung it in the closet.

"Thanks," Stephanie said, and suddenly gave Jane a suggestive look, lifting one eyebrow. "You have no *idea* what I had to do to get that coat."

Jane, unsure how to respond to this, hesitated.

"Hello, hello!" Florence, saving the day, bustled into the foyer from the family room.

Jane introduced the two women to each other.

"It is a true pleasure to meet you," Florence said.

Jane was pleased that Florence hadn't said anything about Stephanie's being Faith Carson's friend. But from the fire in Florence's eyes, Jane knew that was exactly what Florence was thinking about. Jane hung up her own coat and they all went into the dining room, where Florence had set a lavish table. In the center was a large basket that Florence had filled with gourds of all shapes and sizes, bright orange and yellow and green.

"This is lovely, Florence," Jane said.

"Yes," Stephanie said, taking a seat. "Pure Norman Rockwell."

"Norman who?" Florence frowned.

"What a nice compliment," Jane said lightly. "Florence, I'll help you serve."

Jane followed Florence into the kitchen. On the stove was a big pot of soup. Jane looked in and saw cabbage and carrots and pasta shells in a thick tomato broth. "This smells heavenly."

"Missus," Florence whispered, coming up close to her. "Your cousin—I mean Mr. Stuart's cousin—what do you think of her?"

Jane shot her a look. There was no fooling Florence. "Not much so far, to be honest," Jane said softly. "But we have to be nice; we have to look for the good qualities."

"Why?" Florence looked puzzled.

"Because," Jane said patiently, "she's family. Now, what can I do?"

Florence had also made salad and a quiche. She and Jane carried these into the dining room. Then Florence carried out bowls of soup on a tray.

Sitting down, Jane saw that the table was set for three. She considered Florence one of the family and would never have thought twice about her joining Jane and her company for lunch, but after the conversation Jane and Stephanie had had in the car about Daniel, Jane wondered how this would strike Stephanie. Not that it mattered.

Jane watched Florence finish passing soup bowls and then take her seat, a big smile on her pretty face. Stephanie was watching Florence, her eyebrows slightly raised.

"Well!" Florence said with a satisfied sigh. "I do hope this all came out as planned." She opened her napkin, placed it in her lap, and looked up to find Stephanie staring at her.

"Stephanie," Jane said in an effort to distract her, "I think it's so exciting, your coming here for a new job—a new life, really. I hope things work out well for you. It could be such fun."

Stephanie seemed to be having trouble wresting her gaze from Florence. Jane could just imagine what she was thinking: *The help eats with the family,* or some such. Well, that was just too bad for snobby, racist Stephanie—cousin or no cousin. In fact, as far as Jane was concerned, the sooner this cousin was out of the house, the better.

Stephanie took a forkful of quiche. "By fun," she said, smiling urbanely, "I suppose you mean working with Faith Carson."

"No, not at all. I mean going from advertising, which you don't seem to have liked, to this new job in publishing. Kenneth used to say that when he was an editor, he'd had the most fun working for the smaller, more intimate companies. Everybody got to do a little bit of everything. It was a looser, more relaxed atmosphere."

"Mm," Stephanie murmured, seeming not to have heard what Jane had said. She let out an easy laugh. "Everyone's always been positively agog"—she drawled heavily on *agog*— "at the idea of my being best friends with Faith Carson, but they don't understand that to me, she's just good old Faithie, my roommate at Wellesley."

Florence piped up, "She may be good old Faithie to you, but her arrival in Shady Hills has created quite a stir, I can tell you that. You know, a former *queen . . .* "

Stephanie stared at Florence as if surprised that she had dared to speak two sentences in a row. Florence's smile abruptly vanished. She took a deep breath and removed her napkin from her lap. "Missus," she said, "if you'll excuse me, I'm not feeling very hungry."

"Y-yes, of course," Jane said, hurting for Florence, and watched her get up from the table and walk into the kitchen. Yes, the sooner Stephanie left, the better. She turned to her; she looked happier now that Florence had departed.

"So," Jane said, fighting hard to control her anger,

"you said you'll be working for Carson & Hart as an editor?"

"Mm-hm." Stephanie speared some salad. "You'd be surprised at how many different programs they've got going."

At that moment Winky appeared in the archway to the living room. She glared at Stephanie, seemed to make a decision, and leapt onto the table.

"Winky!" Jane jumped up and shooed Winky off the table, but Winky opted for halfway, perching on Florence's vacated chair.

"A cat," Stephanie said. From the tone of her voice it was unclear to Jane whether to Stephanie this was a bad thing or a good thing.

"Yes, Kenneth gave Winky to Nicholas as a kitten. We adore her—don't we, Wink?"

"How sweet," Stephanie drawled. "Which reminds me, Faithie said something about a big new project involving cats." Before Jane could ask for details she went on, "More than that, however, I don't know."

Winky jumped down from Florence's chair, walked around the table, and hopped up onto the empty chair next to Stephanie with a rumbling purr. "Nice little kitty," Stephanie said, reaching out to pet her. Suddenly Winky bristled and let out a vicious hiss. Stephanie snatched back her hand as if it had been burned.

"Winky!" Jane scolded her, and turned to Stephanie. "I don't know what's come over her. No manners at all," she told the cat, and rising to shoo her completely out of the room, she smiled to herself at Winky's shrewd judgment of character. "I'm so sorry," she said, coming back into the room.

"Don't worry about it," Stephanie said with a laugh.

"This is all so charming, really, and I'm just thrilled to be out of boring old Boston. You couldn't have been more correct about my job with that horrid ad agency."

"Advertising's not for you, then," Jane said solemnly.

"No . . . though it took me a long time to figure that out. I must confess I was so bored with my work that I did a terrible job. I mean, can you imagine writing ad copy for cough syrup? Me!" She looked down at her plate. "It was downhill from there. My work was horrid, we lost the client, and I knew I was going to get fired. Which would have been no more than I deserved, I suppose."

"So this opportunity came along just in time."

"Absolutely. What was there to keep me in Boston? I have no ties—no boyfriend, at least not at the moment . . ."

Jane couldn't help thinking of the mink coat.

". . . no husband, no one who needed me. And here was my dearest friend. So I decided to go for it." Stephanie shrugged. "And if, by some chance, things don't work out, maybe I can be of use to you in your little literary agency!"

Jane felt the blood drain from her face. She would rather die. Besides, she had no intention of hiring anyone in addition to Daniel; she hadn't the need, the room, or the money for anyone else.

She just smiled sweetly and took a bite of quiche.

After lunch, Jane showed Stephanie the house. Florence was nowhere to be found. Checking her watch, Jane saw that it was 2:45 and realized that Florence had gone to pick up Nick at school.

Jane took Stephanie outside. Standing in the backyard, gazing up into the pines and then back at the house, Stephanie shook her head in wonder. "It's all so . . . village."

"Yes," Jane conceded, "this is a village."

"You know what I mean. It's got that cozy, everybody-knows-everybody-else's-business feeling. I've had that sense ever since I stepped off the train. And I'm very good at picking up vibrations from places." She shivered—they had come outside without their coats.

"I'll get your coat," Jane said, then had an idea. "Would you like to walk a little around the neighborhood? It'll give us some more time to chat—and get some exercise." She grimaced, rolling her eyes heavenward. "I'm supposed to be on the Stillkin diet, but I haven't done very well so far. I'm either determined not to be on a diet, or I just forget!"

"But you look marvelous. Why do you want to diet?"

"Thanks, but I've got eight pounds I want gone before I go on vacation."

"Gotcha. Sure, let's walk. I'll pick up vibes."

Walking back into the house, Jane resolved to try to get to know Stephanie better, *and* to like her. Surely she had some redeeming qualities Jane simply hadn't found yet.

In the foyer she got Stephanie her mink and put on her own charcoal wool; then they went out the front door, turned right, and started down the hill.

Stephanie stopped and took in Audrey and Elliott Fairchild's massive Tudor across the street. "Now *that's* a house. I needed a house just like that for one of my ad campaigns."

"That's Audrey and Elliott Fairchild. He's medical director of NJRI—New Jersey Rehabilitation Institute."

Stephanie looked impressed. "Are you close friends with them?"

Jane had to laugh. It wasn't really possible to be close to Audrey. "I wouldn't say *close. Friendly* is more like it. Nice people, though," she added quickly. "They have a teenage daughter, Cara."

"That's nice. Houses, houses," Stephanie mused, looking down, her hands shoved deep in her mink pockets. "I've got to find a place to live. An apartment. And the sooner the better. I don't want to be a burden on you."

"Don't be silly. There's an apartment broker down in the village who I hear is quite good. If you like, I'll take you there this afternoon."

"Perfect. If they're willing, I'll look all afternoon today, and if I see something right I'll grab it. Remember, I'm starting work tomorrow. I'd thought about stopping in at the office, but I don't want to bother Faithie and Gav while they're setting up."

Jane nodded. At the bottom of Lilac Way they turned left onto Oakmont, a busier street with a sidewalk. Even with the biting cold edge to the air, it was a glorious sunny day, the sky a hard cloudless blue.

When they reached Magnolia Lane, which climbed back up the hill on their left, Stephanie stopped and gazed upward. "Now this street looks intriguing. More picturesque cottages up there?"

There was at least one: the bungalow that had once been occupied by Roger Haines. That had been during that horrid business with Marlene, Jane's nanny before Florence. Come to think of it, Jane's business with

Roger had turned out equally horrid, teaching her
never to become intimate—at least, not *that* intimate—
with a client again. Jane avoided this street whenever
possible, but Stephanie was clearly intrigued. "We can
go up here if you like," Jane said.

They started up.

"Your friend Faith . . ." Jane began. "As Florence said,
she's creating quite a stir here in town."

Stephanie laughed. "Faith always does. She's one of
those women people either love or hate. But if you really get to know her, you can't help loving her. She's
good people."

Jane doubted whether she would trust Stephanie's
judgment when it came to "good people," but nodded
politely. "You were roommates at Wellesley, you said."

"Mm. Long time ago now. Twenty-one years." She
looked wistful. "You should have seen her then. But of
course you've seen pictures. She was really quite ravish-
ing. That Grace Kelly look. She was the quintessential
Boston debutante."

Roger's bungalow, as Jane thought of it, was coming
up on the right. She looked away. "How did Faith meet
the prince?"

Stephanie gave a tiny shrug. "It was just another
party, really. Just a bunch of us Wellesley girls hanging
around on a Saturday night. One of our friends had invited her boyfriend over from Harvard, and he brought
a whole bunch of other guys. One of them was Ravi.
That was his actual name. Officially, he was called the
Maharaj Kumar—which means crown prince—of Ananda. Do you know much about Ananda?"

Jane shook her head, then remembered what Florence had told her. "Only that some people likened it to heaven."

Stephanie's features softened and her eyes unfocused, as if she were there again. "It really was heaven. A teeny place, smaller than Rhode Island, high up in the Himalayas, between China and India. I can still see those neat little houses climbing the mountainsides, and at the top of the highest mountain of all was the palace, a massive structure all of wood. It was literally in the clouds most of the time. The first thing Faithie said when she saw Ananda was, 'It's Shangri-la.'

"Anyway, Ravi was as handsome as Faith was beautiful, and the two of them fell madly in love on sight. I've never seen anything quite like it. They behaved as if they were destined to be together, and you know"—Stephanie looked directly at Jane—"I believe they were."

"What was Ravi doing at Harvard?"

"Finishing his doctorate studies—he was a few years older than Faith. He was studying political economy at the Kennedy School."

"Ah, an enlightened ruler."

"That was the original plan," Stephanie said uneasily. "His father, the king, wanted Ravi to learn about the world, about business, international trade, those sorts of things. He wanted Ravi to bring Ananda into the twentieth century. But once Ravi laid eyes on Faithie, I don't think he was interested in much besides being with her."

They had reached the top of the hill, where Magnolia Lane veered off into a cul-de-sac and became Magnolia Place. Jane led the way in, thinking Stephanie would find it interesting. Once, there had been only a steep wooded cliff here. In the past year a developer had created a winding road down this cliff's side, and along this road he had built "executive homes"—enormous luxury houses with price tags in excess of a million dollars.

Stephanie glanced down the new road, where the roof of the highest house could be seen through the bare trees. "Money down there. That's an easy vibe."

"You got that right," Jane said with a laugh. "The new money in Shady Hills. Puffy hates it."

"Oh, you know Puffy. Then you know she and Oren own the building Faithie and Gav are moving into?"

"Yes."

"Puffy and Oren were at Faith and Ravi's wedding," Stephanie said, a distant look in her eyes.

"So I've heard. How soon after Faith and Ravi met did they marry?"

"About a year." Stephanie turned with Jane and they walked out of Magnolia Place and back onto Magnolia Lane, continuing through the woods. "It was right after Faith graduated from Wellesley, and Ravi had finished his doctorate," Stephanie went on. "It all worked out just right. And the wedding . . ." She cast up her eyes. "Perfection.

"We all flew to Ananda—which was an experience in itself—and there, among the clouds, in an incredible ceremony, my little Faithie became Her Majesty the Crown Princess. I was her maid of honor.

"Well! The media went bananas. They played the whole thing up as another Grace Kelly, Lisa Halaby, Hope Cooke sort of thing, which I suppose it was. Very romantic. And of course they all pointed out that when Ravi's father the king died, Ravi would become king—

he was an only child, so there was no question about that—and Faith would be his queen. Can you imagine? Queen of Ananda!"

"Unbelievable," Jane said.

"Then came the best part, and I was there to see it. Faithie was afraid to be alone—you know, without someone from home around—so she asked me to stay on for a while, and I did. I stayed four months, in fact. Anyway, after the wedding, Ravi gave Faith something incredible." Stephanie shook her head. "When I think what I had to go through to get this miserable mink coat . . ."

"What was it?"

Stephanie stopped. Her eyes grew huge. "Have you ever heard," she said softly, "of the Star of Ananda?"

Jane was beginning to wish she'd read *Queen of Heaven.* "No."

"I wish you could have seen it," Stephanie said, shaking her head. "The Star itself was a star sapphire, a huge stone, very smooth and round, about the size of an egg. It was blue . . . cashmere-blue is what they called it. And it weighed forty carats."

"Oh my word."

" 'Oh my word' is right! It was over two hundred years old. It had originally been mined in Ceylon, and the King of Ceylon gave it as a gift to Ravi's great-great-whatever-grandfather. *He* had it put on a diamond necklace and gave it to his wife, which was the beginning of the tradition: All the princes and kings of Ananda presented this necklace to their wives, all down through the generations."

"Didn't it still belong to Ravi's mother?"

"Long dead of some disease. There was only his father, the king, the useless old playboy. When Ravi married Faith, Ravi's father gave it to him to give to his princess."

"So romantic," Jane said dreamily.

"Mm, romantic as hell. But there's more. Faith told me that when Ravi gave it to her on their wedding night, he told her it was the perfect gift for her, because the three cross bars that made the star inside the jewel were believed to represent Hope, Destiny . . . and Faith! Could you just die!"

"It's like a fairy tale."

"Exactly! Three months after the wedding, Ravi had Faith's royal portrait painted, and for it she wore the necklace—another tradition." Stephanie shook her head in wonder. "What a life they had. I hated to leave."

"But you were there four months," Jane pointed out.

"I know, but I could have stayed forever. The palace high on the mountain . . . The village clinging to the mountainsides . . . Those sweet, wonderful people . . ." She made a sour expression. "But I had to get back. It was the beginning of fall, and hordes of college grads were flocking to New York and Boston looking for jobs. So, back to the real world I went. I thought I was interested in advertising, idiot that I was, so I used some of my connections—you know what I mean. I got an entry-level job with an agency in Boston, on Tremont Street."

They had reached a section of Magnolia Lane where there were no houses, just woods that stood stark and lonely, close to the sides of the road, rising from a thick brown carpet of fallen leaves.

"But you kept in touch with Faith," Jane said.

"Of course. She was always good at keeping in touch, writing letters—long letters. Her letters surprised me."

"Oh?"

Stephanie looked at Jane. "Faith said she was bored. Frustrated. She said life in Ananda wasn't nearly as glamorous and fun as she thought it would be—as the rest of the world thought it was. She said it really wasn't glamorous at all."

They came to where Christopher Street veered off to the right. If they continued on Magnolia Lane, Jane realized, they would pass Doris's house. Jane led Stephanie down Christopher, which would eventually lead to a way back to Jane's house.

Stephanie was gazing down at the street as she walked. "Ravi's father, the king—his name was Abhay—was a total waste. A dashing devil, but completely useless. He was a widower, and he was always chasing some blonde or other—he worshipped blondes."

"Wasn't he needed to run the country?"

"Nah. Ananda had always pretty much run itself. It was peaceful, very prosperous—no poverty. Anyway, Abhay was always off being the jet-setter. He'd play polo, gamble. He loved Monte Carlo, spent a lot of time there. *Adored* a certain famous blonde there a number of years ago, if you know what I mean." Stephanie wiggled her brows suggestively.

Jane, suddenly understanding only too well, widened her eyes in shock. "With Abhay away, Ravi ran the country, then."

"No, I've just told you, there was nothing to do—at least, nothing for Ravi to do. He served no real function. So neither did Faith! She wrote to me that she'd tried to speak to him about their life, about what they might accomplish together for the betterment of the country, and he laughed at her! He said his plans con-

sisted of nothing more than jet-setting around the
world having fun, just like his father. Ravi had his own
favorite spots, too. Rome, Madrid, London, New York,
Aspen, Hollywood. He told Faith she was welcome to go
with him. But Faith told me the general understanding
on the part of Ravi and the entire country, really, was
that she would soon start having princes and prin-
cesses."

They turned right onto Adams Road; through the
bare forest Jane could see Adams Pond, a grim khaki
color. There was no sidewalk on this street, and they
kept far to the right, though no cars passed.

"As it turned out," Stephanie said, "Faith did go with
Ravi on some of his play trips, but that got boring, too.
And then she did get pregnant, so she was happy to stay
home."

Adams Road opened onto Oakmont Avenue, where
they had started from, and they strolled the short distance back to the foot of Lilac Way and started up the
hill.

Jane said, "That must have made everyone happy."

"Yes, but a sad thing happened at almost the exact
same time. Abhay was in Tunisia visiting some billionaire friend, and he lost control of his sports car on a
winding road at the edge of a ravine. The car smashed
through a guardrail, shot right to the bottom, and exploded."

"How horrible."

"Mm. Sad . . . but interesting for Faith and Ravi.
Because he was king now, of course, and Faithie was his
queen. My little Faithie from Wellesley, Queen of
Ananda! Needless to say, the media had a field day."

They had almost reached Jane's house. As they ap-

proached the space in the tall holly hedge that surrounded Jane's front lawn, a voice called, "Whoo-oo,
Janey-doll!"

Jane turned. Audrey Fairchild stood in the middle of
the road. Her honey-blond hair was piled on top of her
head in a mass of ringlets, and she wore a mink coat of
her own, this one a pale honey color, close in shade to
her hair. She clicked confidently across the street in her
high heels, smiling a wide, scarlet-lipsticked smile.

"Home in the afternoon. My, my," she said, and
laughed, clearly amusing herself. "Now don't let yourself get fat and lazy just because you're doing those big
deals!"

Inwardly Jane winced at Audrey's use of the word *fat*,
but she kept smiling. She opened her mouth to introduce Audrey to Stephanie, but realized Audrey had already turned to her.

Instantly, Audrey's smile faded and her face turned
cold. Her eyes widened slightly in surprise.

"Audrey," Jane said, frowning, "is something wrong?"

"No, no," Audrey said hurriedly, seemingly unable to
tear her gaze from Stephanie.

"I was about to introduce you. Audrey Fairchild—"

"We've met," Audrey said uncomfortably.

Jane, taken aback, said, "You have?"

"Yes, we have," Stephanie said, her expression
equally cold. "So you're Fairchild now," she mused to
Audrey.

"My married name." Audrey touched Jane's sleeve.
"Darling, I've got to run, zillions of things to do. I was
just leaving, in fact." And without a word to Stephanie,
or even a look, she turned and clipped back across the
street, entering her open garage.

Jane led the way up the path to the front door. "Small world," she said, turning to Stephanie. "How do you know Audrey?"

"You remember my sister, Caroline? She couldn't make your wedding, but she was at Kenneth's funeral. She's four years older than I am.

"Caroline was a senior at Wellesley when I was a freshman. Audrey was a senior, like Caroline. They were close friends. Anyway, Audrey got engaged to this guy named Lowell who was going to MIT. Well, Caroline fell for Lowell. You don't know Caroline, but when she sets her sights on something, heaven help anybody who gets in her way. And Audrey was definitely in the way. Caroline got Lowell away from Audrey . . . got Lowell to call off his engagement to her."

"Did Caroline marry him instead?"

"Nah. She got bored with him after about two months. Dumped him."

"Did he go back to Audrey?"

"No. And so," Stephanie said with a sigh, "Audrey has always hated Caroline—and, by association, me!"

"But *you* didn't do anything wrong."

"I know, but you know how people are." Stephanie shrugged, as if to say she couldn't explain it and really didn't care.

They entered the house. A thought occurred to Jane and in the foyer she turned to Stephanie. "Something doesn't make sense. You say Audrey was a senior when you were a freshman. That would make Audrey at least three years older than you, and you're forty-three, right?"

Stephanie winced but then reluctantly nodded.

"That would mean Audrey is at least forty-six."

"Mm-hm," Stephanie murmured. "So?"

"So she's not. She's only a year older than I am. She's forty."

Stephanie gave Jane a pitying smile. "She *says* she's forty. I admit she looks great—I'm sure she's got one of the best plastic surgeons in New York—but forty she's not. Many women lie about their age, Jane. If I remember correctly, Audrey is just a liar in general."

Jane recalled an incident involving her previous nanny, Marlene, in which Audrey had lied repeatedly. Troubled at this thought, she nibbled the inside of her cheek. "Coffee?" she asked Stephanie absently.

"Thanks, but I shouldn't. Gotta get to that apartment broker you mentioned."

"Right. I'll drive you."

In the car, heading down the other side of Lilac Way, Stephanie tapped the door handle, her lips pursed thoughtfully. "So Audrey's name is Fairchild, you said. What was it you said her husband does?"

"Elliott? He's medical director of NJRI. People go there after car accidents and things like that. Famous people, too. It's supposed to be finest place of its kind."

"Mm," Stephanie murmured thoughtfully. "So she's done all right for herself, as it turns out."

"Yes . . . though she and Elliott are working out some problems at the moment." Jane turned left on Grange, heading into town. "They're separated. I hope they can work things out, get back together, if only for Cara's sake."

"So this Elliott, he's not living there?"

"No. He took an apartment in Essex Fells, not far from the Institute. Essex Fells is just a few towns away from here."

Stephanie gazed out the window thoughtfully. "I'm not surprised—about their marriage being in trouble, I mean. Who could live with Audrey Cook—that was her maiden name—for any length of time? That hair, that big mouth, that affected way she has of speaking." She shuddered.

Jane would have liked to point out that it had been Elliott's infidelities that had caused the difficulties in his and Audrey's marriage, but felt it wasn't her place to do so.

"People just don't change," Stephanie said, and with a self-satisfied little smile, she began stroking the lustrous black fur of her coat.

Chapter Six

Jane parked behind her office but they didn't go in. Instead, Jane led Stephanie through the narrow alley beside Jane's building and along the street to The Home Place, the real estate agency and apartment broker she had recommended to Stephanie. Myrtle Lovesey, who owned the agency, was the only person in the office when they entered. The tall, gaunt, elderly woman rose behind her desk with a gracious smile. Jane introduced Stephanie to her.

"A pleasure," Myrtle said. "We miss your cousin very much."

"Thanks," Stephanie said, her gaze darting about.

Uncomfortable, Jane said, "Stephanie's moving here, Myrtle. I thought you'd have some nice apartments to show her."

"Of course!" Myrtle turned and took a thick loose-leaf binder from the credenza behind her chair. "And where have you come *from?*" she asked pleasantly, making conversation.

"Boston." Stephanie's tone, like the little scowl on

her face, made it clear she didn't care to discuss her life changes with Myrtle.

"Ah." Myrtle opened the notebook and looked up at Stephanie. "We do have a number of nice apartments at the moment. I'm short-staffed today, so I'll show them to you myself."

"That's awfully nice of you, Myrtle," Jane said, and felt an overpowering urge to say to Stephanie, as she might to Nicholas, "And what do you say to Mrs. Lovesey?"

Stephanie smiled mildly.

"I'll come back for you"—Jane checked her watch; it was 3:45—"around five?" She looked at Myrtle and Stephanie.

"Sounds good to me," Myrtle said. "You just leave everything to me, Jane." Myrtle invited Stephanie to sit in one of the chairs facing her desk. "Now. First let's get an idea of what you're looking for."

Jane waved good-bye and left. She started back along Center Street toward her office, deep in thought.

Stephanie was decidedly odd. No, more than odd; she was downright rude. And spoiled. A snob—that was it. Stephanie was a snob. Not a very nice person, not at all. Jane didn't like her. But she was Kenneth's cousin, and Jane would do her duty by her. But once Stephanie was a permanent resident of the area, working every day right around the corner from Jane's office, was Jane expected to maintain a relationship with her? Jane didn't think she could bring herself to do that.

She laughed to herself at her own thoughts. *Expected to!* No one expected her to do anything. She would do what she felt was right. Helping Kenneth's cousin get settled, giving her a place to stay, was right. Being her friend afterward was definitely optional.

Daniel had a few phone messages for her when she came in. Tina Blanton had called to see if her signing check had come in yet from Pocket Books, and Daniel had told her it hadn't. Tina had still wanted to talk to Jane—to tell her to nag for the check, no doubt. Looking at the pink message slip, Jane shook her head. Tina wasn't her only client who was always desperately in need of money. One of the first pieces of advice Jane gave writers when they signed with her was that they shouldn't expect to live on their writing, at least not at the beginning, and perhaps never. Yet many writers gleefully quit their jobs as soon as they sold their first books, as if it were only a matter of time before the six-figure checks started rolling in and they could pay off their mortgages.

Yves Golden, Goddess's manager, had also called. And Bertha Stumpf. Jane couldn't deal with Bertha today, not after an afternoon of Stephanie, so as she entered her office she put that slip on the near right corner of her desk—the place she put messages she didn't intend to reply to immediately.

She called Yves Golden first. He wanted to know what Jane thought of the jacket of Goddess's book. Jane said she loved it. Yves didn't seem to know how he felt about it. One thing was clear: He wasn't about to defer to Jane's professional opinion. Sounding uneasy, he said he was going to show it to some other people at his "shop." Jane said that was fine, and rolling her eyes, replaced the phone.

Then she called Tina Blanton.

"At this rate, I'll have the book finished before they pay me for it," she said. "Jane, I've got bills here."

It occurred to Jane that someday she should install a

voice mail system in her agency. *If you would like to whine about a check you have not yet received, press two.*

"Exaggerating a bit, aren't you, Tina? We returned the signed contracts . . . let's see . . ." She consulted a notebook at the left edge of her work mountain. "Two weeks ago. It should be here soon."

"Could you find out for sure?"

"Yes, Tina," she said, like a robot, and as soon as she'd hung up, screamed for Daniel.

"Yes, Jane," his voice came from the intercom. "Jane, why not try the intercom sometime? It's much nicer than screaming."

"I like screaming better. Besides, I don't know how to work that thing. Daniel, would you please call Patsy over at Pocket and ask her when Tina Blanton's check is coming?"

"We just returned her contracts two weeks ago."

She laughed. "I know. But I told Tina I'd check. You know how she is."

"Okay," Daniel said tiredly.

With her calls now returned—or at least all the calls she intended to return for the moment—Jane opened her briefcase and, with a sense of excited anticipation, brought out *The Blue Palindrome*. She had only about fifty pages left, and now found herself reading faster and faster, eager to know the fate of the sad young man who was the novel's protagonist.

Finally, she turned over the final page. The near edge of her desk was covered with wadded-up tissues, and she pressed a fresh one to the corners of her eyes, shaking her head at the depth of this Nathaniel Barre's talent.

At that moment Daniel came in. "Jane, what's wrong?"

"Nothing. It's this book; it's so wonderful. You have to read it."

His eyes widened in excitement. "This is that *Blue* something?"

"*The Blue Palindrome.* Which, by the way, makes perfect sense once you finish the book." She patted the tall stack of pages. "This man is a genius, Daniel."

"Well . . . sign him up!"

"I fully intend to. This is really big." She flipped over the manuscript and found Nathaniel Barre's cover letter, which bore the telephone number of his home in Green Bay, Wisconsin. As Daniel watched, she dialed it. An older woman answered. At first she seemed to think Jane was selling something, and almost hung up on her, but Jane quickly explained that she was a literary agent and was calling about the manuscript Mr. Barre had sent her. At this, the woman identified herself as "Nat's mom" and, her voice growing excited, gave Jane Nat's work number. "He should be there now," Mrs. Barre said.

Jane thanked her and dialed the work number. A young woman answered with the name of a prominent national chain of drugstores. When Jane asked for Nathaniel Barre, the young woman said she would put Jane through to the pharmacy. A man picked up.

"I'm trying to reach Nathaniel Barre, please."

"Speaking." His voice was a monotone.

"Oh, Mr. Barre, it's Jane Stuart. I'm the literary agent you sent your manuscript to."

"Yes."

"I'm calling to tell you I think your book is absolutely marvelous and that I'd be honored to represent you."

"Okay."

Jane frowned and gave Daniel a helpless look.

Nathaniel Barre sounded as if he was on some sort of tranquilizer. "It's . . . it's a work of true genius," she gushed.

"Uh-huh."

"Well. Anyway, I assume you're still looking for representation?"

"Yes."

"And you'll sign with my agency?"

"Yes."

"Good. I'll send you my representation agreement, and in the meantime I'll get started on marketing your book."

"Okay."

"Where shall I send the agreement—to the address on your letter?"

"Yes."

"All righty, then. Expect it in the next few days. I'm very pleased to be working with you."

"Uh-huh."

"By the way, Mr. Barre, I'm just curious. You work in the pharmacy; is that how you know so much about alchemy and drugs?"

"Right. I'm the pharmacist."

"I see. Well, thanks. A pleasure, really. Good-bye."

"Bye."

Daniel was staring at her in bafflement. "What happened?"

She shrugged. "He's signing with us."

"Was he pleased?"

"I don't know. He didn't express any emotion at all."

Daniel nodded. "Probably just not a 'gusher.'"

"That's putting it mildly. He sounds as if he's just come from the lobotomy farm."

Daniel laughed. "You're terrible, Jane! Everyone's

different. He could be pleased beyond words but just doesn't show it on the outside."

Jane shrugged and waved her hand dismissively. "In the end it doesn't matter if his personality is Truman Capote or J.D. Salinger; as a novelist, he's a genius, and that's all that matters." She picked up the manuscript and hugged it to her chest. "Ooh, I'm so excited! Now, who do we pitch it to? We'll auction, of course."

"Of course. I'll get his agreement out."

"Thanks." She handed him Barre's cover letter. "Come to think of it, let's send it by overnight mail."

"Done." He smiled. "This is great, Jane." He jogged out of her office.

Around four-thirty, Jane glanced out her front office window and saw Stanley Greenberg's patrol car pull up to the curb. She smiled. She loved it when he dropped by, an increasingly frequent occurrence lately. She watched him get out of the car and approach the agency's front door, tall, thin, broad-shouldered, his sandy hair falling across his forehead like a young boy's.

A moment later there was a soft knock on her office door and he poked his head in, smiling. She motioned him in and he came up to her desk and kissed her before falling into her visitor's chair.

"Bad day?" she asked.

"Not one of my best. Another break-in today."

"Oh no. Where?"

He looked uneasy. "I hate to tell you this, but since nothing's ever a secret in this town, you might as well hear it from me. It was a house on Oakmont, between your street and Magnolia Lane."

She sat up straight in alarm. "But that's right at the *foot* of my street. There are only two or three houses between Lilac and Magnolia. Do I know these people?"

"I don't think so. Name's Schmidt. She works in the city; he's a lawyer with a firm in Morris Plains. He rushed right home."

"What did the burglars take?"

"Burglars? You've decided it's more than one?"

"It's just a manner of speaking. Who's the word person around here, me or you?"

He smiled. "Jewelry, some cash, an antique clock. They got in through a basement window. Smashed it in."

"Stanley, you've got to catch this person—or persons. This is awful."

"Of course it's awful, but it's not as if we've never seen this kind of thing before. What are you getting so upset about?"

"They're getting closer and closer to *my* house; that's what."

"Yes," he said solemnly, "I'm certain that whoever is behind this has a map of Shady Hills and is methodically zeroing in on Nine Lilac Way. It's only a matter of time."

"Smart ass."

"Actually, we do have some ideas about who's behind this. Ideas," he added quickly, "I'm not authorized to share with you."

She remembered that poor Stanley had been reprimanded for allowing her to become too involved in the case of the girl found hanging from a tree behind Hydrangea House. Jane had found this reprimand amusing: It had been she, in the end, who solved the case, yet Stanley should not have let her help.

"How's your day going?" he asked, clearly trying to change the subject.

"Good and bad. Good because I've discovered a marvelous new novelist, a true genius. I don't think I've been this excited about a book in years."

"That's great!" His expression turned thoughtful. "You know, I really should finish that police thriller I've been working on."

"Yeah, yeah." She'd heard this countless times before. "I've come to the conclusion that this famous book you keep referring to doesn't really exist. It's like a man's etchings."

He laughed. "It does exist. It's just that I'm too insecure to show it to you."

"I see. Well, when you trust me enough to expose yourself to such vulnerability, I'd be more than delighted to read it and give you my thoughts. And I promise I'll be honest but gentle."

"Thank you, Jane. Now what's the bad part of your day?"

She made a sour face. "Stephanie. Stanley, I've tried my hardest to like her, but she's just awful. She's a supercilious, superficial snob. I can't believe she's related to my poor Kenneth."

"They were cousins, not brother and sister. Even brother and sister can be as different as night and day."

"True. And that would explain why Kenneth barely ever talked about her. He must not have liked her. But I still feel I owe it to her as family to help her out here. I've left her with Myrtle for the afternoon to look for an apartment."

"She's not wasting any time."

"No, and that's fine by me. The sooner she's out of my house, the better. She was unforgivably rude to poor

Florence, and I'm sure Nick will despise her. Besides, she starts her new job tomorrow. She wants to settle her living arrangements as soon as possible."

"On the way over here I saw Myrtle driving another woman. Black hair, long sharp nose?"

"Right. Mink coat. That's Stephanie."

A movement at the corner of her eye made her look out her front window at the green. She had expected to see Ivor, but instead saw a young mother holding the hand of a toddler, leading him along one of the paths toward the green's far side. Ivor was nowhere in sight.

She leaned forward, frowning. "Daniel said he saw you speaking to Ivor out front this morning."

His face darkened. "Yeah," he said sadly. "Poor old guy slept on the sidewalk right in front of your office all night."

She shook her head. "I don't think he's as old as you think. Why on earth would he have slept out there? It must have been forty degrees last night."

"It seems old Kevin forgot to leave the waiting room at the train station unlocked."

"Forgot? I wonder. Stanley, what can we do to help this poor soul?"

"The best thing for him would be to get into a shelter . . . and to get sober. I've tried several times to talk to him, find out something about him, get him to trust me, but all he'll say is that he came out from New York on the train because he had to get out of the city. I suppose I could take him in for vagrancy, but what good would that do?"

"It would give him a place to sleep, for one thing. A jail cell is better than the sidewalk."

He lowered his gaze, as if unsure of his thoughts.

She said, "Do you know of any shelters near here, any place he could go?"

"There is a place I've been thinking of, a shelter in Paterson."

"Then let's drive him over there," Jane said, sitting up.

"I've already offered and he refused. There's no point in forcing the man, because as soon as we drop him off he'll leave. At least here we can keep an eye on him."

"I suppose . . . But in that case, we'd better make sure he always has a place to sleep. We've got to speak to Kevin and make sure the station waiting room stays unlocked. The nights are getting colder and colder."

"Yes, Jane. I'll find Kevin and speak to him. And in time maybe Ivor will trust me enough to let me help him."

"Yes, that's it. I'll keep trying, too."

Stanley leaned back in his chair. "Jane . . . this company your Stephanie is going to work for. Are you aware who owns it?"

"Sure am. Faith Carson and her husband, Gavin Hart. I've been getting the story from all sides. Stephanie is Faith's best friend from Wellesley. Stephanie and I went for a walk today—in fact, we must have walked right past that house that got burglarized—and I got a lot of the Faith Carson story."

He nodded, though he didn't look much interested. "They're taking the space Tim Kruger had."

"Know that, too."

There was a knock on her door and Daniel looked in. "Puffy Chapin just called and asked me to remind you about her party tonight in honor of Faith and Gavin."

"Oh," Jane moaned, holding her head. "I'd forgotten. Are you going?" she asked Daniel.

"Absolutely! I'm taking Ginny. We wouldn't miss this for anything. This is Faith Carson!" He gave Jane a shrewd look. "Now, Jane, you really can't get out of this one."

Jane put a splayed hand to her chest, the picture of innocence. "Who said I wanted to get out of it?" She would have given anything not to go. "Stephanie is my late husband's cousin. She's going to work for these people." She gave one assured nod. "We'll be there."

"We?" Stanley said.

"Oh, didn't I tell you?" Jane asked pleasantly. "You're taking me."

He opened his mouth to speak, then closed it and smiled. "It will be my pleasure."

"For tonight's dinner," Florence announced proudly, "I have prepared not one special surprise, but two!"

Jane, at the head of the dining room table, grinned. Bless Florence. "What marvels have you worked?"

"Yeah," Nick chimed in at Jane's left. "What's up, Flo?"

Florence gave him an aggrieved look. "Now you know I don't like that name Flo."

"I know," Nick said with a silly shrug. "That's why I use it!"

"Naughty little man." Florence smoothed the bottom of her peach-colored sweater over her brown slacks—fancier clothes than Jane could remember seeing her wear for a long time—and looked at Stephanie. "First, I will be right back with the first of my special treats for our very special guest."

Stephanie smiled a tight smile, though her brows wrinkled slightly as if she were worried.

"Don't worry, Stephanie," Nick said. "Florence is a great cook. I'm sure her surprise has something to do with the food."

Stephanie nodded, her eyes fixed on Florence's retreating figure as she went through the swinging door into the kitchen.

"Here I come!" Florence called, and pushed back through into the dining room carrying a large tray. On it were Jane's best soup tureen, a ladle, and four soup bowls. "I have made my very own favorite Trinidadian meal," she said, beaming. "Something I want to share with our new family member. I hope you like it, Stephanie."

Stephanie just continued to smile. *Say something, damn it,* Jane thought, but Stephanie said nothing.

Florence set down the tray and removed the lid from the tureen. Inside was a dark soup of some sort, great puffs of steam rising from it.

"Mm," Jane said. "Florence, that looks marvelous."

"Thanks, missus. It's Trinidad black bean soup. This recipe is from my father's grandmother. It's black beans, flavored with corned beef, onions, and lots of garlic. It was always a favorite in our house." She began to spoon soup into a bowl. "First, Miss Stephanie." She held out the bowl to her.

Stephanie looked at the bowl's lumpy contents and her mouth opened in dismay. Then she seemed to snap to, and took the bowl, forcing a smile. "Yes. Thanks." She set it down before her and sat primly, her mouth tightly shut.

Florence filled another bowl and Jane held out her hand, but Florence passed it instead to Nick. "Oh no, missus, for you I have the second surprise! Be right back."

She disappeared into the kitchen again and reappeared with a plate full of food. "This," she announced, "is for your special eating plan." She came around the table and placed the plate before Jane. "I must confess I borrowed your Stillkin book to get the recipes, missus. There you have green beans, Stillkin style—sautéed in a bit of oil and lemon juice and then sprinkled with bran! Also there is Stillkin chicken, made with cabbage and more bran! And then Dr. Stillkin's special rice, cooked in fish broth."

"Yuck," Nick said, and gulped a spoonful of black bean soup. "Florence, this is *good.*"

"I am so happy you like it," she said, and indeed she was beaming with pleasure. Then she turned to Stephanie, whose bowl sat before her, untouched.

"You don't like black beans?" Florence hazarded.

"It's . . ." Stephanie began, smiling what she must have thought was a polite smile but which looked just plain snotty to Jane. "It's not my sort of thing. And we do have Puffy's party tonight. I'm sure she'll have lots to eat."

It was as if the air had been drained from Florence. Her shoulders sank. "I see." Briskly, smiling her own version of a polite smile, she hurried over to Stephanie's place and quickly took away the bowl. "I'm sorry."

Jane wanted to die. How could anyone be so incredibly rude? She noticed that even Nick was watching Stephanie; his gaze darted to Florence and then to Jane.

Jane looked again at her plate, so lovingly prepared. "Florence, I can't thank you enough for this. You are a wonder."

Florence set Stephanie's bowl at her own place and sat down, unfolding her napkin in her lap. She smiled her beautiful smile at Jane. "You are most welcome, missus. It was my pleasure to help you with your program."

"So!" Jane said, and took a bite of chicken. Like the Stillkin shake, it tasted like a barnyard. Which was not, of course, Florence's fault; Jane was certain she'd followed the recipes meticulously. "Stephanie," she said briskly, "how did it go today with Myrtle? Find anything that might work?"

"Oh!" Stephanie said, rolling her eyes in delight. "Did I ever! A darling place, in a new complex at the north end of town. Hart Run, I believe it's called."

"Ooh, fancy-shmancy," Jane said.

"Exactly. My kind of place, I must admit. Pool, health club, tennis courts, the works. I've already said I want it, but I can't move in till the first of December." She looked uneasy as she said this, and Jane knew why, because it made her feel uneasy, too, to put it mildly. This meant Stephanie would be their houseguest for several weeks. But what, Jane asked herself, had she expected? Stephanie would never have found a place she could move into any earlier.

"I hope you'll be able to put up with me until then," Stephanie said with a little laugh.

"Of course," Jane lied.

But in ten days I'll be somewhere in the Caribbean, she thought gratefully.

"Then you'll be with us for Thanksgiving," Florence said brightly. "I was going to make a traditional Trinidadian feast—much grander than this one—but I think I will go American instead. Turkey, dressing, mashed potatoes, cranberry juice—"

"Sauce," Nick corrected her. "Cranberry sauce."

"Yes, sauce. Won't that be nice?" Florence gazed warmly at Stephanie.

"Thanks," Stephanie said, this time not even bothering to smile, "but I'm not sure yet."

"Not sure yet?" Florence echoed, her face blank.

"I may be spending the holiday with Faith and Gavin."

"I see." Florence shot Jane a look before rising from the table. "I'll go check on the rest of our dinner."

"What is it, Florence?" Nick asked.

"Trinidad pelau, one of my favorites. It is a chicken and rice dish."

"Stephanie won't like it," Nick said casually, and took another spoonful of black bean soup.

Florence darted a look at Stephanie, who had turned to Nick in surprise.

"No, perhaps not," Florence said, turning toward the kitchen. "Perhaps not."

Chapter Seven

_____

"I hate this party," Jane whispered fiercely.

Stanley stopped in his tracks and looked at her. "We're not there yet!"

She shrugged. "I still hate it."

She and Greenberg were making their way up the many steps that climbed Puffy and Oren Chapin's gently sloping lawn to their majestic French château-style manor at the top of the hill. Stephanie was a good ten steps behind, an expectant smile on her face.

"I've never been up here," Greenberg said softly to Jane. "That's some place up there. How'd they make their money, do you know?"

"They didn't. It's Old Money, the only kind that matters, in Puffy's book." Jane looked back and saw a veritable parade of people climbing the steps behind Stephanie. "I actually think Puffy invited the whole town."

They reached the wide front steps and climbed them

to the door, which stood open to reveal a welcoming glow from inside.

Jane realized that although she and Kenneth had once explored this area of Shady Hills—Puffy and Oren lived on Fenwyck Road, off Highland, in the oldest part of town—she had never actually been inside this house, either.

There was already quite a crowd inside—people wearing everything from thick sweaters to cocktail dresses, laughing and chattering away. As Jane, Greenberg, and Stephanie stepped farther into the foyer, looking for a place to put their coats, Puffy hurried up to them.

"Darlings!" She took Jane's hands in both of hers and squeezed them (Puffy never kissed), then turned to Stephanie. "Good to see you, dear. Welcome to Shady Hills."

Stephanie smiled. "Where's Faith?"

Puffy, a bit taken aback, threw a glance backward into the living room, where Jane could see a fire blazing behind the crowd. "In there," Puffy said with a laugh, "surrounded by admirers. I know she'll be eager to see you."

Without a word to Jane or Greenberg, Stephanie departed, slipping off her coat.

"See you later . . ." Greenberg said softly after her.

"Now behave," Jane said with a phony smile. Then, under her breath: "See what I mean about her? Rude as hell. Where *do* we put our coats?"

A woman Jane had never seen before overheard the question and said, "In the sunroom, at the back of the house."

Jane thanked her, and she and Greenberg found this room and added their coats to an already mammoth heap on a sofa. Jane spotted Stephanie's mink, care-lessly tossed.

"Champagne's sure flowing freely," Stanley com-mented as they made their way back to the front of the house. He located filled flutes on a table in the dining room and grabbed one for him and one for Jane. They sipped, looking around at this house that must once have been opulent but which now looked in need of some TLC. A frayed lampshade, a threadbare chair . . . Everything was a bit scruffy, as if even Puffy and Oren's Old Money wasn't enough to keep the place in good re-pair.

"I don't see a soul I know," Jane said in a low voice. "That means if we leave, no one will care."

"We can't leave. Stephanie came with us."

"Exactly," Jane said wickedly.

Greenberg gave her a scolding look. "Besides, we haven't met the guests of honor."

"Probably won't, either. Take a look." She pointed into the living room across the foyer, where a mass of people had gathered around a woman with light brown hair swept back from her face, and a trim, darkly hand-some middle-aged man. For a moment the crowd shifted and Jane was able to get a full-length look at Faith Carson. In face and figure she was as beautiful as her photographs, though older, of course. Jane thought her wispy golden cocktail dress must be reminiscent of the garments she had worn as Queen of Ananda. Jane noticed also that Faith Carson's manner seemed re-served, as if she were allowing herself to smile a little, but never actually to laugh. Gavin, on the other hand, laughed uproariously, throwing back his head.

"Hello, you two." Stephanie had appeared as if from nowhere. She was glowing, as if in her element. "I want to introduce you to Faithie and Gav, but there's a huge crowd around them. I could barely get through myself! Let's wait a little while and try then."

"Sounds good," Greenberg said, his face serious.

"Can't wait," Jane said, watching Stephanie walk away.

She turned and gazed at Puffy still meeting people in the foyer. The older woman's manner was the same with each person who came in; the same squeezing of hands, the same warm yet somehow aloof greeting. It occurred to Jane that perhaps no one really knew Puffy very well. Certainly, average Shady Hills people like Jane and Greenberg whom Puffy had invited would barely know her, if they knew her at all, because Puffy always kept to her "own kind." Jane would have guessed that so far only Faith, Gavin, and Stephanie fit that category.

Daniel and Ginny appeared at the door, all smiles. Daniel, who always knew the right thing to do or wear, had on a navy blazer, gray flannel trousers, and a white shirt open at the neck. Ginny wore a pretty red cocktail dress Jane had never seen before.

Daniel had had his hand squeezed by Puffy and moved into the foyer. He spotted Jane and Greenberg and waved, then turned to tell Ginny. When Puffy was finished squeezing Ginny's hand, they hurried into the dining room.

"Coats in the sunroom," Jane told them. "Then you can come back and have as much fun as we're having."

Daniel gave Jane a stern look. "Now, Jane, make the best of it. You're doing this for Kenneth."

He was right. Duly abashed, Jane nodded, took a sip of her champagne, and made an effort to look pleasant.

In a few moments Daniel and Ginny returned, champagne in hand.

"Isn't this fabulous?" Ginny bubbled. "I don't think I've ever been in a house like this." She turned to Daniel. "Bet you have."

Jane knew that Ginny was referring to the fact that to Daniel, son of one of the richest men in America, such homes were quite familiar.

"Actually," he said, looking around, "it reminds me of a house my father owned in Maine. You know—big old sprawling place, zillions of rooms. My friends and I used to get lost in them—we had to call for the nanny to find us."

They all laughed and sipped.

"Hello, hello!" It was Rhoda, sweeping in, wearing a fawn skirt and sweater set. She was holding the hand of Adam Forrest, her boyfriend, whom Jane had met only once before. He was a small, quiet man, mild-mannered, a good complement to Rhoda's often raw outspokenness.

"How are you, Adam?" Jane asked.

"Fine, Jane, thank you," he said, and smiled as he accepted a glass of champagne from Rhoda.

"Hotter'n hell in here, don't you think?" Rhoda said, taking in the thickening crowd around them. "Let's find someplace quieter to talk." She led the way out the rear door of the dining room, down the hall, and into the library, where only two couples stood chatting with each other.

"Much better," Rhoda said, and sidled up to Jane. "So what do you think of the house?"

"Uh . . . big."

"Exactly." She turned and ran a finger along the

front of a bookshelf, then held the finger aloft to display a thick coat of dust.

"Rhoda!" Jane cried, scandalized.

Rhoda giggled.

Ginny said softly, "Maybe the Chapins aren't as rich as everybody thinks."

"No, no, it isn't that," Rhoda said. "You don't get it. This isn't 'look at my gorgeous house' money; this is old goyish money!"

"Old goyish money?" Ginny repeated, looking confused.

"That's not nice, Rhoda," Jane said. "I've told you I hate that word."

"Well, it's true."

"What's *goyish?*" Ginny asked.

"Gentile," Rhoda said. "Not Jewish. Puffy and Oren," she explained, "are of a type. Don't let this place fool you. There's plenty of money, more than anyone here will probably ever see. But people like Puffy and Oren don't spend it on new furniture and cars and clothes and vacations, because they don't care about things like that. They're also not interested in showing off their wealth. They invest their money. All very quietly. There's money, all right," she repeated. "It's just not liquid."

At that moment Jane saw Faith Carson in the hall, warmly greeting an older woman, taking her hands and moving close to her. The older woman, who appeared to be in her early seventies, was elegantly dressed and coifed. She was also, it occurred to Jane, exactly what one means when referring to a woman as "dripping in diamonds." Huge glittering stones adorned her ears, an intricate necklace blazed against her eggplant silk blouse, and on her fingers were an emerald and a ruby the size of jelly beans.

"Who's she?" Jane whispered.

Rhoda took in the older woman with a knowing look. "That's Lillian Strohman."

"Who's she?"

"She lives down the street. A widow. Her husband owned the MegaFood supermarket chain."

"How do you know her?" Daniel asked.

Rhoda shrugged. "She's a member of my synagogue. The richest member. Always giving money for this and that charity or foundation, and of course to the temple itself."

Ginny said, "I guess Faith Carson knows lots of people like that—I mean, considering the circles she moves in."

Rhoda gave her a look of skeptical scorn. "Don't you kid yourself. Sure, they know a lot of people like Lillian, but this party is as much for Faith and Gavin to make new contacts—to meet *more* people like Lillian—as it is to welcome them to Shady Hills."

Daniel looked baffled. "What do you mean? Why would Faith and Gavin need to make new contacts?"

"Ah," Rhoda said, casting up her eyes, then looking at Daniel pityingly, "you're so young, so handsome, so rich . . . yet so dumb. Sweetie," she explained, as if to a child, "society matrons like Lillian are the primary source of Faith and Gavin's income."

Now everyone looked at Rhoda in confusion.

Rhoda addressed them all. "Just think about what Carson & Hart publishes."

Jane shrugged. "Come to think of it, I have no clear idea of *what* they publish."

"Well, I do," Rhoda said. "Nearly all of their books are written by people like Lillian Strohman. Autobiographies, people's accounts of their safaris, their adventures in Italy and Yugoslavia, the occasional novel. These books are nothing more than glorified vanity jobs!"

"You mean like a vanity press?" Ginny hazarded.

"Now you got it. These 'authors' underwrite their own publication by contributing to the 'promotion' budget. Then they buy huge numbers of copies to give to their family and friends. It is *exactly* vanity publishing." Rhoda winked knowingly. "Lillian is a perfect mark for them. She was a starlet in Hollywood for about fifteen minutes. And then of course she married Sheldon the supermarket king. They traveled extensively, mostly to look for new charities to throw money at. You mark my words. She'll soon be working with Faith and Gavin, writing her memoirs."

"But I don't get it," Ginny said. "Why would someone like Faith Carson need to do something so . . . sleazy?"

"Money, what else?"

"But isn't she rich? I mean, she was a *queen!*"

"Queen, shmeen. She's just some chick who found herself a great sugar daddy . . . till he got his head blown off."

"Till he what?" Jane said.

But before Rhoda could respond, Stephanie appeared in the doorway and hurried up to the group. Her cheeks and chin were pink and her demeanor seemed looser, as if she'd had a lot of champagne.

"You naughty antisocial people! What are you all doing in here? I was looking for you," she said, looking at Jane, "to introduce you to Faithie, but I couldn't find you anywhere."

"But I've been here all the time!" Jane said innocently, and when Stephanie looked confused by this remark, gave a tiny smile.

"Anyway," Stephanie said, "now it's too late—Faithie and Gav are positively *mobbed* with admirers. That's good, though. They could use some positive attention. They've been through some rough times."

"What rough times?" Rhoda asked avidly.

But Stephanie seemed not to have heard. "Anyway, I'll come back for you when Faith and Gavin are ready."

Jane felt as if Stephanie was preparing to present her to royalty—which, Jane realized, was in effect what was happening. Jane giggled at the thought that she hadn't worn elbow-length gloves, as one must when one is introduced to Queen Elizabeth.

"You do that," she told Stephanie seriously, and Stephanie hurried away.

Daniel said to Rhoda, "What were you saying about Faith's sugar daddy getting his head blown off?"

"Shhh. You know, the king. He was assassinated."

"Oh, right. I forgot."

"Yeah," Rhoda went on, "that was the beginning of the end for poor little 'Faithie.' She had to get the hell out of Dodge with her two brats. Ended up marrying 'Gav,' who'd been her husband's chief adviser or something like that."

"Rhoda," Jane said, "how come you didn't know all this stuff last night at our knitting meeting?"

Rhoda shrugged. "I vaguely remembered—you know, from when it all actually happened. But you got me so interested that I went to Barnes & Noble this morning and bought Faith's autobiography. They had it in paperback. *Queen of Heaven*, it's called. 'Of course, she puts a certain 'spin' on everything that happened, but it's not hard to read between the lines."

"Rhoda," Adam said, speaking for the first time, "how do you know so much about Faith and her husband's publishing company? *That* wouldn't have been in her autobiography."

"From Lillian!"

"From Lillian?" everyone said.

"Sure. Lillian's a crafty old broad. She's got no illusions. She knows all about Carson & Hart because so many of her friends have published books with them." She nodded. "Lillian told me all about it last Friday night at Shabbat services. The vanity part of it doesn't matter in the least to her—she could buy the whole damn company if she wanted to. She just wants someone to make a book about her life. And the books Carson & Hart produces *are* quite beautiful. Lillian said doing a book would be an absolute hoot—and those were her words."

Daniel turned to Jane. "Doesn't look as if Carson & Hart will be a market for any of our projects."

Jane, remembering the remarks Doris had made the previous night about the books Jane handled, had to nod in agreement.

"I'm hungry," Greenberg said suddenly. He held up his champagne flute. "Can't drink champagne all night. Anybody seen any food around here?"

Rhoda threw back her head and laughed. "Hon, you can search all twenty-five rooms of this joint, and I doubt you'll find more than a few stale Saltines. I told you—the goyim!"

"Rhoda . . ." Jane began.

"It's true, Jane. They're far more interested in drinking than in eating. There's a beautifully stocked bar, and then there's a table with brie and some crackers—in fact, I think they *were* Saltines!" She laughed again.

"Well," Jane said, getting restless and eager to leave, "I'd like to pay my respects to Faith and go. It's been a long day."

Greenberg nodded, and he and Jane bade the rest of the group good night. Greenberg led the way out of the library and down the hall to the living room. The crowd around Faith and Gavin was even bigger than before. Jane spotted Stephanie deep in conversation with Lillian Strohman, their foreheads practically touching. She went up to the two women and waited politely to be noticed.

Stephanie looked up. "Oh, Jane. Have you met Lillian?" When Jane shook her head, Stephanie said, "Lillian, I'd like you to meet my dear cousin Jane."

Inwardly Jane cringed. "Jane Stuart." She took Lillian's hand.

"Lillian Strohman. So you're cousins?" she asked with a bright smile. Jane noticed that her makeup was perfect, as if a professional had applied it, then recalled that Lillian had spent time in Hollywood.

"Stephanie is my late husband's first cousin," Jane told her.

Lillian frowned sympathetically and nodded. "I'm a widow, too. I'm so sorry. When did you lose your husband?"

"Three years ago."

"Very sad," Stephanie said briskly. "But the family sticks together."

This comment stunned Jane. She had met Stephanie precisely twice—at her and Kenneth's wedding, and at Kenneth's funeral. If Faith Carson and her husband hadn't moved their company to Shady Hills, if Stephanie had not gotten her job with them, Jane probably would never have laid eyes on Stephanie again.

"Nice, very nice," Lillian said sweetly, and Jane just nodded.

"Stephanie," Jane said, "Stanley and I have to go. Is there someone who could give you a ride? I assume you're not ready to leave."

"The party's just getting started!" Stephanie exclaimed. "But I understand. No problem, I'm sure I can find my way back. Just let me make sure I've got your address right. Twelve Lilac Way?"

"Nine."

Stephanie nodded, then made a little moue of disappointment. "I never did introduce you to my little Faithie."

"That's okay. They'll be around, right? Working in town. I'm sure I'll bump into her at some point. At the 7-Eleven."

"Okay," Stephanie chirped, and returned her attention to Lillian.

Jane found Greenberg and then they both found Puffy and Oren and thanked them for their hospitality. Puffy was clearly three sheets to the wind.

"Oh, my darling," she lockjawed, once again taking Jane's hand in her two hands and squeezing hard. "Thank you *so* much for coming. I'll see you soon?"

Jane had no idea what that meant. She certainly hoped not. Maybe in ShopRite, near the bran.

"Absolutely. Good night. Good night, Oren. Wonderful party."

She took Greenberg by the arm and propelled him to the front door. "Come on," she said through her teeth, "let's get the hell out of here while we can."

Once outside, on the long stairway, he chuckled. "I don't think I quite fit in at parties like that."

"You mean," Jane said, "at parties in honor of former royalty?"

"No, parties where so much bull is being slung."

They both laughed. Reaching the road—there were no sidewalks in this old part of town—they walked alongside the line of cars until they found Greenberg's.

"I am positively starving," Jane said, getting in. "I do believe Rhoda was right."

"Yeah, feelin' a mite empty myself. I could go for one of Giorgio's veal parmesan heroes right now. What about you?"

"You're on," she said, taking his arm as he pulled the car away from the curb. Then she had a thought. "Wait. I can't have food like that. It's not Stillkin."

He looked at her, waiting, his expression saying nothing.

"Aw, screw it," she burst out. "I'll trade you half of your veal parm for half my eggplant parm."

"Deal."

Chapter Eight

In her study late that night, by the glow of her desk lamp, Jane added to her list the name of an editor at Simon & Schuster, then considered the name for a moment, shook her head, and crossed it out. She wrote in its place the name of another editor at the same company. Yes, this person would be right for *The Blue Palindrome*, would better appreciate it.

From the window over her desk she saw headlights coming up Lilac Way. The car, a white BMW, pulled into her driveway, one of its rear doors opened, and Stephanie got out. She leaned into the car, talking animatedly with whoever was inside, shut the door, and started up the walk.

Jane had left the front door unlocked for her. Much as Jane would have liked to ignore her, to let her come in and go up to her room, Jane felt obliged to greet her, especially since this was Stephanie's first night as Jane's guest. She left her study, crossed the living room, and reached the foyer just as Stephanie was coming in. Seeing Jane, Stephanie gave her a smile that could only have been described as dopey. Jane noticed that her face had gone from pink at the cheeks and chin to allover red.

"You missed a really good tiiime," Stephanie said a little sloppily in a singsong voice, emphasizing the last word like a mother telling a child she'd made an error in judgment. "Should have stayed later."

Jane, feeling superior, gave a tight smile of her own and a slight shrug. "I'm glad you had a good time. You must be tired after such a busy day."

"Actually, no. I feel . . . energized. I was just telling that to Faithie and Gav, saying how excited I am to be starting at their company in the morning."

"They gave you a ride?" Jane asked, surprised. "That was Faithie—I mean Faith and Gavin in the car just now?"

"Yeah," Stephanie replied lightly.

For some reason Jane found it amusing that former royalty should have pulled into her driveway, seen her house. How silly, she told herself.

"I wish you'd had a chance to meet them. It's strange. . . . You go to a party in their honor and never even get up close to them."

Was she reprimanding Jane? Jane couldn't be sure. "I'm sure the opportunity will present itself again. Do you think they enjoyed the party?"

"Oh, definitely." Stephanie slipped off her mink and hung it up in the foyer closet. "But it wasn't just fun; it was also profitable." She turned from the closet and gave Jane a sly look. "Faithie and Gav and I stopped for coffee on the way home. They explained to me how their company works. There was some good business for them at that party tonight, starting with that supermarket woman, Lillian Strudel."

"Strohman."

"Right. She's going to do a book with them—her memoirs. In fact, tomorrow Faithie's going to Lillian's house to discuss the project over breakfast."

"Terrific," Jane said with gusto, remembering what Rhoda had said about Carson & Hart.

"Well, nighty-night." Stephanie yawned mightily and started up the stairs.

"Good night, Stephanie." Then Jane remembered something. "Oh, Stephanie."

Stephanie turned, her eyes sleepy slits.

"I'd like to take you to lunch tomorrow if you're free. To celebrate the beginning of your new job."

"Oh," Stephanie said vaguely, "that's nice."

"Then you're free?"

"Um, yeah, sure." Stephanie continued up the stairs.

"Don't do me any favors," Jane mumbled under her breath.

She returned to her study to work on her submission list for *The Blue Palindrome*.

Chapter Nine

———————

Jane checked her watch, though she'd just done so a minute earlier. It was 12:45. She and Stephanie had agreed Jane would pick up Stephanie at her office at 12:30. Jane had offered to come up, which she felt would have been more polite anyway, but for some reason Stephanie had discouraged that, insisting instead that she'd "pop out" at half past twelve.

Jane blew out a great gust of air. She really didn't have time for this. She'd spent the morning calling editors about *The Blue Palindrome,* and the responses had been uniformly enthusiastic. Even now Daniel was taking the manuscript to the Mr. Copy on Route 46, where he and Jane had all of their heavy photocopying done, to have the manuscript duplicated. She could be working on her cover letter—something Jane always put a lot of thought into—instead of sitting here at the curb in front of Puffy and Oren's office building, alternately feeling angry and foolish.

She looked up and saw Greenberg coming toward

her in his car. She waved and he made a shrugging gesture, his hands out, as if to say, "Where is she?"

She shrugged back and waved him on.

It was her own fault. She was the one who'd invited Stephanie to lunch. Why? She knew why. For Kenneth. It would be over soon. Stephanie would get the apartment she wanted, or another one, settle into her new home and her new job, and she and Jane would probably see each other only seldom. Stephanie certainly wasn't the kind of person Jane could be friends with.

Jane decided that if Stephanie didn't come out in the next five minutes, Jane was going in. But just as she had this thought, Stephanie appeared at the side of the building in her mink. She seemed preoccupied, elsewhere, frowning, her head down. She looked up, saw Jane, and waved with a forced little smile. Then she seemed to sink back into a deep preoccupation as she made her way down the front path between carefully tended beds of mixed yellow and orange chrysanthemums.

Stay cheerful, Jane told herself; *be nice.* Stephanie reached the car and got in.

"Hi!" Jane said. "Busy day, huh?"

"Mm." Stephanie stared straight ahead, as if she'd just given directions to a cabbie and was waiting for the car to move.

Jane pulled away from the curb and headed along Packer Road, turning right onto Highland. *"I've* certainly had a busy morning." She was making herself sick with her falsely bubbly voice. "Did I tell you about the wonderful manuscript I'm submitting? *The Blue Palindrome?"*

"Wh—excuse me?" Stephanie turned to her as if

she'd just been somewhere far away. "What did you say?"

"Nothing. Just chattering. Stephanie, is something wrong? You don't seem yourself. Don't you like your new job?"

"No, no, it's not that. It's fabulous, really."

"It must be fun to work with your old friend." Jane took a left onto Cranmore. They passed the Senior Center on the right, and just after it, Shady Hills Cemetery.

"Isn't that where . . ." Stephanie began.

"Yes. Where Kenneth is buried." Jane glanced at the black wrought-iron fence and the grass and gravestones rising on the gently sloping hill beyond. The old trees that shaded the graves so comfortingly in the summer gave the whole place a grim, stark feeling now, and Jane looked away. Following the curve in the road, she crossed the railroad tracks, then turned left into the parking lot of Eleanor's, the best restaurant in Shady Hills.

The quaint former gristmill sat on the bank of the Morris River, which looked cold and murky on this gray day.

Inside, Jane asked for a table in the restaurant's small back room, which looked out on the mill wheel and millpond. They both ordered salads. Stephanie gazed out the window, as if transfixed by the gray-green water.

"Stephanie," Jane said gently, "I don't know you very well, but it's easy to see something's bothering you. Do you want to tell me?"

Stephanie turned to her, her mouth slightly parted. "I was just thinking about Faithie. She behaved so strangely this morning . . ."

"Strangely? How?"

"She came in late because of her breakfast with Lillian Strohman. You remember, that woman from the party last night who's going to do a book with Faithie and Gav?"

"Yes, I remember."

"Faith was . . . I've never seen her that way. She looked as if—as if she'd seen a ghost. Totally preoccupied, wandering around the office but not knowing what she was doing. It was as if she was—I don't know, trying to work out some complicated puzzle in her head. At one point Gavin asked her if something was wrong, and she snapped at him that she was fine. But I know Faith Carson, and she was anything but fine."

"What do you think it was? Something Lillian had said to her?"

Stephanie shook her head quickly. "What could she have said? They were just meeting to discuss Lillian's book."

"Maybe Lillian had changed her mind. That might have upset Faith."

"It wasn't that. I heard Faith asking Sam—that's her son; he works there—to get a contract ready for Lillian."

Jane hadn't thought about Faith's children. If Jane remembered correctly, she had a son and a daughter, who would of course be grown up now.

"Anyway," Stephanie said, shaking herself a little as if to clear her mind, "we'll probably never know what it was. Maybe something between her and Gavin, a private thing. But it sure wasn't what I expected on my first day at Carson & Hart."

Their salads arrived and Jane speared a forkful. "So what's it like there?"

Stephanie pondered. "It's an odd setup. Of course, there are still boxes everywhere, and things are a little up in the air—you know, confused—because of that, but I could still pretty much see how things work.

"Faithie and Gav run the place, of course. They work on all of the bigger projects, the real moneymakers. Then there's Sam, whom I just mentioned, and his sister, Kate."

Jane frowned. "For some reason I thought the children's names were different."

"They were. Sam's real name is Surya. He's twenty now—hard to believe. And Kate is really Ketaki. She's nineteen. When Faith and Gavin and the kids came to the States, Faith encouraged them to take on American names."

"I see," Jane said. "It hadn't occurred to me that Faith's children would be working at the company."

"I was surprised, too. Neither one of them was interested in going to college, even after the expensive educations Faith had given them. They've both been a source of great disappointment for Faith. She's told me she believes that Ravi's laziness, his lack of ambition, was passed down to them.

"Anyway, Sam seems to be nothing more than a glorified secretary. I hadn't seen him in a few years, but now that I see him as a grownup, I can tell that Faith is right—he has zero ambition. He's odd, too."

"Odd? In what way?"

"It's hard to explain. He seems to think he's some kind of lady-killer. He's very good-looking, I'll give him that, but he behaves as if he has the power to make women swoon at his feet, when he really just comes off like some kind of . . . lounge lizard!"

"*Very* odd."

"Now Kate, she's a different story."

"What is she like?"

"Solid. Quite serious. She's always been like that—intense. She's managing editor at the company. She's also quite a talented photographer. She's got an actual studio set up in the office to take pictures for the jackets of the company's books."

"Interesting. Is that the whole staff?"

"Pretty much. There's a young guy named Mel, I think, who works in the mail room. And an older Hungarian woman named Norma, who's the cleaning lady, but not just for Carson & Hart. She cleans the whole building. Not all at once, of course."

Jane maintained a cheerful countenance, though in truth she was bored senseless. The rest of the meal was an endurance test, Stephanie blabbing on and on about the apartment she'd loved so much and how she just *had* to get it. Not once did Stephanie ask anything related to Jane or anyone in her world. Stephanie, Jane had come to realize, was a true narcissist, and narcissists are boring.

Mercifully, as soon as the waiter had taken away their plates, Stephanie looked at her watch and announced that she'd better get back to work. "Wouldn't want to take too long a lunch break on my first day." She put her bag on her lap, brought out a compact and lipstick, and got to work on her face. Meanwhile, Jane paid the bill.

A few minutes later, pulling up in front of the office building, Jane offered to come in. "I'd love to get a look at this place. And of course I want to meet the famous Faith Carson."

"You will," Stephanie said, pushing open her door, "but not today." She got out, slammed the door, and scurried up the walk, not looking back for either a good-bye or a thank-you. Jane had expected neither.

"Missus, what the devil have you got on?"

Florence stood at the foot of the stairs, staring up at Jane, who had just put on an iridescent orange nylon running suit.

"I'm going jogging," Jane said matter-of-factly, though she felt anything but matter-of-fact. She couldn't say the Stillkin Diet wasn't working, because she wasn't really on it. Tonight Florence had offered to make another Stillkin recipe for Jane's dinner, but Jane had thanked her and declined, choosing instead to eat spaghetti and meatballs with garlic bread along with everyone else. The answer, she decided, was exercise. She would jog every night until her vacation, and even during her vacation she would spend at least an hour each day in the hotel's gym.

Florence laughed. "I need sunglasses to look at you in that! I didn't even know you owned it."

Jane shrugged, growing irritated. "I've had it for a year, bought it at Sports Authority." She left out that the running suit had fit much more loosely when she'd bought it—and that this was the first time she'd ever worn it.

"Oh my!" came Stephanie's voice behind her.

With a little roll of her eyes, Jane turned, forcing a smile. "I'm going jogging." She headed for the front door.

"Ooh, can I come?"

Jane stopped, surprised.

"I jogged a lot in Boston. If you'll wait a second, I'll put on my sweats."

"Okay," Jane said, deeply disappointed that she wouldn't have this time alone, away from Stephanie, after all.

Stephanie ran upstairs. A moment later Nick wandered into the foyer, Winky in his arms, and looked at Jane as if she were from another planet. "Mom, you look like a carrot."

"Now, that is not a nice way to speak to your mother," Florence said, suppressing a smile. "And what have you two been up to?"

"Winky and I were doing homework. Now Winky wants to go outside."

Lately they had been allowing Winky to go outside from time to time. At first Jane had resisted this idea, but for some time Winky had made it clear by scratching at the doors and windows that she wanted to go out. Jane had spoken to Dr. Singh, Winky's veterinarian, about the idea, and Dr. Singh had said it was fine to let Winky out because she had her claws. Another point in Winky's favor was that Lilac Way was a quiet street, heavily wooded, with only a few houses on it.

Nick opened the front door and Winky shot out.

"Ready!" Stephanie announced, descending the stairs. She wore a gray sweat suit that fit her snugly. Jane had to admit she had a nice figure—shapely but not fat, just right.

"All right, ladies," Florence said, sounding like a gym teacher, "I want you to work up a good sweat."

"You got it, coach," Jane said, running in place, and led the way outside.

It was a mild evening, more like late September than November. Jane took a deep breath of the sweet air. "Lovely."

"Mm," Stephanie agreed, hopping in place beside her.

Jane went through the space in the holly hedge and to the left, down the street toward Grange Road. Stephanie jogged alongside her.

"Well," Jane said, feeling as if she should make conversation, "how did the rest of your first day go?"

"Fine." Stephanie sounded thoughtful. Then she turned to Jane with a bright expression. "I've already been put in charge of a special project. It's that cat book I mentioned to you."

"That's terrific. Congratulations."

"Yes, I'm very pleased. It's called *Mew's Who's Who.*"

Jane turned to her with a frown. "It's called what?"

"*Mew's Who's Who.*" Stephanie's tone was quite serious. "It's a biographical directory of cats. You've heard of *Who's Who* for people. Well, this one's for cats!"

"But how—" Jane began, not understanding.

"Here's how it works. It's very clever, really." Stephanie slipped a stiff lock of black hair behind her right ear. "The company buys lists of cat owners—you know, from cat magazines, cat organizations, that kind of thing. Then they mail out about a zillion questionnaires. It's a riot," she said with a chuckle. "People fill out the questionnaire so their cats can be *considered* for the directory. Of course, every cat gets in. And most important, practically every cat *owner* buys a directory."

Jane found this kind of vanity directory publishing offensive but smiled politely. "And you're in charge of this project?"

"That's right," Stephanie said proudly. Then her mouth opened and she looked at Jane. "I just thought of something! Kate says she needs a cat to pose for the jacket. How about Winky?"

Jane stared at Stephanie. "Winky?"

"Sure. Wouldn't that be priceless? I bet Nick would love it."

"That's true." Jane turned right onto Grange Road. She smiled. "I guess it would be kind of fun."

"It would be perfect!" Then Stephanie seemed to have a thought and looked troubled. "I wonder if Winky is the sort of cat Kate has in mind?"

"What do you mean?" Jane asked, as if someone were insulting her child.

"She is kind of . . . funny-looking."

"Funny-looking?"

"Yes, her fur is all those mixed-up colors."

"She's tortoiseshell. That's how tortoiseshell cats are supposed to look. *Mottled.* Stephanie," Jane said solemnly, "Winky is a beautiful cat."

"All right, then." Stephanie sounded convinced. "I'll speak to Kate about it first thing in the morning."

"Don't forget to mention to Kate that Winky has been in *People* magazine," Jane said, referring to an article the magazine had run about Jane's finding her previous nanny, Marlene.

"That's right." Stephanie threw back her head and laughed. "Winky the star."

They jogged a bit farther on Grange; then Jane suggested that they turn around, or else they would have to go a considerable distance to get home by way of Packer and Oakmont.

After a brief silence, Jane said, "So, did Faith seem more herself after you got back from lunch?"

Stephanie's face grew troubled. "Actually, just as I was coming in, she was rushing out. She told me she had an appointment in New York. She was in a big hurry. Gavin was standing behind her and he asked where she was going, but Faith was already out the door and didn't answer him."

"I imagine she has lots of appointments in New York."

"True. I think Gavin was asking her because of the way she was acting—so hurried and troubled. Something was still not right with her."

They jogged back to the house in silence. It was completely dark now, the streetlamps casting dim circles of bluish light. Between the lamps there was virtually no light at all, and Jane resolved to buy some reflective gear for her future jogs. She couldn't remember the last time she'd jogged and was becoming out of breath, but she tried hard to hide this from Stephanie, who didn't appear winded in the slightest.

As they approached the hedge in front of Jane's house, Winky appeared on the strip of grass running between the driveway and right edge of Jane's property, where a low juniper hedge grew. She let out a quiet mew to make the women aware of her presence, but Jane had already seen her. She hurried up to the cat and scooped her up in her arms.

"Winky, you're going to be a star!"

Stephanie looked a little uncomfortable. "If Kate says it's okay."

"Oh, right." Jane looked back into Winky's eyes. "We need final approval, Wink, but it looks good." Jane led the way into the house, where they found Nick putting on his coat.

"Where are you going?" Jane asked.

He saw Winky in Jane's arms and grinned broadly. "Nowhere now. I've been calling Winky for ten minutes. Where did you find her?"

"By the driveway," Jane replied with a shrug. "I'd say

she found us. Hey, wait till you hear this." She glanced mischievously at Stephanie. "It's not a hundred percent final, but Stephanie may get our Miss Winky on the jacket of a book!"

"Wink!" Nick cried, taking the squirming cat from Jane's arms, and he kissed her so hard on the top of her head that she let out a yowl. "My star cat! First *People* magazine, now this. Hey, Mom, maybe Winky could star in a movie!"

Florence appeared from the family room, smiling broadly. "I couldn't help overhearing. Winky," she said, taking her from Nick's arms, "you are going to be a movie star." A mirror in a gilt frame hung on the wall of the foyer, and Florence began stepping slowly and dramatically toward it, holding Winky's face up close to her own.

"We're ready for our close-up, Mr. De Mille!" she said in a low Gloria Swanson voice, then threw back her head in joyous laughter.

Chapter Ten

"Why would I take twenty thousand for two books when I wouldn't take ten for one?" Jane barked into the phone, and rolled her eyes. Sometimes she wondered if editors had to take a special idiot test as part of their job applications.

At the other end of the line, Arliss Krauss, executive editor at Millennium House, made a sound of impatience. "Because we're making more of a commitment, *obviously*. Your author will have the security of knowing we believe in her enough to agree to two books now."

"Bullshit. If the first book doesn't sell well enough for you, you'll find a reason to cancel the second one. If Peg delivers ten minutes late you'll use that as your excuse. Or you'll just say it's due to 'market conditions.' Stop wasting my time. One book at fifteen thousand or good-bye."

"Why only one?"

"Because frankly, Arliss, Peg and I aren't sure we want to commit to two books with any publisher."

"Confident, aren't you," Arliss observed smugly.

"You're that sure you can just find her another publisher? For yet another down-home Southern novel?"

"I'm not sure of anything, not in today's publishing climate. Next week we'll probably be able to read every book ever written on a handheld device receiving signals from satellites."

"Hmm, not a bad idea," Arliss said, showing uncharacteristic lightheartedness. "Anyway"—her voice grew serious again—"would we have a deal at fifteen thou?"

"Fifteen thou, North American rights only."

Arliss was silent for a moment. "Okay," she said at last. "You got it."

"Not yet, I haven't. I've got to run it past Peg, remember?"

"Oh, right. Then get back to me. Thanks, Jane."

"Mm," Jane said, unable to bring herself to say "You're welcome," and hung up. The moment she did, her intercom buzzed.

"Jane," Daniel said, "Florence called about five minutes ago. She asked you to call her, says it's important."

Jane dialed the house.

"Missus, thank you for getting back to me. I hate to bother you, truly, but I really have to talk to you. Are you busy at lunchtime? Is there any way you could come home?"

"Of course. What is it, Florence? Are you all right?"

"I'm fine, missus. But . . . I'd rather explain it to you when you get here."

"Sure, sure. I'll be there in five."

She grabbed her bag and went out to the reception area. Daniel looked up, concern on his face. "Everything all right?"

"Don't know," Jane said, troubled, taking her coat

from the closet and putting it on. "Florence is in a tizzy. I'll have lunch at home, shouldn't be gone long."

Florence was waiting for Jane in the back hall, just inside the door from the garage. "Thanks for coming home, missus."

"Of course. Now what's wrong?"

Florence wrung her hands as she walked with her into the kitchen. "Do you want coffee?"

"No, thank you, Florence." Jane sat down at the kitchen table. "Why don't you just tell me what's wrong."

"All right." Florence sat down facing her. "Missus, I need for you to make me a promise."

"A promise?" Jane frowned.

"What I am about to tell you—you must promise me you won't repeat to Detective Greenberg."

What could Florence possibly want to tell her? "Now you've got me really scared!" Jane said, trying to sound less concerned than she felt. "What'd you do, Florence, kill someone?"

"No, missus!" Florence cried, taking her quite seriously. "Do you promise?"

"Yes, yes, I promise—against my better judgment. Now out with it."

"All right. All right. Missus," Florence said, her large, pretty brown eyes looking directly into Jane's, "have I ever told you about my friend Una, who is also from Trinidad?"

Jane thought. "Una . . . I don't think so."

Florence shook her head. "I don't think I've ever mentioned her to you. She's kind of a new friend for me. Anyway, Una works as a maid here in Shady Hills."

"I see. Who does she work for?"

"A Mrs. Strohman."

"Lillian Strohman?" Jane sat up. "How interesting."

"Do you know her?"

"I met her at Puffy Chapin's party Wednesday night."

"A very rich lady. A widow. Her husband owned a chain of supermarkets."

"So I've heard."

"Anyway, late this morning I got a phone call from Una. She was hysterical; I've never heard her like that. Something happened earlier today, something awful, and she didn't know who else to tell about it. She told me, and I'm going to tell you, because I don't know what to do about it, but something should definitely be done."

"What happened?"

"Well." Florence tried to compose herself. "Quite early this morning, while Mrs. Strohman was out of the house—she goes to her health club every morning—Una was in Mrs. Strohman's bedroom suite, putting away some clothes she'd just ironed. All of a sudden she heard a funny sound, and when she looked up, she saw a man outside the window, getting ready to climb into the room!"

"Good heavens!"

Florence nodded quickly. "He was standing on a roof that runs just outside this window, and he was working very hard prying open the window."

"Did he see Una?"

"No, thank God. She's sure of that. Very slowly she put down the clothes and hid in one of Mrs. Strohman's closets."

"Why didn't she just scream or something?"

"I asked her that. She said she was afraid that if he

saw her he would shoot her or come after her. She was alone in the house."

"I see. Go on."

"The closet Una was hiding in has louvered doors, so she could see into the bedroom, through the slats. So she watched. This man, this burglar, he got the window open and climbed in. Then he crossed the room and went right into Mrs. Strohman's dressing room. Una said it was odd . . ."

"What was odd?"

"The way the man walked right to the dressing room, as if he knew exactly where it was. He also knew exactly where Mrs. Strohman's safe was in the dressing room."

"He opened her safe?"

Florence's head bobbed up and down, her expression one of horror. "He had a *tool* with him, some kind of drill. From the closet, Una could only see him partially, but she says it was a drill and that it was quite loud. He used it several places—"

"The hinges," Jane said.

"Yes, I suppose, and then he got it open. Una saw him take out Mrs. Strohman's jewelry box. Then he took a sack, like a big pillowcase, out of his pocket and emptied the whole jewelry box into it."

"And then what did he do?"

"He hurried back out the window."

"Did she see his face?"

"Oh, yes. Twice. He had to pass the closet to get to the dressing room. Una says he was young, with black hair. Not thin but not too fat—he had a little roll of fat around his middle, over his belt.

"Una was so scared she thought she would have a heart attack. Now she feels terribly guilty."

"She certainly shouldn't feel guilty. She's right—he

might very well have hurt her. Happens every day. But what I don't understand is why I had to promise not to tell any of this to the police?"

Florence looked down, as if ashamed on Una's behalf. "Because, missus, Una is in the United States illegally. No one knows she's here, that she works for Mrs. Strohman. Una won't even tell Mrs. Strohman what she saw, because Una knows that Mrs. Strohman would tell the police that Una saw the burglar, and that the police would force Una to tell them what she saw. Then the police would do some checking up on Una, and she would be sent home. You know how strict they are about these things nowadays."

"True."

"So you see, missus, why we are in such a dilemma? Una asked me what I thought she should do. I said I would speak to you, in confidence. Poor Mrs. Strohman doesn't know yet that her jewelry is missing. Una is even afraid Mrs. Strohman might think *she* took it!"

"Well, *that's* just ridiculous," Jane said dismissively. "You really think Lillian would believe Una would do such a thing? And if she would, that she would actually take a drill to the hinges of the safe?"

"Perhaps not."

"I see why you wanted me to promise not to tell Detective Greenberg about this, and now I'm sorry I made that promise."

"Oh, please, missus, don't tell him. There has to be some other way to help Mrs. Strohman without getting poor Una in trouble. She has family in Trinidad and sends money to them every month. Without her salary they would starve."

"There's got to be some way—"

"But I haven't told you the whole story," Florence said.

"There's *more?*"

"I am afraid so, missus. A *lot* more. As soon as the burglar went back out the window, Una hurried downstairs and looked out a window overlooking the back lawn. The man ran into a narrow strip of woods. Una rushed out the back door of the house and went to the edge of these woods. The man had reached the other side of the woods, where there is a road. A dark car pulled right up to where he was standing. A woman got out of the car and spoke to the man. He had the sack tucked into his trousers. He took it and opened it up and let the woman look inside. She rummaged around in it and pulled out something. It must have been a big piece of jewelry, because Una said it flashed very bright in the sun. The woman took her purse out of her bag and handed the man some money. He tucked the sack back into his trousers and ran across the road and into the trees there. The woman got back in her car and drove away."

Jane sat transfixed, imagining this scene.

Florence's eyes grew immense. "Missus, the woman, the woman in the car. Una knew who she was! She knew who the woman was because she went to Mrs. Strohman's house yesterday for breakfast. But even if she hadn't, anyone would have known her."

Jane waited. "Who?"

"Faith Carson," Florence said hollowly, her eyes wide.

"But how can that be?" Jane scoffed. "It's ridiculous! Faith Carson, commissioning burglaries?"

"I know, it does sound ridiculous, but it is true."

"I can't believe it," Jane said, dumbfounded.

"What should we do?" Florence asked pleadingly. "What can Una do?"

"She must go to the police."

"But she can't. I've just told you that, missus; she can't. She would be shipped right back to Port of Spain."

Jane leaned forward on the table. "Florence, I won't break my promise; don't worry about that. But I want you to reconsider. At the very least, consider this: What if I were to speak to Stanley, tell him *what* was seen, but not who saw it?"

"Well . . ." Florence nibbled the inside of her bottom lip. "He would know it was Una because she was the only person in the house at that time. The cook, Yvette, was out buying groceries. There's a man who does the outdoor work, sort of a gardener. Una doesn't know where he was—outside somewhere. There's another maid, a girl named Britt, but she was out grocery shopping with Yvette."

Jane thought for a moment. "Florence, I'll speak to Detective Greenberg, but as my friend. I'll make him promise not to do anything about Una if I tell him what she saw. Then he can tell us what he thinks we should do."

"Do you think you can trust him, missus?"

"Stanley? Absolutely."

"All right, if you think so. I suppose it's the only thing we can do."

Rising, Jane patted Florence's hand. "That's some story, Florence. Looks as if publishing isn't the only business Faith Carson has come to Shady Hills to conduct."

* * *

Greenberg paced behind his desk, then leaned against the back wall of his office, cinder blocks painted gray. "Unbelievable."

"Don't forget your promise."

"Which I should never have made."

"But you did, and if you break it I'll never speak to you again."

"You know I wouldn't."

"I know," Jane said, smiling. "So what do we do?"

"Mrs. Strohman reported the burglary about an hour ago. We sent a couple of guys over there. They said it looks like a professional job. We can certainly look for a man fitting the description Una gave Florence, and we sure as hell are going to keep a tight watch on Faith Carson." He shook his head in wonder. "This woman was a princess!"

"A queen!"

"And now she's fencing jewelry."

"Hey," Jane said with a smile, "a girl's gotta do what a girl's gotta do."

He laughed. "Guess business isn't very good at Carson & Hart."

"Guess not."

Stephanie wasn't her usual gabby self at dinner that night. She stared for long moments at nothing in particular, preoccupied as she had been at lunch.

"Miss Stephanie," Florence said softly, "can I get you something else to eat?"

Stephanie glanced down at her plate of broiled pork chops, rice pilaf, and peas—one of Florence's favorite Friday dinners—as if it had just materialized before her.

She gave Florence a too-sweet smile. "No, thank you, Florence. This is delicious."

Jane frowned and noticed that Florence did, too. How could Stephanie know her dinner was delicious? She hadn't touched it.

Nick, as if sensing a need for conversation, spoke up. "Scott's dad heard some more about the bum down in the village."

"I've told you not to call him that," Jane said.

"That *gentleman* down in the village," Nick said punctiliously, and Jane gave him a warning look. "He escaped from a loony bin."

"What!" Florence said.

"That's right. He's schizo—" He struggled with the word. "Schizophrenic. He hears voices. He's crazy—I mean mentally ill, but he doesn't have his medicine."

"How ridiculous," Jane muttered, cutting her pork chop.

"You never know," Stephanie murmured, surprising everyone. They all looked at her. "You can think a person is a certain way . . . you can think it for years . . . and they turn out to be someone else entirely. No matter how well you think you know someone, you never really do, not *really.*"

Jane slid her a speculating look. Did she know about Lillian Strohman's jewelry and Faith?

They all waited for Stephanie to continue, but she slipped back into her reverie.

"More rice, Mr. Nicholas?" Florence asked cheerily.

"No. I hate the rice. It has onions. I've *told* you not to put in onions, Florence."

Florence looked guilty. "Can't you learn to like them?"

"I don't mind how they taste, but they're slimy."

Nick, apparently bored with this subject, turned to Stephanie and tilted his head pensively. "A penny for your thoughts!"

"Hm?" She sat up, startled. "I beg your pardon?"

"A penny for your thoughts," Nick repeated.

She gave him a kind smile. "All right. My thoughts were kind of a riddle."

"I love riddles!"

"Good. Here it is. How can the light change in a room with no windows?"

Jane frowned, bewildered.

"I know!" Nick cried. "Turn off the light!"

"Good guess, but it's not the answer."

Nick thought for a moment. "Okay, I give up. How can the light change in a room with no windows?"

They all waited. After a moment, Stephanie looked up and gave a little shake of her head. "I don't know!"

Nick's mouth dropped. Florence caught herself staring in puzzlement and busied herself with her dinner.

Jane watched Stephanie out of the corner of her left eye. Odd, she thought; decidedly odd. Stephanie may not have known the answer to her own riddle, but she knew something.

Yes, she knew something . . .

Chapter Eleven

In her study, Jane drew squiggles and curlicues on the margin of her notepad, next to the draft of her submission letter for *The Blue Palindrome*. She gazed out the window above her desk. On the front lawn, Nick and his friend Aaron tossed a football back and forth, laughing and calling each other silly names. She smiled, wishing Kenneth could see this.

The phone rang. It was Greenberg.

"Are we still on tonight?" he asked.

"Sure, if you want to." She knew she didn't sound enthusiastic, but she couldn't help it. She was still deeply troubled by what Florence had told her about Una the day before. She also knew Stanley was upset with her for telling him what she had but insisting that he keep most of the important details to himself. She didn't particularly feel like going out, but she thought she should make an effort to see Stanley, especially since she'd be leaving for her vacation in a week.

"Sure I want to go out," he said, his tone flat.

"You don't sound any more enthusiastic than I do," she joked.

"Sorry. We found something today, something bad."

She sat up. "What?"

"A body. In Adams Pond."

"What!" Adams Pond was across the street from Nick's school, Hillmont Elementary, and not far at all from Jane's house. "Who is it—was it?"

"A local small-time criminal type, a character by the name of Roy Lynch. Young guy," Greenberg said, a meaningful note creeping into his voice. "Black hair, *a roll of fat around his middle . . .*"

Jane swallowed. "I see."

"Yes, I thought you would. Sounds familiar, huh?"

"Was it . . . an accident?"

There was a silence as he hesitated. "I get into trouble for telling you things, but I'll tell you this because you should know. It appears he was stabbed, then held under the water. Someone was taking no chances."

"Who found him?" Adams Pond was completely surrounded by woods.

"Three little boys chasing a runaway dog. The body had washed up at the edge of the pond."

"How awful."

"We're looking into his background and already know a lot. I'd actually heard about this guy. He was a professional thief with a history of convictions for various acts of larceny. Lived in Boonton," he said, referring to a town that bordered on Shady Hills. "We searched his apartment and found jewelry—a lot of it. Many of the pieces are the ones stolen from Mrs. Strohman, but she says there's still a piece, a very important piece, missing."

"Stanley, I—"

"You've put me in a very difficult position, Jane. I'm sorry," he said, sounding downright angry now, "but I think I can't make it tonight. I'll talk to you soon." And he hung up.

Slowly putting down the receiver, Jane frowned, deeply troubled by this conversation. A man was dead, perhaps because of her. Outside, Nick, cradling the football, plowed headlong into Aaron and collapsed on top of him. They both howled with laughter, struggling on the brown grass. Their image faded, and Jane saw the bloated body of a young man lying half out of the water of Adams Pond.

With sudden resolve, she got up from her chair and went in search of Florence.

Florence often went out on weekends, but today she was in her room. Jane heard her moving around inside. She knocked softly on the door.

"Yes, come in," Florence called.

Jane poked her head around the door. Florence was sitting up in bed reading *Queen of Heaven*. She smiled at Jane. "Morning, missus. Is something wrong?"

"Florence, we have to talk. May I come in?"

Florence's face grew concerned. "Of course. Is something the matter with Nick?"

"No, he's fine. It's not about him." Jane entered the room and sat down on Florence's bed. "Florence, I just spoke with Detective Greenberg and he told me something upsetting. I'm going to tell you what he said, in total confidence, because it's important for you to know it." She repeated everything Greenberg had said: the little boys finding Roy Lynch in Adams Pond, Lynch's physical description, the jewelry found in his apartment.

Florence put a hand to her mouth. "It's the man Una saw."

"Without question. Florence, you *have* to speak with Una again, try to get her to tell the police firsthand what she saw."

Florence set down the book on her night table. "Yes, of course you're right, missus. I'll call her now." There was a phone on the night table, and Florence picked up the receiver and dialed.

"Una, it's Florence. Something has happened, something bad. It has to do with what you saw yesterday . . . I don't want to tell you now; I want to come over there and speak with you. Mrs. Stuart and I, we both want to speak with you . . . I'll tell you when we see you . . . No, you won't get in trouble—Una, stop screaming! . . . Yes, you can trust her; I promise you that. She is a good person . . . Good. Can we come over now? . . . All right, we will. We're coming over there just now."

Hanging up, Florence turned to Jane. "She says we should come over right now. Mrs. Strohman isn't home. That makes things easier."

"All right," Jane said, already at the door, "let's go. I'll tell Nick he has to wait for us inside and that Aaron has to go home now. We'll drop him off on our way to Mrs. Strohman's."

"Can't Miss Stephanie watch him for a little while?"

"She's not here. She's off with Myrtle Lovesey, the real estate agent, looking at apartments. Apparently the one she wanted fell through."

* * *

Lillian Strohman's house, which was built of pale stone and resembled a castle, made Puffy's look like a cottage. A wide drive made of paving stones climbed the slope of an immense lawn and passed beneath an arched porte-cochere in the house itself.

When they were halfway up the drive, Florence said, "Una asked us to come around to the back door, so we should go through here." She pointed to the archway. "There's a place to park in the back."

"Why does she want us to come to the back?"

"Because that's the door to the kitchen, and she's working in there right now. Or she might be in the laundry room, but that's right off the kitchen. She didn't want us coming to the front door, all public—you know."

Jane drove through the porte-cochere, and they emerged onto a wide paved area behind the house.

As they got out of the car, Florence said, "Sometimes Una doesn't hear the doorbell when she's in the laundry room, because the washer and dryer make a lot of noise, so she said she would leave the door unlocked for us."

"Okay." Approaching the kitchen door, Jane noticed that some construction work was in progress. The ground between the paved area and the door itself had been torn up—chunks of concrete lay off to one side— and a wooden frame had been put in place, the kind of frame used to contain poured concrete. The floor of this frame consisted of exposed earth as well as large amounts of white dust from the broken-up concrete.

"Oh," Florence said, seeing this mess and remembering, "Una said to watch where we walk. Mrs. Strohman is having this part replaced."

"So I see," Jane said, irritated that no boards had been put down between the concrete that was still intact and the door. Carefully she and Florence picked their way across. Jane's feet sank into the earth and concrete dust; she could see white powder collecting on her shoes.

The door had a window in it, but it was covered with a shirred white curtain, so they couldn't see into the kitchen. Jane turned the knob and the door opened. She was about to enter the house when Florence placed her hand on Jane's.

"Missus, I'm thinking it would be best if I go in first and speak to Una, tell her again that you're okay. Would that be all right? It will only take a minute or two."

"Yes, if you think so," Jane said, and stood aside so Florence could go in. With a nervous smile, Florence stepped into the kitchen, which Jane could see was large but old-fashioned, as many of the kitchens in these old mansions were. Florence left the door ajar.

Jane turned away from the door and gazed up at the house. From here it was clear that the building was a jumble of levels at various heights; she could easily see how a burglar might have climbed up and used the roof of one level to gain access to Lillian Strohman's bedroom.

"Missus!"

Jane jumped. It was Florence, shrieking in terror, shrieking as Jane had never heard her shriek. Jane spun around and pushed open the door. It nearly hit Florence, who had been running toward it. Her face was twisted in terror and tears streamed down her cheeks.

"Missus—" Panting, she leaned on Jane, apparently unable to say any more.

Jane's heart pounded. "What is it? Florence, what happened?"

"Missus," Florence gasped. "It's Una. She's . . . dead!"

Chapter Twelve

"Dead?" Jane echoed. "But—how?"

"Come see," Florence said, and as she led the way across the kitchen toward a room Jane could see was the laundry room; she walked slowly, cautiously, as if afraid of someone lurking in the shadows.

At the door to the laundry room she stood aside. "In there."

Jane looked in. She saw a washer and dryer, a table for folding clothes, an ironing board and iron, several lines hung with bags of clothespins. "Florence, there's no one in here."

"On—on the door, missus," Florence said, gesturing to Jane that she should look on the other side.

Taking a deep breath, Jane did—and froze. "Oh dear God."

Una, whom Jane had never seen before, had been a petite woman. Her short slim body in a white maid's uniform hung on the back of the door like some article of clothing on a hook. Indeed, it must have been a hook she hung from, her arms dangling at her sides, her shoes—white Nikes—two feet off the floor.

From the center of Una's chest protruded the dark wood handle of what appeared to be a kitchen knife, a large kitchen knife. Glossy red-brown blood soaked the front of her white blouse around the blade. Jane looked at Una's face. Her eyes were shut tight, as if she still felt the pain of the blade entering her chest. Her mouth was set in a little tight-lipped line. Jane couldn't help noticing that Una had been a pretty young woman, with a flawless coffee-colored complexion and short-clipped curly black hair on a well-shaped head.

"Missus . . ." Florence stood off to one side, where she could see Jane but not Una. She held both her hands to her mouth, as if she were about to be sick. "What do we do?"

Jane sprung to action, taking charge. "We get out of here, for one thing. Come on, Florence," she said, taking the younger woman by the arm and leading her firmly out the kitchen door. "Now, I want you to go sit in the car and wait for me." Florence hesitated, her expression questioning whether this was the right thing to do. "Go ahead," Jane urged. "I'm going to call Detective Greenberg."

Florence obeyed, walking with a sort of weak limp, as if she'd been injured herself, and getting laboriously into the car.

Jane took her cell phone from her bag, dialed the police station, and asked for Greenberg.

"He's out, Jane," Buzzi at the desk told her. "I'll tell him you—"

"It's an *emergency*, Buzzi. Put me through to him."

Buzzi must have immediately understood the gravity of the situation, because he said, "All right, I'll patch you through," very quickly; there was a brief pause and then Greenberg came on the line.

"Jane?" His voice sounded hollow. "Jane, what's the matter?"

"Stanley, I'm at Lillian Strohman's house. There's been a murder."

"A murder! Who? Mrs. Strohman?"

"No, her maid, Una. Stanley," Jane said, and burst into tears, "it's horrible. She's been stabbed and hung on a door like a towel and I—" She stopped, a thought occurring to her, and looked around the yard, at the dark forest encircling the small yard. "Stanley, what if the person—"

"Jane, I want you to listen to me. Where are you?"

"I told you!" she screamed into the tiny phone. "At Lillian Strohman's."

"I know that," Greenberg said patiently. "But where, exactly."

She forced herself to calm down. "In the back, near the kitchen door."

"Where's your car?"

"Over there."

"Where?"

"In a parking area right in front of me. Florence is with me. Una is—was her friend. Stanley, Una's the one who—"

"I know who she is, Jane. Is anyone else in the house, that you know of?"

"I don't think so, no. Everyone's out. Or at least they were a little before we got here. Everyone except Una."

"Okay, here's what I want you to do. Get in your car and lock your doors and drive back down to the road. Park in front of the house next door and wait for me. I'm on my way; I'm already on Highland."

"All right, Stanley, I'll do that." Still holding the phone to her ear, Jane ran to the car and got in beside Florence, who sat crying, her face in her hands. "Florence, lock your door. Lock the back doors."

Florence looked up, nodded quickly, and complied, reaching behind her into the backseat.

"Jane," Greenberg said, "you can hang up now; I'm just turning onto Fenwyck. The important thing is that you and Florence get out of there."

"Okay, we're getting out," Jane said, and in her agitation she clicked off the phone, tossed it onto the console between her and Florence's seats, and started the car with a roar. She backed up in a K-turn so fast the wheels screeched, then drove back under the archway.

"Where are we going, missus?" Florence asked, looking about them as they plummeted down the driveway.

"He said to wait in the car in front of the house next door. That's over there," Jane said, pointing to a smaller Tudor across the street and a little to the left. She pulled onto the road, turned into the Tudor's driveway, and backed out so she was facing in the other direction, the direction from which Stanley would come.

At that moment his car appeared. "Thank God," Jane breathed, and she and Florence flipped up their door locks and jumped out of the car. He squealed to a stop on the other side of the road, at the foot of Mrs. Strohman's lawn, and got out.

Jane rushed up to him and cried against his chest, felt his arms fold around her. "Stanley, it's horrible; you won't believe it."

"My poor little friend," Florence said a few feet away.

A car, a midnight-blue Mercedes, appeared from the opposite direction. Jane saw that its driver was Lillian Strohman. With a look of consternation, she stopped the car where Greenberg and the two women stood and rolled down her window. "What's going on? What's happened?"

Greenberg went up to the car. "Mrs. Strohman, I have some upsetting news. Your maid, Una, has been murdered."

"Murdered!"

He nodded. "Mrs. Stuart and Miss Price here found her."

The old woman's face went from a healthy rosiness to the white, it occurred to Jane, of a maggot, a yellow-white. She took a deep breath, swallowed. Great beads of sweat broke out on her brow, and her eyes began to close; clearly she was about to pass out.

Greenberg, seeing this, spun around and said to Jane, "You and Florence go and wait for me at the station. I'm going to call for an ambulance for Mrs. Strohman." He ran to his car.

"Come on, Florence," Jane said, and with a reluctant glance back at poor Mrs. Strohman, she got into her own car, waited for Florence to shut her door, and started the engine once again. She raced down the street.

"Oh, missus," Florence said, and to Jane's surprise there was a note of anger in her voice. "First the burglary, now this murder . . . Una told me Mrs. Strohman was going to write a book for Faith Carson's company. You see what it is, don't you? Don't you?"

"What?" Jane asked, distraught.

"It's your cousin, that awful woman Stephanie! All of these terrible things started to happen because of her coming to town. She's terrible trouble, missus—I'm sorry to say it, but she is. She should never have come here!"

Chapter Thirteen

"I'm sorry, missus, I should not have said those terrible things. I'm just so upset about my friend . . ." Florence hastily set down her coffee cup, placed her chin in her hand, and began to cry again.

Jane came around the kitchen table, put an arm around her, and squeezed her tight. "I know, and you don't have to apologize. It's horrible what happened to Una. I only hope the police can figure out who did this to her."

"Why would anyone have killed her?"

Jane sat back down. "That's easy. Because of what she saw—the burglar in Mrs. Strohman's bedroom, Faith Carson taking jewelry from him, paying him . . ."

Jane shook her head. "But no one knows she saw any of that—except for you, me, and Detective Greenberg."

"Yes, that's true." Florence quickly shook her head. "I blame myself. I do. If we hadn't wanted to speak to her, she wouldn't have left the back door unlocked, and whoever did that to her wouldn't have been able to get in."

"You can't blame yourself. Besides, in that case I'm just as responsible. I wanted to speak to her, too. And it was for her own good; don't forget that. How could we have known?"

A thoughtful look coming over her face, Florence looked at Jane. "You know, Una was my friend, and she was from Trinidad, which gave us something special that we shared . . . but she was not always a good Christian."

Jane made a little frown. "What do you mean?"

"She did some not-so-nice things. I remember she told me that one day when she was vacuuming upstairs, she walked into Mrs. Strohman's bedroom and found her in bed with a man—a much younger man. Later Una found out that the man was the son of one of Mrs. Strohman's best friends. Una . . . well, she didn't exactly blackmail Mrs. Strohman, but she told her in a roundabout way that she intended to keep Mrs. Strohman's secret and that Mrs. Strohman didn't have to worry. She told her there was no need to thank her for her discretion. Well, Mrs. Strohman got the message and gave Una a raise."

Jane lifted her brows. "I'd say that comes pretty close to blackmail. Una just had a subtle way of doing it. No," she agreed, "not so nice."

"God forgive me, I'm not telling you this to blacken poor Una's character, but just to say that maybe she did it again. Maybe she tried to blackmail Faith Carson!"

Jane gave her a wildly skeptical look and set down her coffee. "But that would suggest that Faith Carson murdered Una to keep her from telling anyone what she'd seen. That's crazy!"

"Is it, missus? Is it any crazier than paying a burglar

for stolen jewelry? It's all"—she pressed her lips together, her eyes welling with tears—"it's all too bizarre!"

With a sudden movement she pushed her chair away from the table, and as she did, something on the floor caught her eye. "Oh, missus, look at your shoes."

Jane pushed back her own chair and looked. They were covered with mud and plaster dust from the unfinished paving outside Mrs. Strohman's kitchen. "Yours, too," she told Florence.

Florence looked down. "You're right. Give me yours and I'll clean them for both of us."

Jane removed her shoes and handed them to her. She put her arm around the other woman again. "I'm so terribly sorry about your friend. Why don't you do something nice for yourself. You shouldn't be cleaning shoes. It's your weekend, after all."

"Thanks. I don't know what I'll do with myself. Maybe I should go and speak to the Reverend Lockridge."

Jane gave her an uneasy look. "Florence, I'm pretty sure Detective Greenberg wouldn't want you talking about this to anyone."

"Yes, you're right." Florence raised her shoulders and shook her head, at a loss. Carrying both pairs of shoes, she went out to the back hall, where Jane could hear her open a cabinet; then she heard the sounds of brisk brushing. With a deep sigh, Jane went to check on Nick.

She found him in the backyard, tossing a Frisbee with Stephanie, who looked happy and lighthearted in jeans and a baggy tan turtleneck sweater. She saw Jane and waved. "Good news!" she called. "I've got an apartment."

Thank you, Lord. "Why, Stephanie, that's wonderful! Tell me about it."

"Time out," Stephanie told Nick, tossing him the Frisbee.

"Aw, Stephanie, come on!" At that moment Winky emerged from the woods and ran up to Nick, distracting him. He swept her up in his arms and squeezed her, at the same time spinning around. "I'm gonna make you dizzy, Wink!"

Stephanie ambled over to Jane. "It's a real find," she said in her languid way. "You'll adore it."

Jane would adore any place that would allow Stephanie to end her stay as a houseguest. "Tell me about it." She forced a bright smile.

"It's not in Shady Hills. It's in Mountain Lakes, right at the Boonton border. The complex is called Boulevard Heights—the main street in Mountain Lakes is called just Boulevard, you know."

Jane, who knew, nodded.

Stephanie rushed on, "It's a one-bedroom, which is smaller than I would have liked, but it's what I can afford on what I'll be earning at Carson & Hart. I'm going to use part of the living room as my home office. All the windows look out on woods except for the bedroom, which has sliders onto a tiny deck with a view of one of the lakes! It's heaven—so peaceful. Best of all, I'll be right near Faithie and Gav. You know they've bought a house in Mountain Lakes, right?"

"No, I wasn't aware of that." Interesting, Jane thought, that this couple who had run into financial trouble had bought a house in one of the most affluent towns in New Jersey. "That *will* be nice for you."

Stephanie gave Jane a funny look. "Jane, is something wrong? You're acting oddly."

Lowering her voice, Jane said, "Actually, something

awful has happened. Just a short while ago Florence and I went to see Florence's friend Una. Coincidentally, she works as a maid for Mrs. Strohman. Anyway, we found her . . . dead. Murdered, actually."

Stephanie's features grew very still; it was impossible to read her face, hard as Jane tried. "That's horrendous," Stephanie said at last, her voice low.

"Yes, it is."

"How—how was she—killed?"

"I really shouldn't talk about it. The police have asked us not to," Jane lied. "While they're investigating."

"I see," Stephanie said slowly.

"Stephanie!" Nick hollered, at the same time releasing Winky onto the ground; she shook her head repeatedly, no doubt in an effort to abate her dizziness. "What about our Frisbee game?"

"Oh." Stephanie forced a little smile. "Yes, all right." She jogged back into the middle of the yard.

Jane turned and started back toward the house. She happened to glance up and saw Florence standing at the kitchen window, staring hard at Stephanie, her eyes narrowed to slits.

The last thing Jane felt like doing was running errands, but she realized she wouldn't feel comfortable doing anything else; Una's murder had given the day a surreal quality.

She ascertained that Florence would be in all day and asked her to keep an eye on Nick. Then she drove down into the village and made her first stop a place she'd been avoiding all week—Up, Up and Away.

She was surprised and relieved to find Barbara Kaplan's desk occupied today by an attractive young blonde woman, who asked if she could help Jane.

"I've been working with Barbara on a trip I'm planning," Jane told her.

"She's off today—family emergency. I'll be happy to help you."

"Thanks," Jane said, and added with a smile, "as long as Barbara will still get her commission."

The young woman laughed. "Boy, I wish all our customers were as considerate as you!"

"I work on commission, too," Jane explained, "so I understand how important they are."

"Have a seat. I'm Pauline—people call me Paulie. I'll be happy to help you, and yes, Barb will get her commission. I'm helping her out today, covering for her, as a favor."

"Very nice," Jane said, sitting in the visitor's chair, and bringing Paulie up to date.

Recognition dawned on Paulie's face. "Oh, you're the one who can't make up her mind!"

Jane laughed, feeling herself blush. "I've never heard myself described that way, but I suppose in this case it's true."

"Well, have you?"

"Have I what?"

"Made up your mind?"

"Yes. Anywhere. I want to go anywhere I can get in at this late date. I know it's all my doing. I suppose I couldn't settle on a place because I wanted it to be perfect. Now I just want it to be *away*."

"Now you're talkin'," Paulie said, turning to the computer, and her fingers flew over the keyboard.

Jane said hesitatingly, "Barbara did say there was an opening at Neptune's Palace. Someone had canceled."

Paulie looked at Jane, threw back her head, and roared with laughter, as if someone had just told her the funniest joke she'd ever heard. Jane simply stared at her, nonplussed.

Apparently what Jane had said was so inane as to not even deserve a response, because except for laughing, Paulie ignored it. She reached down into Barbara's file drawer, flipped through tabs, and pulled out a file. "Here we go," she said, opening the file folder. "Barb has a list jotted here. I take it these were the places you were considering? Antigua, Barbados, and Neptune's Palace."

"Those were my first choices. But at this point I'm flexible."

"Okay, let's see." Paulie typed, studied many screens, and made a couple of phone calls. Half an hour later, Jane was thanking her, standing with a travel folder of her own tucked under her arm.

"You're gonna flip over Antigua," Paulie said. "My ex-husband and I went there on our honeymoon—of course, he wasn't my ex-husband then!"

"Of course," Jane said, thanked her once more, and left.

She walked four stores down to the dry cleaner, another place she'd been meaning to stop for over a week. Enough of her wardrobe was now there that she couldn't put off this errand any longer.

There were two counters in Village Green Cleaners. There was a customer at the right counter, so Jane stepped up to the empty one on the left.

"Well, howdy there, doll!"

Jane turned. The customer at the right counter was Audrey Fairchild, her blonde hair in a ponytail, wearing tight jeans and a pink angora turtleneck sweater that fit snugly over her ample breasts.

"Hi, Audrey. Guess we're both catching up!" Jane fished a handful of cleaning tickets from her bag.

Marie, the store's owner, appeared and hung a blouse and a woman's suit on the rack next to the counter where Audrey stood.

"Are you kidding!" Audrey said with an upward roll of her eyes. "I'm here every day."

"Really? Even without . . . Elliott's things?"

"Absolutely. Cara's clothes alone keep me running in here constantly."

"Her school clothes?"

"Mm-hmm," Audrey said firmly. "You know my Cara, always wants things just right. This is a suit she wore to an awards ceremony her business club had the other night, but even her jeans—those, too, must be dry cleaned."

Jane chuckled. "Has Cara ever heard about that wonderful invention, the iron?"

Audrey just smiled; like Paulie, she thought Jane was making a joke. Audrey paid Marie for her cleaning, thanked her with a huge crimson-lipped smile, and approached Jane, coming, as she always did, closer than Jane would have liked—invading her personal space, as Jane had once heard it described.

Marie had come to stand at Jane's counter, but apparently Audrey didn't care, because she said in a low voice, "Janey, babe, I'm sorry if I was . . . you know, not myself Wednesday when you and Stephanie appeared outside my house. It's just that I couldn't believe it. You—with *her!* Is it true? She's Kenneth's cousin?"

"That's right. First cousins. You didn't see her at the funeral?"

"No," Audrey said thoughtfully. "Unbelievable." Her face turned bitter. "I don't suppose Stephanie told you anything about our—history. Hers and mine, I mean."

"Actually, she did." Jane felt awkward discussing this. "I was sorry to hear it. I don't really know Caroline, Stephanie's sister, at all."

Audrey looked baffled. "What does her sister have to do with anything?"

Now it was Jane's turned to be confused. "She told me—well, that Caroline—well, um, ended up with—"

Audrey gasped, her eyes growing huge. "Stephanie told you it was her sister Caroline who stole Lowell away from me?" Her mouth fell open and she shook her head, looking about her in disbelief. "What a bitch!" she finally said with great gusto. "Unbelievable."

"You mean it's not true?"

"*No,* it's not true. Jane, my darling," Audrey said, coming even closer and putting a hand on Jane's wrist, "it was *Stephanie* who took Lowell away from me. She set her sights on him, devised a scheme to seduce him, and did." She thought for a moment. "Yes, it makes perfect sense."

"What does?"

"That Stephanie would lie, of course. She did an awful thing, Jane. I loved Lowell. I'd probably be married to him today if she hadn't done that to me. And the other thing to remember about Stephanie, of course, is that the woman is simply a liar. That's what she is, a pathological liar."

Jane stared at Audrey in surprise.

"What shocks you, that she took my guy or that she lies like a rug?"

"Well—" Jane blustered. "Both!"

Audrey nodded simply. "You watch out for her, Jane. Get rid of her as soon as you can. She's trouble. She's a lying, conniving bitch, and she'll do you wrong as fast as she did me if it suits her purposes." She finally turned and lifted her cleaning off the rack. "Unbelievable," she muttered, and without a good-bye—unusual for Audrey—she walked out of the store.

Jane turned back to the counter, where Marie still stood, patiently waiting. From Marie's expression, Jane could tell she'd heard everything.

Jane realized she hadn't put down her cleaning tickets. She handed them to Marie.

"Thanks, Mrs. Stuart," the older woman said, and suddenly stared at the store's plate-glass window. Jane turned, following her gaze, and jumped.

On the other side of the glass, Ivor stood perfectly still, watching them. Recognizing Jane, he smiled. She gave him a tentative little smile back.

"Please, Mrs. Stuart," Marie said in a rush. "Don't encourage him. He's always here—on the sidewalk, on the green—bothering people, asking for money. I've complained to the police, but they don't seem to want to do anything." She looked at Jane's ticket, then looked up again at Jane. "You're still seeing that nice Greenberg fellow, aren't you?"

"Yes . . ." Jane said, surprised.

"Put in a word, will you?" Marie said, and headed toward the back of the store to find Jane's cleaning.

Chapter Fourteen

"It sounds like a remarkable book, Jane," said Hamilton Kiels, executive editor at Corsair Publishing. "When did you say you're closing?"

"Tuesday, December fifth. That gives everyone enough time even with Thanksgiving—and it gives me time to go on vacation."

"Got it. Can't wait to read it."

"You're gonna love it. Watch for it tomorrow morning."

Jane hung up and went out to Daniel's desk. Next to his computer was a large stack of phone messages—not unusual for a Monday morning, even this early. Looking up, he pointed to a box he'd placed on a table against the far wall that they used for collating materials and preparing submissions.

"Ten copies of *The Blue Palindrome*, ready to go. I'm just finishing up the cover letters."

"Great. Thanks. I feel really good about this project. I think it's going to go big."

"From your mouth to God's ears," he said, turning

back to his computer and resuming typing. "Oh," he said, looking up again, "your messages." He handed her the pile of slips. She flipped through them. The calls were nearly all from clients; there were a few from editors to whom she'd already pitched *The Blue Palindrome*. One was from Arliss Krauss, probably calling to get some idea of whether any other publishers had expressed interest. Jane had made it clear that everyone would receive the manuscript at the same time, but Arliss probably hadn't believed her. Jane would call her first.

She finished returning her calls a little before noon. She had no lunch plans today and went out to ask Daniel if he'd like to go to Whipped Cream with her. He'd get to see Ginny that way.

"Thanks, Jane, but Ginny and I actually have plans already." He looked down shyly. "We've got an appointment to look at an apartment."

"I *see*," Jane said, beaming. "How wonderful. I hope you like it."

"Thanks, Jane."

She got her coat from the closet, wished him luck, and went out, starting across Center Street toward the green.

"Jane! Jane!"

Stephanie, in her mink, a newspaper under her arm, approached rapidly from the right. Apparently she'd walked from her office around the corner. From her expression it was clear she had something important on her mind.

"Stephanie—what's the matter?"

"Jane," she said, reaching her, "Jane, are you free for lunch? Can I take you out for lunch?"

Stephanie's offer to treat was all the evidence Jane needed that Stephanie needed to talk.

"Yes, I'm free. Are you okay?"

Stephanie opened her mouth to speak, closed it, opened it again—clearly she didn't know where to begin. "I'll tell you at lunch. Where should we go?"

"Whipped Cream?"

Stephanie frowned, glancing across the green at the café's quaint brick front. "Where your friend Ginny works?"

"Yes, but she won't be there now."

Stephanie considered this, then shook her head. "Too . . . popular. Where else?"

"There's Giorgio's," Jane said, pointing to the left. "Good pizza, sandwiches, but nothing fancy."

"It's fine." Stephanie had already started along the sidewalk.

Seated in a booth in the storefront restaurant that had a gigantic mural of Italy on one wall, Stephanie set down the newspaper she'd been carrying, slipped off her coat, and laid it beside her on the seat. "Jane, something happened at the office today, something strange, and I wondered if I could confide in you about it. I don't know who else to talk to."

"Of course," Jane said, dreading whatever it was. She'd had enough "strange" to last her several years. "Now, what happened?"

"It was a little after I got to work this morning, not long after you and I drove into the village together. I'd picked up a *New York Times* at the newsstand before I walked over to the office, and I was sitting at my desk reading it, and I noticed something odd."

A young man in a white apron appeared with menus.

Jane didn't have to look—she wanted a slice of broccoli-olive pizza and a Diet Coke and ordered it. Dr. Stillkin be damned.

"Same," Stephanie said. The minute the young man was gone, she continued. "Anyway, I noticed something odd in the paper. It was a small story about a jewelry dealer in New York City who'd been found murdered."

Jane chuckled cynically. "Nothing unusual about that."

"No," Stephanie said, shaking her head impatiently, "hear me out. The reason it struck me as odd is that the name of the man was familiar to me, but I couldn't remember how I'd heard it."

"What was his name?"

"Wachtel. Irwin Wachtel. It's not a common name."

"No," Jane agreed. "I wonder how you'd heard it."

"It drove me crazy, but finally I remembered. Yesterday Faith and I were helping Kate with a jacket shoot, and Faith needed something from her office. She asked me to get it for her. I found it on her desk. While I was picking it up, I noticed that Faith's Rolodex was open to a card with that name on it. Just the name and a New York phone number. I didn't think anything of it, of course; it meant nothing to me. Until this morning, when I found the story saying he'd been murdered."

Jane laughed skeptically, though the image of Faith Carson taking jewels from Roy Lynch flashed into her mind. "Are you saying Faith murdered Mr. Wachtel?"

"No! It's just that it is an amazing coincidence; you have to agree that it is. When Faith came in this morning, I mentioned it to her in passing. I showed her the story in the *Times,* and then I told her that when I'd gotten those papers for her I'd noticed his name in her Rolodex."

"What did she say?"

"She denied ever having heard of him!"

Jane frowned. "How strange . . . Maybe she'd dealt with him once briefly a long time ago, written his name on a Rolodex card, and forgotten. It happens. In fact, it sounds like something I might do."

"True. Anyone might do that. I just shrugged it off, figured something had happened like you just said— she'd known him once for some reason and forgotten. And I chalked the whole thing up to coincidence. I said something to that effect to Faith, expecting her to go along with it, but she was quite adamant. She *did not* know this man, she said, and *she never had.*"

Stephanie's face still looked troubled.

"And something more happened?" Jane ventured.

"Mm. I shouldn't have done this—I don't like to snoop—but I couldn't help myself. Faith went to the ladies' room and I went in her office and checked her Rolodex. Wachtel's card was gone."

"Gone?"

"Gone. Faith must have taken it out, and she must have done it between yesterday and this morning. But why? Jane, it *has* to have something to do with Wachtel's murder."

The young man brought their order. Jane took a bite of her pizza. "What are you saying?"

"I . . . I don't know. Jane . . ." Stephanie wrinkled her brow in troubled concentration. "Don't you see? All that's happened? Faith comes to town, meets Lillian Strohman, Lillian agrees to do a book with Faith—and Mrs. Strohman's maid gets murdered! I see Irwin Wachtel's card in Faith's Rolodex, he's murdered—and the card vanishes! Something's going on up there, Jane."

Jane had to agree that these coincidences didn't look good. Stephanie wasn't even aware of what Una had seen. But what did Stephanie want from Jane? She asked Stephanie.

"Jane, I think Faith is involved in something bad. I've known this woman for twenty-five years—known her well—and I would never have thought this possible, but I think she's involved with these two murders. I do."

"And . . . ?"

"If only you could see this place, Carson & Hart, for yourself . . . You know publishing, Jane; you'll know better than I could if something is up."

Jane frowned, not just at what Stephanie said but also because she'd found an olive pit on her slice. She removed it from her mouth and set it to one side of her plate. "What does my knowing publishing have to do with the possibility that Faith Carson is a murderer?"

"No, I don't mean that; I'm not being clear. What I mean is, you know publishing and could fit in at Carson & Hart quite convincingly. You could find out if something is wrong without my—my having to take my suspicions to the police. After all, she's my oldest friend, my best friend. She's an international celebrity. How would it look for me to start throwing around accusations involving murder?"

"Stephanie," Jane said, out of patience now, "just come out and tell me what it is you want me to do."

Stephanie picked a burned piece of broccoli off her pizza slice and set it on the edge of her paper plate. Then her gaze met Jane's.

"I want you to work at Carson & Hart. I want you to go undercover."

Chapter Fifteen

———————

"Go undercover! What are you talking about?"
"Look." Stephanie picked up the *Times*—presumably the one that carried the story of Irwin Wachtel's murder—and turned to the Help Wanted section. An ad was circled in red. Stephanie turned the newspaper around and pushed the ad in front of Jane.

ADMINISTRATIVE ASSISTANT
Small publishing company seeks ambitious, organized assistant for administrative. Must have office/ computer skills and, preferably, some experience in publishing. We offer competitive salary, benefits & friendly, supportive environment. Fax resumé to . . .

There was a phone number with a Shady Hills exchange. Jane stared at Stephanie. "You don't want me . . ."
"Why not? It's perfect. You could apply for the job as someone I know; I'll vouch for you. Then, as I said, you'd be in a better position than I am to know whether

something's going on. You know, you could snoop around . . ."

"But, Stephanie, this is outlandish! I have a job of my own."

"But it would only be for a short time. I think you could get to the bottom of this within a few days."

"I'm going on vacation this Saturday—that's five days from now."

"I know. I'm certain you'll have discovered whatever there is to discover by then. And then you can just quit!"

Jane shook her head, regarding Stephanie as if she'd gone mad. "This is the craziest thing I've ever heard. No, Stephanie. I'm sorry, but it's just not something I'm willing to do."

Stephanie's gaze dropped to her pizza slice and a tear fell from her cheek to the edge of her plate. She grabbed a paper napkin from the dispenser and wiped her eyes.

"Please, Jane, I'm begging you. You've . . . investigated things like this, I know you have. That business with your nanny, and Florence told me how you helped find out who that girl was hanging behind the inn. Am I asking so much? A few days of your help. And if you tell me nothing's wrong up there, that everything's on the up and up, we'll forget all about it and that will be that. Jane," she said, looking into her eyes, "Faith Carson is the only friend I have. I *need* to know what's going on. Please."

Thoroughly put out, Jane cast her glance away, taking in the floor-to-ceiling refrigerator containing soft drinks at the far end of the restaurant, the mural of Italy, Giorgio tossing pizza dough into the air.

And then she saw him.

Kenneth.

He was sitting in a booth, alone, and he was turned all the way around, his arm on the back of his seat, looking at her. Her mouth opened; she stared.

Do it, Jane, he was urging her. *For my cousin. I know she's a jerk, but she's my cousin and she needs help. I'd help her if I could, but I'm not here anymore so I can't. She needs you, Jane. Please. Help her.*

She looked back at Stephanie, who was taking a sip of her Diet Coke.

"How would this work?" Jane asked.

Stephanie looked at her eagerly. "Well," she said breathily, "I'll just go back now and say I thought of someone who might like the job. I'll say you're an old family friend. You'll have to make up a name. You'll come in tomorrow, interview with Faith and maybe Gavin—though I doubt he'll get involved at this level—and I'll talk you up. You'll tell them you can start right away. Once you're up there, you'll look around, see what you can find out. I'll help you as much as I can, of course, but I'm convinced you'll find things I wouldn't."

"But someone will know me," Jane protested. "I live right here in town."

"No, I've thought that all through, Jane. Don't you remember? At Puffy's party, you never got a chance to meet Faith and Gavin. When they drove me home and I asked them to come in, they said another time. They don't know you!"

"What if someone who does know me comes in?"

"No one goes up there! Faith always meets with her socialite writers at their homes. So no one will blow your cover."

This was insane. Jane took a deep breath, glanced back at the booth where she'd imagined seeing Kenneth. He was gone, but she could still hear his voice, soft, urging. *She's my cousin. Help her out. She needs you, Jane.*

So, it occurred to Jane, did Florence. Her dear friend Una was dead, and perhaps Faith Carson *was* somehow involved.

"All right. You'd better let me have that ad." She shook her head. "Daniel's going to think I've gone all the way over the edge."

"Oh, thank you, thank you," Stephanie said, squeezing Jane's hand. "But do you think you should tell Daniel what you're doing?"

"Daniel is like family to me. I could trust him with my life. I'm telling him. I'm also telling Stanley. Heaven knows what *he'll* think."

"Okay, okay." Stephanie pushed the paper closer to Jane. "Take this, and I'll go back now and say I've thought of this wonderful person I know who would love the job." She stood up, her pizza barely touched, her soda cup still nearly full, and started to leave. Suddenly she turned back to Jane. "What's your name?"

"What?"

"Your make-believe name. What shall I say your name is?"

"I don't know," Jane said impatiently, and for some reason a picture of Audrey in her pink angora flashed into her mind. The sweater girl.

"Lana."

"Lana?"

"Yeah, like Lana Turner. Lana's a pretty name."

"All right. Lana what?"

Jane let her gaze move around the table. She saw the olive pit at the edge of her paper plate.

"Pitt. Lana Pitt."

"Eew," Stephanie said. "What an awful name."

Jane gave her a warning look meant to tell Stephanie not to push her luck.

"Okay, okay. Lana Pitt. Thanks, Jane, really. Kenneth would be proud of you." And Stephanie ran out of the restaurant.

Jane reread the ad in the *Times* and couldn't help laughing. The last time she'd been an assistant was when she'd been assistant to Kenneth at Silver and Payne, seventeen years before. She rose, tucking the newspaper under her arm, and started to go when she remembered Stephanie hadn't treated her to lunch after all. Shaking her head, she tossed a few dollars on the table and went up to the register to pay.

Chapter Sixteen

"Stephanie really likes you, Lana." Faith Carson glanced at Stephanie, who sat beside Faith's desk in the small, windowless office. She set down Jane's application and gave her a frank look with those famous violet eyes beneath thick light lashes. "Where do you see yourself in five years?"

Jane nearly burst out laughing. This was that cliché of a question she herself used to ask people she interviewed, people in their early twenties, just starting out in their careers. Here she was, thirty-nine years old, being asked the very same question. Quickly she thought back to how those young people had answered her.

"I would hope to move up," she said, her voice earnest. "Maybe some day—perhaps not in five years—I could even be an editor."

Faith gave a nod, equally serious. She referred again to Jane's application. "You've put down that you have experience with literary agencies. You worked for Silver and Payne in New York years ago, and more recently you've worked for a . . . Jane Stuart, right here in Shady Hills."

"That's right."

"Didn't that work out?"

"It wasn't that. I just felt I needed a change—you know, wanted to try something new. I'd like to see how it is on the other side."

"You mean inside a publishing company," Faith said with a modest smile.

As if, Jane thought, Carson & Hart were a real publisher. But she nodded solemnly.

"Stephanie," she said, turning to her friend, "I think I share your enthusiasm for Mrs. Pitt." She turned to Jane with a smile. "Let's do it."

"Great! Thank you so much," Jane said.

Faith merely gave a quick, insincere smile. "Can you start right away? Today?"

"Absolutely."

"Good. Stephanie will show you the ropes." Faith directed her attention to what looked like a set of page proofs that lay before her. Clearly, Jane and Stephanie were dismissed. Stephanie gave Jane a meaningful look and a tilt of her head that meant she'd talk to her outside.

As Stephanie closed Faith's door, she said loudly enough to be heard, "I'll show you where your desk is, Lana, and we can go over your work." Then, when the door was completely shut, she whispered, "You did great." She led the way to the left, down a corridor whose sides were stacked with boxes. Very soon on the right-hand side this corridor widened enough to accommodate two desks. One, the farthest one, was empty. At the nearest desk sat a young man whose gaze shot up at the sound of their approach. He gave both women the kind of appraising up-and-down look Jane hadn't experienced in years. As gauche and obvious as it was, it made Jane blush, for this was one of the handsomest young men she had seen in a long time. This, she thought, must be Faith's son, Sam—the lounge lizard, Stephanie had called him.

"Well, hello, hello," he said in a deep mellow voice, and stood up. He was of medium height and slim, in black slacks and a gold shirt that looked as if it were made of silk or rayon, open at the collar. To Jane these clothes seemed more appropriate for a Saturday night out than for the office, but then, he was Faith's son, and traditional office rules could not be expected to apply to him.

He didn't look at all like his mother; Jane couldn't see Faith in him at all. His features were strong and regular—a hard clean jawline, a deep cleft in his firm chin, prominent cheekbones, a low forehead under crisp, curly black hair. His skin was a flawless gold color, as if he had a perpetual tan, which made his eyes especially striking. They were a very pale blue, the kind of eyes that were so light that Jane found them unnerving. These eyes, she reasoned, must be from his mother.

Clearly he was waiting to be introduced. Jane turned to Stephanie, who looked bored. "J—Lana, I'd like you to meet Sam."

"Hello, Sam," Jane said, extending her hand.

"Lana . . ." he breathed, as if tasting the name, and gently he brought her hand to his lips and kissed it. Lounge lizard indeed!

Suddenly he glanced quickly from Jane to the empty desk next to his. "Are you my roommate?" he asked eagerly, and when she nodded, he said, "Oh, we're going to have a *good* time."

Jane had a bad feeling in the middle of her stomach. She wanted to run away from this young man who was obviously as obnoxious an office neighbor as she could have hoped to find. Then she reminded herself that she had agreed to this insanity for only a few days at most. She supposed she could put up with anything for that amount of time.

Stephanie showed Jane to her desk, on which sat a messy stack of papers about a foot high. "Filing," Stephanie said with an embarrassed grin.

"No problem," Jane said cheerfully. "Just show me where."

"These cabinets here." Stephanie indicated a bank of horizontal file cabinets about two yards from Jane, perpendicular to the two desks. "The filing's backed up, as you can see. The files are arranged alphabetically by author, so you'll need to look at each piece of paper to see who it's about."

"I think I can handle that," Jane said, and smirked.

Stephanie grimaced uncomfortably and mouthed the word "Sorry."

Jane shook her head to say it was okay, then set to work.

"All right, then," Stephanie said briskly, "see you later."

Jane watched her enter an office just opposite her own desk. This was the layout of the office, then, Jane thought: Stephanie, Faith, and the last office, which opened off the far end of the corridor, she guessed belonged to Gavin, whom Jane hadn't yet seen.

"Good morning," came a booming voice behind her, and she jumped, spinning around.

A good-looking middle-aged man stood in the corridor, smiling at her. Unlike Sam, he was dressed for business in an expensive-looking charcoal suit, a white shirt, and a maroon-and-gold rep tie. His hair, neatly trimmed, was black, with touches of gray at the temples. He put out his hand. "I'm Gavin Hart, Faith's husband. You must be Lana."

For a second she just stared at him; then she remembered that Lana was her "cover."

"Uh—yes! Lana, Lana Pitt," she said, flustered, and took his hand. His handshake was warm and firm. Nice-looking man, she thought, now that she saw him up close, though not the kind of man whose looks one would necessarily remember for a long time. Perhaps that was the best kind of husband for a former queen.

"I hope you enjoy working with us," Gavin said, then looked at Sam. Jane followed his gaze. Sam was playing tic-tac-toe with himself on a yellow legal pad. "Sam," Gavin boomed, "I trust you'll help Lana with her work, showing her how things work at Carson & Hart?"

"Mm-hmm," Sam said, not looking up, still making *X*'s and *O*'s.

Gavin threw him an irritated look, then returned his gaze to Jane and smiled warmly. "If there's anything you need, don't hesitate to ask any of us." He gave her a sporty wink. "Glad to have you aboard."

"Thanks," Jane said, and watched him walk to the last office, the one she'd guessed was his, and go in, closing the door behind him.

At that moment Faith emerged from her office and went into Stephanie's. Jane heard Faith asking Stephanie a question, then Stephanie's response. Seconds later Faith emerged, looking impatient, and walked up to Sam's desk. Still he did not look up.

"Sam—"

"Mm."

"Sam, Stephanie says the reason the *Who's Who of American Gardening* direct-mail piece hasn't gone out yet is because she's still waiting for you to give her the labels. Where are you with that?"

"Labels?" At last he looked up at his mother, a vague and slightly irritated look on his face. "I'm printing them."

"You are? Then where are they? Why didn't you give them to Stephanie?"

He drew a deep breath and lolled back in his chair, one arm dangling over the side, as if his patience had run out. "I *can't* give them to her because they're not complete. You said not to bother giving them to her until they were complete."

"Why *aren't* they complete?" Faith said, as if speaking to a simpleton.

"Because," he replied reasonably, "I didn't key in the names and addresses from the bird-watcher mailing."

"And why not?"

His face darkened. "Because, *Mother,* I really haven't felt like it!" He leaned forward defiantly, waiting for her response.

Faith opened her mouth, then shut it tightly. She appeared to compose herself. "I want you to give the whole thing to Lana, do you understand?"

"Perfectly."

She continued to stare at him, as if she just couldn't stop. At last she pulled her gaze from him and turned to Lana. "You'll help us out with this, won't you, Lana? Sam will show you what needs to be done. That computer over there"—she indicated a machine against the corridor wall across from Jane's desk—"that's where we key in names and addresses for our mailings."

"No problem," Jane said crisply.

"Thanks." Faith gave her a tiny smile, which promptly vanished as she passed Sam's desk and returned to her office.

Sam looked up from his legal pad. "No problem," he mimicked, and gave her another up-and-down once-over.

What an obnoxious young man, Jane thought, and knelt to resume her filing.

"Tell me, Lana," Sam said dreamily, leaning way back in his chair again. "What's an old broad like you doing in a place like this?"

She stared at him over the file drawer, her mouth agape. "How dare you speak to me like that!"

He laughed—an extremely pleasant, almost musical laugh, she had to admit. "How dare I? Sweetcakes, that was my *mommy* just now. The *Queen of Ananda!* I can basically do whatever the hell I like, and I'll still get a paycheck. In fact, I could stay home and watch reruns of *The Andy Griffith Show* all day, and I'd *still* get my paycheck. So. Let's start again. What's a beautiful girl like you doing in a place like this?"

She found his candor alarming yet also refreshing. She couldn't help smiling. "A minute ago you said 'old,' not 'beautiful.'"

"So I did. You have to remember—to a twenty-year-old, a woman your age is old. How old are you, by the way?"

"None of your business, but I'll tell you anyway. I'm thirty-nine. What am I doing here? Earning money to feed my ten-year-old son." Jane had always believed that the best way to lie was to stick as close to the truth as possible.

"A son," he said thoughtfully. "Married, are we?"

"A widow."

"Mm." Not the usual "I'm sorry"; just "Mm." He doodled happy faces on the edge of his legal pad. "You're beautiful, too, do you know that?"

"Yes. My husband used to tell me that all the time."

"He was a lucky man." He gave her yet another appraising look, but this one was more respectful, more admiring. "That's some head of hair you've got there. I love redheads."

"Auburn."

"What?"

"I'm not a redhead. My hair is auburn."

"Okay," he said, humoring her. "I love auburn-heads."

She lifted her shoulders in a carefree little laugh, closed the drawer she was working in, and opened the one below it. "Love whatever you like." Her gaze met his. "Just leave me alone."

He sat up straight. "My, my! A woman with spirit! I love that. Lana . . ." he said, savoring the name. "Hey, Lana," he said, lowering his voice and looking around to make sure no one heard, "are you seeing someone? I mean, you got a boyfriend?"

"Sam!"

They both jumped.

A stocky woman, around the same age as Sam, stood in the corridor near Jane's desk. She wore a navy pantsuit and had shoulder-length black hair. Her complexion was olive, like Sam's, but unlike Sam, she was not, in Jane's estimation, at all attractive, with an almost perfectly round face and tiny, piglike eyes.

"Sam, get back to work," she barked at him, then turned to Jane. "You're the new woman," she said briskly. "I'm Kate."

She didn't put out her hand, so Jane didn't put out hers.

"I'm sorry about my brother. He thinks we're all here to play."

Sam sat up suddenly, as if startled. "You mean we're not?"

Kate rolled her eyes and started down the corridor toward Gavin's office. A door not far from Sam's desk opened and a young man emerged with a mail cart. He looked about nineteen, wore baggy corduroy trousers and a T-shirt with writing on it Jane couldn't make out, and had a mop of light brown hair over a long, acne-spotted face.

"Mel," Kate called to him. "Come here."

Mel walked his cart down to her, casting an uninterested look at Jane.

"Mel, this is our new person, Lana. Lana Pitt, is that correct?" she asked Jane.

"That's right."

Kate turned back to Mel. "Now you know who she is if any mail comes for her."

Mel nodded once, leaned into his cart, and hefted out an enormous pile of mail, which he dropped into Sam's In box. Then Mel walked away, Kate right behind him.

"You've certainly got your work cut out for you," Jane observed.

"Just because they put it on my desk doesn't mean I'm going to do it." With a suave smirk, he skimmed a few pieces off the top and flung them into a wastebasket that stood behind his desk in the corner.

Jane opened her mouth to protest, then stopped herself. He was like a child, being outrageous, incorrigible, trying to get a rise out of her. She wouldn't give him that pleasure. Besides, she wasn't here on this insane mission to bother with his silliness. Stephanie had asked her to try to discover whether anything odd was going on at Carson & Hart, and Jane intended to do that and get out.

Shortly before noon, the door through which Mel had come opened and an elderly woman appeared. Dressed in the light blue uniform of a cleaning lady, she walked with a stoop and carried a spray can and a dusting rag. She stopped to wipe off the computer table, then moved on, paying no attention to either Jane or Sam. As she passed, Jane noticed that her face was extremely wrinkled; this could be an extremely old woman, Jane thought. The woman's hair, however, was a glossy chestnut, teased into a neat bouffant.

When she reached Sam's desk, he growled lustily at her.

Jane observed this with horror, but the woman who was the subject of Sam's disrespect seemed to take no notice, continuing down the corridor, stopping to dust the edge of a bookcase.

Jane couldn't keep silent any longer. She regarded him with repugnance. "You are truly the most obnoxious person I've met in a very long time. Do you work at it?"

He laughed, as if she were joking. "Talk like that really turns me on, you animal. Besides," he said, indicating the old woman now at the opposite end of the corridor, "Norma's nearly deaf and doesn't speak a word of English. Only Hungarian."

"I'm sure she knows you're making fun of her."

He shrugged, unconcerned. "She's lucky I take any notice of her at all."

Jane had to get out of here. She checked her watch. It was a little after noon. "Lunchtime!" she said brightly, setting down her filing on her desk.

"Care to join me?" he asked suggestively.

"Thanks, but no. I've got some errands to run."

"Tomorrow, then. This is only Tuesday. I've got all week to make you mine."

Jane grabbed her coat from a closet not far from their desks and hurried through a doorway between Faith's and Stephanie's offices to a small reception area with no receptionist. She passed from this room into the second-floor corridor and took the elevator down to the lobby.

The building's entrance was at its back, opening onto a long, narrow parking lot. This was fortuitous, allowing Jane to avoid being seen by anyone who knew her true identity. She had parked her car not here but in the parking lot behind her own building around the corner, also to avoid any risk of being identified, but also because each morning she would be stopping in at her own office to touch base with Daniel before hurrying over here.

She walked along the lot, then down a drive that ran alongside the building toward Packer Road and provided access to and from the parking lot. There was a dark green Dumpster at the edge of this drive, pushed as far to the side as possible. Jane peeked in and saw only a few scraps of plasterboard and an old wooden desk chair. Someone in the building must have started a remodeling project, she thought.

She walked around the corner to the village green. When she entered her own office, Daniel looked up and laughed in disbelief. "You're actually doing this!

You actually worked at Carson & Hart all morning as Lana Pitt?"

"Yes," she said, falling into his visitor's chair, "and I ought to have my head examined."

"That bad, huh?"

"Definitely weird—on that score Stephanie was right. My desk neighbor is Faith's son, Sam, the most repulsive young man I've ever met, hands down."

"Really? Repulsive how?"

"Lazy, arrogant, thinks he's God's gift to women. Ugh!" She shuddered.

"And how's the mission going? Notice anything amiss?"

"Not yet, too soon. I think I've met everybody, though." She told him about Faith, Gavin, Kate, Mel, and Norma.

"What is Faith like?"

"Very refined, all business. As beautiful as her pictures, maybe a little heavier than I expected. She's got no patience for Sam; I can tell you that. Who would!"

Daniel shook his head. "You deserve some kind of medal for this."

She shrugged it away. "I told you why I'm doing it— for Kenneth." She pondered for a moment. "And for Florence. If her friend Una was telling the truth about what she saw, then this Faith Carson *needs* investigating. Now," she said briskly, "how's today's mail?"

He handed her a blessedly small pile. On top was the latest issue of *Romantic Times,* the leading magazine for readers and writers of romance fiction. As an agent who represented a large number of romance writers, Jane felt it vital to read this magazine carefully each month. Casually she flipped back the cover and drew in her breath. At the bottom right-hand corner of the first page was a photograph of Jane posing with her clients

Bertha Stumpf and Elaine Lawler at the annual convention of Romance Authors Together in New York City in May. Beneath the photo was a caption that read: *Literary agent Jane Stuart took a moment to pose with two of her leading ladies of romance, Rhonda Redmond and Elaine Lawler.*

"How did the magazine get this?"

"You told me to send it to them."

"Oh." She considered, then laughed. "What am I worried about? I sincerely doubt that anyone at Carson & Hart reads *Romantic Times*."

"I'm sure you're right. Your secret is safe."

She flipped through the rest of the mail. There were two rejections from editors, a small check due one of Jane's clients on acceptance of a manuscript, and the rest were query letters from writers seeking an agent. Nothing urgent here; she handed it all back to Daniel to handle.

"Any calls?"

He nodded eagerly. "Ham Kiels called about *The Blue Palindrome*. He loves it, wants to talk to you about it, see what your plans are."

"What my plans are! I told him, I've set a closing for December fifth. What else is there to tell him?"

Daniel shook his head.

"Playing games," Jane muttered. "I should have left him out. Can't stand that company, anyway."

"I said you'd get back to him," Daniel said.

"I will when I can."

"Okay. I'll call him back and say you're out of the office for the rest of the day."

She checked her watch. "Ooh—almost one already. Better get back. My lunch hour's almost up!"

Daniel shook his head and laughed as she hurried

out. She realized she was hungry. She considered crossing the green to Whipped Cream for a muffin or something, which would also give her an opportunity to see Ginny; but then she rejected this idea. It would take too long. Besides, she'd realized that morning that she'd virtually abandoned her Stillkin diet, and that there wasn't much time left to shed those extra pounds for her vacation. She stopped in at the deli a few doors down from her office and bought two apples—highly recommended by Dr. Stillkin—which she would eat at her desk.

When she arrived at Carson & Hart, Stephanie was not in her office. Both Faith's and Gavin's doors were closed, so Jane couldn't tell if they were in or not. Sam was in. He had his back to Jane, busily applying something to the wall beside his desk. He heard her sit down and turned to her with a devilish grin.

"Couldn't stay away. I knew it."

She rolled her eyes. "My lunch hour was over." She plunked the two apples down on her desk. Then something on Sam's wall—presumably what he'd been putting up—caught her eye, and she looked at it more closely. She realized, to her horror and amazement, that it was a photograph of a human head on what appeared to be a refrigerator rack. At the bottom of the photo, someone had written in crude capital letters, SERVING SUGGESTION.

"What on earth is that?" she breathed.

His eyes gleamed. "Isn't it funny?"

"I said, what is it?"

"It's Jeffrey Dahmer's fridge."

She made a sound of shocked disgust. "But where did you get it? Why do you have it?"

"I know someone who knows one of the cops who was on that case. In Milwaukee."

"I know where. But why," she asked, "have you put it on your wall?"

"I find it . . . interesting."

"Who wrote that at the bottom?"

"I did." He laughed.

She could only turn away. This was one sick puppy. She'd ignore him to the fullest extent possible. She grabbed another stack of papers and returned to the file cabinet. As she filed, she thought about how she might go about finding out if, as Stephanie believed, there was more to Carson & Hart than met the eye.

"Sam!"

She jumped, turned.

Gavin stood at Sam's desk, staring with a look of revulsion at the grisly photograph on the wall.

Sam sat up straight in his chair in mock attention. "Yes, Mr. Hart, sir!"

"Stop that. Take that down immediately." Gavin glanced at Jane with a look of embarrassment, then returned his attention to Sam. "You seem to think this is some kind of . . . playland! This is a *business*. If you aren't interested or don't feel you want to—"

"Blah blah blah," Sam said, and Jane glanced over furtively to see him wave Gavin away dismissively and go back to whatever he had been doing.

Gavin's jaw dropped. He shot another look at Jane. Then he shook his head in resignation and walked away toward his office.

"What a supreme asshole," Sam said, and not at all softly. He looked up at Jane. "He's right. I really oughta quit this dump."

Jane made no response, just raised her brows inquiringly.

Sam went on, "Look at me! My mother *owns* the company, and I'm a—flunky!"

"Like me," Jane quipped.

"Right! But you're not a crown prince. I am. I shouldn't have to work at all."

"Then why do you? Why *don't* you quit?"

"Why?" he said searchingly. "Because Mommy Dearest would never let me hear the end of it. Because, as she has reminded me so many times, we're not in Ananda anymore—those days are long over. We're in America, just regular people, and we have to earn our livings." He shook his head in disgust. "If she'd played her cards right, we'd be so rich we wouldn't have to work."

She narrowed her gaze, interested. "What do you mean, if she'd played her cards right?"

"She should have handled things differently with my father. She should have—"

Jane's phone rang. She frowned. The only "outsiders" who knew she was here were Florence, Stephanie, Greenberg, and Daniel.

It was Daniel.

"Jane, I'm sorry to call you there."

"No, it's not really a good time," she said, irritated. She'd told him never to call her there.

"It's okay, Jane, I asked for Lana. I won't keep you. I just wanted you to know that Hamilton Kiels called again about the Nat Barre book."

"Again? Did you tell him you gave me his message?"

"Yes, but he says now he wants to make you a preemptive offer for the book. You really have to talk to him, Jane."

"All right. Thanks. I'll call him as soon as I can."

When she hung up, Sam was looking at her. "Not bad news, I hope."

"No." She gave a little laugh. "It's my mother. She lives with me. Sometimes she's so helpless."

"Where do you live?"

Why was he asking her this? "Here in town," she said vaguely. She wanted to get back to what he was saying about his mother. But first she had to find a way to call back Ham Kiels.

"I've got to go to the ladies' room," she said, picking up her bag.

He looked at her strangely. "Permission granted."

She laughed. "Thanks."

The rest rooms were located at the end of the corridor nearest Jane's and Sam's desks. There was no one in the ladies' room. She locked herself into a stall, took out her cell phone, and called Ham Kiels.

"Jane, hello!" Ham Kiels was always pleasant, but he spoke now in the tone he used when he was interested in a project. "Hard person to get hold of."

"Yes, sorry about that."

"Why are you whispering?"

"Am I? I think I'm coming down with a cold or something. Sore throat."

"Oh. Well, take care of that. Anyway, this *Blue Palindrome* is truly magnificent, Jane. I gave copies to Jack Layton and Ellen McIntyre," he said, referring to the company's editor in chief and director of publicity and promotion, respectively. "They flipped. I was thinking of taking a floor," he said, referring to a starting bid in a book auction, "but Jack wants me to preempt."

A preemptive bid was one designed, by virtue of its

size, to induce an agent to make a deal and withdraw the project from all other potential bidders.

"I'll listen, Ham, but it had better be big."

"A hundred thousand."

"What!" she screamed, then remembered to lower her voice. "What?" she whispered.

"Jane, it's a first novel. That's excellent money for a first novel."

"Not for this one. I haven't seen something like this in years, and neither have you. If you want to preempt, you're going to have to quadruple that."

"No way."

"Fine. I'll consider that floor bid you mentioned."

"I'll have to speak to Jack," he said peevishly. "You'll be around?"

"Actually, no. I'm not even at my office now. You'll have to leave a message with Daniel."

"You have a cell phone, don't you? I'll call you on that."

Of course that made perfect sense. But she couldn't have her cell phone ringing at her desk; she'd had it turned off until she'd made this call.

"No . . . there's something wrong with it. I'm having it fixed."

"Aren't you on it now?"

"No. I'm at a pay phone."

"Oh." He sighed. "All right. After I speak with Jack, I'll leave a message with Daniel."

Encouraged by Ham's avid interest in Nat Barre's novel, she hurried out of the ladies' room and back to her desk.

"You okay?" Sam asked.

"Fine. Why?"

"I heard you scream in there. It sounded like you were saying, 'What!' "

She laughed. "I saw a big spider. Hate spiders." She went back to the file cabinet. Glancing at her desk, she noticed that someone had left a fresh stack of papers in her In box.

He saw her looking. "Mumsy left that for you. She also left you these lists that need to be typed. When you're done, you need to get Gavin to initial them; then give them back to Mumsy." He pointed to the communal computer across the corridor and smiled sourly. "Aren't we having fun?"

She smiled back and kept filing. But filing was growing tedious and she decided a change of pace was in order. She sat down at her desk and picked up the lists Sam had said needed typing. These seemed innocuous enough. Written in a loopy handwriting she assumed was Faith's, they were actually the company's publication schedule for the coming year. At the very end was *"Stars in My Eyes,* Lillian Strohman, hardcover, $28.95." The date was the following November.

Jane tapped the papers on her desk to straighten them and was about to rise to cross to the computer when she heard a familiar voice. It was coming from the far end of the corridor, near Gavin's office. It was a woman's voice, cultured, with a familiar lockjaw quality. "I think you've done *wonders* with the place, dear," the voice was saying.

It was Puffy Chapin. Glancing down the corridor, Jane could see her just emerging from the door perpendicular to Gavin's office—Kate's office, apparently.

Thinking fast, Jane put a hand quickly to her ear. "Oops!" she said, and slid down her chair and under her desk, like a snake. "Dropped an earring," she said, not too loudly.

Crouched under the desk, she could see Kate's and Puffy's feet approaching. They walked slowly past. "I don't want to bother your mother," Puffy was saying. "Just let her know I came by to make sure everything was all right. I think we've got that heat thing licked, but she should call me if there's the *slightest* problem."

"All right, I'll let her know. Thanks," Kate said graciously, and Jane heard the door to the reception area open and close.

Jane turned to crawl out from under her desk.

A pair of male trousered legs blocked her way. Sam's expensive black slacks, cuffs resting on black loafers that were covered with dust and could have used a shine.

Why was he standing there? His hand went to his fly. "Let's get started, Miss Lewinsky; I haven't got all day."

With an impatient groan she pushed his legs away. "Let me up!"

He was laughing. "What were you doing under there?"

"I told you. I lost an earring."

His face uncomfortably close to hers, he peered at her ears. "Both earrings seem to be there," he said in a seductive, breathy voice.

"That's right," she chirped and smiled tightly, "because I found it." She waited, not moving, staring him down.

He nodded and returned to his desk. His shoulders rose in a quiet chuckle. "I did *not* have sexual relations with that woman!" he said in a raspy voice.

A decidedly strange young man.

It took about twenty minutes for Jane to type up the

lists Faith had left for her. She printed them out and started toward Gavin's office.

Sam looked up quickly. "I wouldn't, Lana. Not quite yet." He smirked. "He's *with* someone."

Jane frowned, confused, but Sam did not elaborate. Jane put the lists on her desk and continued with her filing. Approximately ten minutes later, she heard a door open and looked up. At the far end of the corridor, someone was emerging from Gavin's office. It was Stephanie. As Jane watched, Stephanie glanced back into the office and gave a quick smile— a smile, it seemed to Jane, that implied a high level of intimacy. Standing in the doorway, Stephanie straightened her jacket and smoothed her hair. Then she walked toward her office, a pleased look on her face.

"Lana . . ." Sam whispered in a singsong voice. "You're staring . . ."

She glanced at him sharply. He wiggled his eyebrows suggestively. She knew what that meant. Could he be right?

Stephanie and Gavin? Stephanie was Faith's best friend. No, Jane decided, Stephanie appeared to be of questionable character, but she wouldn't go this far.

Stephanie had closed Gavin's door behind her. Five minutes later it opened again, and Gavin came out. Looking quite unruffled, he headed straight for Jane's desk.

"Mrs. Pitt, may I speak to you in my office, please?"

She looked at him in alarm. She heard Sam snicker and shot him a sidelong glance. "You're next," he murmured. She didn't think Gavin heard him.

She nodded, rose, and followed him into his office. As he closed the door, he invited her to sit down on a sofa that was part of a self-contained meeting area to the far left, in a sort of alcove. There was the sofa, two matching upholstered chairs, and a glass-and-metal coffee table. It occurred to Jane that this area might have been where Dr. Kruger, the office's previous tenant (for clearly this had been his office), met with his patients.

"A psychiatrist had this space before us," Gavin said pleasantly, as if reading her thoughts. "Attractive room, don't you think?" He sat down in one of the chairs, smiling affably. "He left his furniture—sold it to Puffy, actually, which made moving that much easier for us."

"Didn't you have furniture of your own?"

"Some, but not as much—we had much less space in New York."

It was an attractive room—airy, spacious, its east wall occupied mostly by a window that looked out on woods. Though boxes stood stacked against the far wall, Gavin had already put up a few of pieces of art: several watercolors, a vivid abstract painting of a butterfly that Jane guessed must have appeared on a Carson & Hart book. Most striking about the room was its contrast to Faith's small, windowless office. Faith may have been the former queen, but it was clear who ruled at Carson & Hart.

"May I get you some coffee? Tea?" he asked.

"No, thanks very much." She waited. What did he want?

He frowned for a second, as if gathering his thoughts. "Mrs. Pitt . . ." he finally began.

"Please call me Lana."

He nodded appreciatively. "Lana. I think you're going to like it here at Carson & Hart. I can tell already that you'll fit in nicely. And you seem to know what we're all about here. Faith showed me your resumé, and I noticed that you have some very good publishing experience."

She inclined her head graciously, still waiting for him to get to the point.

"Lana, I'm sure you've noticed already that Sam is . . . that Sam needs . . ." He drew a deep breath, seemingly at a loss for the right words. "Sam," he started again, "needs help."

"Help?"

"Yes—he needs a direction in life. You've heard the things he says, seen the way he treats his mother and me, the way he feels about working here."

"Yes."

"I sense that someone like you could be a very positive influence on Sam. Especially with your experience in publishing. Obviously you appreciate this business. I wonder if you could try to—instill some of that appreciation in Sam. Act as, well, sort of a mother figure to him."

"Mother figure?"

"Oh." He seemed to realize suddenly that Jane might have taken offense at his choice of words. "Not literally, of course—I didn't mean that you're old enough—I just mean that I think you could be an excellent influence on him, and I'm giving you complete freedom to speak your mind to him and to let him know when you feel he's off base."

So he wanted her to baby-sit Sam? "I always speak my mind—tactfully, of course. And you're right; Sam does have problems. He's . . . scornful of this place, of his mother and you. He doesn't like working here, doesn't like *working*. I'll do what I can," she said with an assuring smile, "but have you and his mother considered therapy for him? I believe his troubles are far more serious than just a lack of ambition or direction in life—if you'll forgive my saying so."

"Of course, of course—I want to know your thoughts. Actually, Sam has been in therapy for years. He's always been a troubled boy—you know I've been acquainted with his mother for years; I was her husband's assistant in the old days in Ananda."

"Yes, I know."

"Sam has shown himself capable of some pretty shocking acts—as I'm sure you've seen."

She thought of the photo he'd tacked up over his desk, his Lewinsky joke when she'd been under her desk. "Yes."

"Anyway," he said, rising, "I don't mean to take up so much of your time. I realize you have a lot to do. I just wanted you to know we appreciate having a person of your experience here, and that we hope you'll feel free to share your obviously positive outlook with Sam."

She followed him to the door, anxious to get out.

Opening the door for her, he said, "I think you could go far in this company, Lana. I really do." He gave her a patronizing grin. "Great to have you aboard."

She grinned back and started down the corridor toward her desk. Passing Stephanie's office, she looked in just as Stephanie looked up. Stephanie's features were completely impassive, her gaze calculating.

Taking her seat, Jane saw the publication lists on her blotter and realized she'd forgotten to have Gavin initial them. She made an impatient, "Tsk."

Sam looked over. "I was going to remind you, but you seemed to have a lot on your mind already. You could always go back in—if you're ready so soon."

Looking at him in horror, she gathered up the papers and rose. "For the rest of the day," she said with a tiny smile, "I would like you not to speak to me. We'll get along much better that way."

He stared at her, dumbfounded. She turned and headed back toward Gavin's office.

Good influence be damned. Let his therapist keep trying to straighten him out. That wasn't in her job description; besides which, in a few days she'd be gone from this bizarre place.

Chapter Seventeen

At five, Jane gathered her things and got her coat from the closet. Sam rose from his desk at the same time. "Day's over," he said seductively. "Am I allowed to speak now?" He had, in fact, honored her request and kept silent for the rest of the day.

She couldn't help laughing. She shook her head. "Say what you like," she said lightly. "I'm going home."

"I'll walk out with you."

Jane and Stephanie had agreed to leave the office separately each day, but Jane glanced into her office just the same. The small room was empty. Then from Faith's office came the sound of women's voices. Stephanie must be in there.

Jane and Sam left the building together. It was dark and cold, the tall lamps of the parking lot casting an unnatural greenish light.

"Where's your car?" he asked.

He had caught her off guard. "Um . . . around the corner, in the municipal lot."

He looked puzzled. "Why did you park there?"

"Exercise," she answered, thinking fast. "I'm trying to lose weight and need to get more exercise. So I intentionally park a good distance from the office so I can get my walking in."

"Good idea." He looked her up and down. "Though I hardly think you need to lose any weight."

"Thanks," she said, eager to lose him. "Where's your car?" They had already started down the narrow drive beside the building, where the Dumpster stood. Obviously Sam's car wasn't in the lot behind the building, either.

"Over there," he said, pointing back at the lot. When Jane frowned in bewilderment, he said, "I'm not going home just yet. I'm going to grab a bite of dinner at that little pizza place on the green around the corner, then maybe I'll walk around the village; I don't know." Suddenly she saw him as lonely, a sad young man who didn't know where he was going—or, at least, didn't like where he was expected to go.

She decided that if he kept walking with her, she'd disappear into the municipal lot, wait till he was out of sight, then sneak around to the lot behind her office, where her car was really parked.

At the far end of the Dumpster, a tall shadow loomed up. Jane and Sam stopped, taken aback. The figure walked slowly toward them; Jane's heart pounded.

"Spare a dollar?"

It was Ivor. Jane relaxed her shoulders, at the same time opening her bag. She gave him a dollar.

"God bless," he said, and met her gaze. "I know you. You're the lady from around the corner on the grass."

"That's right," she said uncomfortably, and she and Sam walked on.

"Do you make a habit of befriending the local bums?"

"Please don't call him that."

"Ah, a liberal!" he said, nodding. "What did he mean?"

"That he's seen me before, obviously," she said, keeping her tone casual. "I was walking across the green and gave him some money."

"Oh. I never give bums—I mean, beggars—money."

She wasn't sure she liked *beggar* any better than *bum*, but decided to let it go. "And why is that?" she asked tiredly, already knowing the answer.

"Because when you give money to people like that, you're hurting them more than you're helping them."

She looked at him, surprised. "How so?"

"Because it's enabling." He gave her an arch look. "Is my therapy showing? Anyway, you're helping him buy more liquor, which is the last thing he needs. What he needs is rehab."

"I agree, but I'm not in a position to help him get that. And you—you don't even want to acknowledge his existence. Until he can get the kind of help he really needs, isn't it our duty to help him buy some food?"

"He won't use that money for food, Lana, and you know it. Best to just ignore him."

She shook her head. They had come out onto the street. She hadn't wanted to be seen with him, in case someone she knew drove by and blew her cover, but now she realized it was so dark here, the streets so inadequately lit, that there was little danger of that. She found herself glad to be able to walk with him a little more. She felt sorry for him now, and regretted having told him not to speak to her.

Glancing across the street at the police station, she wondered if Stanley was still at work. Then she looked quickly away, starting along the curving sidewalk and returning her attention to Sam.

"Gavin wanted to talk to you about me, didn't he," he said. It was more a statement than a question.

She opened her mouth to respond, but he broke in.

"You don't have to deny it. I know it."

"How do you know?"

"Because I know how he thinks. I can tell he likes you. You're the kind of person he would want me to learn from, to be like."

She was silent for a moment, then said, "It must have been hard for you and Kate, not having a father."

He looked at her in the dimness, shrewd, assessingly. Then he nodded. "Even when we had a father," he said, his eyes distant now, a little sad, "we didn't have much of a father."

She turned to him inquiringly.

"You know that until my grandfather died, my father basically had nothing to do in Ananda. He was . . . well, I suppose he was like me! Not needed for anything."

She was about to protest, but he went on.

"My grandfather died before I was born. My mother was pregnant with me, actually. Grandfather was also pretty much a good-for-nothing type, always jetting around to play with his rich friends. Anyway, one of his favorite spots was Tunisia."

"Yes, I know."

"You do? How?"

"I read your mother's book," she lied, knowing that fact must be in there.

"Ah, the book." His shoulders rose in a short laugh. "Quite a fairy tale, that book. You wasted your time reading it. It's hardly the real story."

Then you tell me, she thought, and waited.

"You know, then, that Grandfather's car went off a cliff into a ravine and exploded. He had been drinking.

All night, in fact. I can't imagine who let him drive in that condition. I can only think that subconsciously he wanted to die. But," he said, shaking his head, "we'll never know." He shoved his hands deep in his coat pockets. "Suddenly my father was king.

"I know from my mother—and maybe this is in her book, I don't know—that when my father became king, she expected his behavior to change. She expected he would take his responsibilities seriously and use his expensive Harvard education to improve his country." He laughed. "That was like expecting your bum—I mean, your homeless person to stop drinking. It just wasn't going to happen. Nothing changed. He was still fun-loving, carefree, content to let Ananda continue to run itself. And why not? For years there had been peace and prosperity. What was there to improve?"

There were more streetlamps here as they neared the village center. Packer Road was busier here, too; a number of cars had to stop here to turn left onto Highland. Afraid someone would see her, Jane turned from the road, quickened her pace.

"So your father was a disappointment to your mother," she said.

"Absolutely." He grew more animated. "And as it turned out, my mother was right. Ananda did need leadership. The country was in trouble."

"What do you mean?"

He frowned mildly. "It's in her book. Don't you remember? One night, a small band of men—just people from down in the city, if you could call it a city—a group of men slipped past palace security—if you could call it security! They actually got into the palace and found my father's rooms; my parents always had separate quarters. They attacked him in his bed. One of them stabbed him. My mother came running, hugely pregnant with me, at the sound of the commotion. There was a lot of blood, blood everywhere, but as it turned out, the blade only pierced my father's side, and the wound was deep but not especially serious."

"What happened to the men who attacked him? I don't recall from the book." She should have read this book, she realized.

"The palace guards caught them quite easily. The police interrogated them. After quite some time, they confessed to being members of a secret group that for years had been plotting to overthrow the Anandese government so China could annex the country. You see, China had had its eye on Ananda for some time. Now we knew that many Anandese were in favor of this annexation, believing life could get even better if this happened."

They neared the railroad tracks.

Sam went on, "As I said, my father wasn't really hurt, not badly, but he was afraid. For once, he showed some backbone and insisted my mother return to the States, at least until she had me, and the rebels could be taken care of. But you've met Mumsy. She's got enough backbone for three people. Not only did she refuse to leave Ananda, but she blamed my father for what had happened. She said if he hadn't been such a lax king, this traitorous group would never have been able to form in the first place. Which is nonsense, of course, but try telling that to my mother. She told him that if he didn't have the balls to run the country, *she* would.

"Everything changed. She gave orders to strengthen security, not just in the palace but also at the borders. Until that time, Anandese, Chinese, Indians, and Nepalese had pretty much passed freely. Mother also commanded Ananda's little police force to ferret out 'the insurgents,' as she called them, and bring them to speedy trial." He grimaced. "I understand it was horrible. Dozens of men—and women—were executed for the crime of treason. This, in a country where no executions had taken place for hundreds of years."

Ahead Jane could see the municipal lot on the right, the village green across from it. Now there was a good chance someone she knew might see her with Sam—which, she reasoned, might not matter, but it wasn't a risk she could take, someone calling out or speaking to her as Jane. She wanted to hear more of this story, but she had better separate from him soon.

"Everyone hated her," Sam was saying. "She became this . . . this *monster*. I know this from Gavin."

"From Gavin?" she asked, surprised. "Why would he tell you these things about your mother?"

"Because he knew I'd hear them, and he wanted me to know the truth. He saw all of this firsthand, because it was at this time that my father hired Gavin as his official secretary."

"Where had he come from?"

"He'd worked at the United Nations. He'd known my father since their undergraduate days at Oxford." He laughed, kicking a stone off the sidewalk. "Gavin told me my mother said hiring him was the only smart thing my father ever did. She was right, in a way. Gavin started doing the things my mother wanted my father to do. Meanwhile, she played the queen role to the hilt—even while she was expecting me.

"Her schedule had never been busier. She was traveling, throwing lavish parties for foreign dignitaries, including royalty. She told Gavin that because she was hosting royalty at the palace, she expected to be hosted in kind by these people at *their* palaces—which did actually happen in some cases. But it was ludicrous, really. Ananda was barely a country, and the 'palace' was a huge old rustic . . . *lodge.*

"She began using the regal 'we' and demanded visitors and servants treat her with 'the deference due royalty.' She was to be addressed as Your Majesty or *'Chogyal,'* which was the ancient Tibetan title for 'ruler.' She distanced herself from my father and from the people—these people who had always had full access to their king and queen. She made Gavin deal with the public; she said that was beneath her.

"During this time an article about Ananda in *Time* magazine referred to my mother as 'a Himalayan Marie Antoinette.' A friend of Gavin's in the States sent him the article. When he showed it to my mother, she laughed and walked away."

They had reached the entrance to the municipal lot. "Well, this is me," she said.

He looked disoriented for a moment, as if he were still in Ananda—though everything he had told Jane so far had occurred before he was born. "Right," he said, glancing at the lot. Fortunately, there were still a number of cars parked there.

"See you in the morning, then," Jane said with a smile, and started into the lot. "You said you were going to Giorgio's, right? It's over there, at the farthest end of the green."

"I know. I've already been there a few times."

"Really? Who do you go there with?"

He laughed, looked at her strangely. "Who do you think? Nobody. Who would go with me?" And, his hands still deep in his coat pockets, his shoulders slumped, he waved good night and crossed the road to the green.

She watched him for a moment, feeling sad, and made her way to a row of four cars parked in the municipal lot. Standing next to one of the cars, she made a business of fussing in her bag, in case he turned around and looked at her. But he didn't. She watched him cross the middle of the green, not something she would do in the dark, even in peaceful Shady Hills. When he disappeared in the shadows of the great oaks, she started out of the lot and headed toward the lot behind her office.

The lights were out in her office. Daniel had gone home, or perhaps out with Ginny. Jane wondered if anything else had happened today regarding *The Blue Palindrome,* wondered whether Hamilton Kiels had reconsidered his preemptive bid. She'd call Daniel's apartment when she got home, and if he wasn't home, she'd leave a message. He'd call her back tonight, wouldn't put her off.

She could always count on Daniel.

Chapter Eighteen

Stephanie had already come in. She was in the family room with Nick, Florence, and Winky. They were watching one of Nick's cartoon shows; he was explaining each character to them. Stephanie, eyes narrowed in fascination, looked up when Jane appeared in the kitchen doorway.

"Hello, all," Jane said. "Am I missing something good?"

"It's *CyberWarriors,* missus." Florence was brightly animated, but Jane could tell this was the result of a great effort on Florence's part. She was, of course, still horrified, devastated, about what had happened to her friend Una, what she had seen. That was something she could never forget.

"Dinner will be ready in about twenty minutes, missus."

"Great. Thanks." Jane crossed the family room, excusing herself when she walked in front of the TV. In the foyer she hung up her coat. Suddenly Stephanie appeared.

"Well?" she whispered. "Anything?"

Jane frowned. "Anything what?"

"Have you discovered anything? At Carson & Hart? What do you think?"

"I've learned a lot," Jane said, "but nothing you don't already know. I need more than a day if I'm going to find out anything meaningful."

"I see," Stephanie said. "All right." Though from her face Jane could tell that Stephanie didn't feel this was all right at all.

Watching Stephanie return to the family room, Jane recalled the image of her emerging from Gavin's office, that smug look on her face. Did Stephanie really want Jane to find out everything that went on at Carson & Hart?

After dinner, she called Daniel and found him at home.

"I was going to call you, 007," he said with a laugh. "I've got some things to report about the Nat Barre book."

"Shoot, shoot. On second thought, let me buy you a drink."

"*Tonight?*"

She laughed. "Daniel, you are such a fuddy-duddy. Yes, tonight! Can you meet me at Eleanor's in half an hour? I promise you'll get home by bedtime."

"Very funny. All right, Eleanor's in thirty minutes."

When she arrived, he was already at a table for two in the restaurant's bar. Always the gentleman, he rose as she approached. He was smiling but looked uncomfortable.

"What's the matter?" she asked.

"It's smoky in here. I hate that. Doesn't it bother you?"

She shrugged, hanging her coat on the back of her chair. "Can't say I noticed it. You want to sit someplace else?"

"We can't because we're not having dinner."

"Ah." She gave a flip of her wrist. "We'll live. Now tell me what's been going on."

He shook his head, gave a little laugh of disbelief. "How long are you going to do this? It's . . . insane."

"No, it's not," she told him reasonably, "it's a good deed. I'm helping Stephanie, who is the cousin of my late husband. Besides, it's fun in a surreal sort of way."

"What's it like there?"

She puzzled over this question. "It's a strange place, not corporate at all, definitely a family business. Each personality exerts a strong influence."

He nodded, though he looked bewildered. "And have you found out anything—anything Stephanie would find useful?"

"No, but I intend to do some serious snooping as soon as I get the opportunity."

At this he just cast his eyes upward. Then he reached down to the floor for a spiral-bound notebook. "Let me tell you what's been happening with the Barre book."

Five of the editors to whom Jane had submitted the novel had called to say they planned to participate in Jane's auction on the fifth. Two editors had passed. Ham Kiels had not called about putting down a floor bid.

At this news, Jane shrugged. "I doubt he will, then. He'll wait for the auction and take his chances. I probably wouldn't have accepted his measly floor anyway."

"How do you know it would have been measly?"

"Because it's Corsair! *Measly* is their middle name."

"Yeah, you're probably right." He closed his notebook.

She looked around. "Isn't someone supposed to take our drink order, or don't they do that at bars anymore?"

"Yes, of course they do," Daniel said, casting his gaze around the dark-paneled room, "but it's very busy. I'll go up. What would you like?"

"Mm . . . a champagne cocktail, I think." She smiled at him. "Thanks." She watched him thread his way among the tables and stand at the bar, waiting for the bartender. All the stools at the bar were full—men and women chattering away, laughing, whispering intimately. Idly Jane scanned these people, wondering if she knew any of them.

And blinked.

Two stools down from where Daniel stood sat Stephanie. She no longer wore the simple suit she had worn at the office. Before coming out she'd put on a slinky black dress.

But who was Stephanie with? It was a man, that much Jane could tell in the dim light, and whoever he was, Stephanie knew him well, because their faces were only inches apart. Jane squinted—and blinked again. It was Gavin Hart. Jane looked away, wishing she could crawl out.

"Here we go." Daniel appeared, placing her drink before her. He frowned down at her. "Is something wrong?"

"Sit, sit." She leaned across the little table toward him. "At the bar," she whispered. "Stephanie and Gavin Hart."

"Who's Gavin Hart?"

"Shhh!" She slid a glance toward the bar to make sure

Gavin hadn't heard his name. Apparently he hadn't, still engaged in his tête-à-tête chatter with Stephanie.

"Who's Gavin Hart?" Daniel repeated softly.

"Faith Carson's husband! Don't you remember? You saw him at Puffy's house."

He looked over. "Oh, yes . . ." He looked back at Jane. "So he and Stephanie are having a drink together. They work in the same office. She's new. What's the big deal? *We're* having a drink."

"True, but I wasn't alone in your office for an hour today, and I didn't come out looking like I'd swallowed the canary."

An unfortunate reference, Jane reflected, but was distracted by Daniel's wide-eyed look of surprise. "You mean they're—"

She nodded avidly. "An office item. Don'tcha love it?"

"No," he said, looking quite serious, "I can't say I do, Jane, with all due respect to Kenneth and his cousin. It's sleazy."

"I completely agree. And," she said, turning her chair, "not something I want Stephanie to know I know about. Besides, she's a grownup. What she does is her business, and I have no right to judge her."

Jane took a sip of her drink at the same time that Daniel put his to his lips, and when their eyes met they both burst out laughing.

"What?" she said, all innocence.

"You have no right to judge her—but you will! You always do."

"True," she said reflectively. "And I should stop that, shouldn't I? I wonder if I've been a member of the Defarge Club for too long."

"Jane," he said impatiently, "you are a member of the

Defarge Club because you are a gossip. You are not a gossip because you are a member of the Defarge Club."

"Very good, Daniel!" She gave a large shrug. "Let's move on, shall we? I really appreciate your holding down the fort while I've been spying. But you have to remember not to call me there unless it's a dire emergency. And you have to ask for Lana Pitt."

"That's what I did," he began to protest.

"I know, I know. You handled it fine. I'm just reminding you. But tomorrow, wait for me to call you. I'll sneak off at lunchtime and call you on my cell phone."

"Why can't you just come to the office at lunch?"

"Because that's when I intend to do my snooping!"

Movement at the bar drew her attention. Stephanie and Gavin were leaving. Jane returned her gaze to Daniel and wiggled her eyebrows. "She'll be coming in late tonight!" Then she turned pensive. "I wonder what Gavin will tell Faith . . ."

Snug in her bed, leaning against the headboard with her knees up, Winky a purring furball under the covers at her feet, Jane turned slightly to look at her bedside clock. Half past midnight. Stephanie still hadn't come in, but though Jane found that fact interesting, it wasn't why she was still awake. The reason was the book propped against her knees, *Queen of Heaven* by Faith Carson, which Jane had borrowed from Florence.

She'd been reading it practically since she got home from Eleanor's, after a quick shower. Faith's story of the fairy-tale-turned-nightmare phase of her life was engrossing, but to read it after meeting a number of the story's key players made it unputdownable.

She'd reached the point in the story when Ravi had just hired Gavin as his official secretary. "Energetic, darkly handsome Gavin Hart," Faith called him. Jane pondered those words for a moment, considered the possibilities . . . Then she continued reading.

> *I felt an instant affinity to Gavin. I believed he and I were uncannily alike in our outlooks and ambitions— very possibly because we were both American. Ravi was immediately pleased with his friend's work, and took to calling him Johnny-on-the-Spot, a nickname Gavin clearly disliked but was too polite to object to. I found it demeaning, incredibly insensitive on Ravi's part, and told my husband that I took offense at the sobriquet on Gavin's behalf and that Ravi was to stop using it immediately.*
>
> *Not long after Gavin joined our staff, I gave birth to my first child, a boy. I named him Surya, which is the Hindi word for "sun." At this time the official demands on my time were greater than ever before, and, sadly, I was forced to remand Surya largely to the care of nannies and servants, always plentiful.*

Jane looked up sharply. She'd heard a noise downstairs. Stephanie coming in, no doubt. Jane heard the sliding of the closet door in the foyer and imagined Stephanie hanging up the ever-present mink. Then came slow footsteps on the stairs, then down the hall, approaching Jane's bedroom. But they didn't continue past her door; they stopped, and there came a soft knocking.

"Jane?" Stephanie whispered through the door, which was open a few inches.

Jane sat up and, without knowing why, shoved the book under the covers. "Yes, Stephanie, come in," she said pleasantly.

Stephanie poked her head around the door. Her black hair was mussed the way hairsprayed hair gets mussed, and her makeup was gone. She'd probably washed it off rather than leave it smudged, a good idea, but the result was that Stephanie looked pale and haggard. The large black-haired head with its sharp features reminded Jane more than ever of a gigantic rat.

Forcing this image from her mind, Jane realized from Stephanie's pinched expression that something was wrong.

"Come in, come in," she said. "Everything all right?"

Stephanie came into the room. Her dress was torn at the sleeve, as if someone had tried to rip it off.

Jane sat up straighter. "What happened?" Had Gavin done this?

"Oh, Jane . . ." Stephanie sat down on the edge of Jane's bed and gave her an imploring look. "I can confide in you, right?"

"Of course."

"There's something you should know. It's about me and Gavin. We're—well, we're having an affair."

Nice thing to do to your best friend, Jane thought, but only nodded, keeping her expression neutral.

"He and I went out after work tonight. We had drinks at that restaurant you took me to by the river— Eleanor's?"

"Right."

"Then we had dinner there. After that we . . . went back to the office. Gavin has a sofa in his office."

Jane found it hard to continue keeping her expression neutral, but she did, and gave a little nod.

"When we were—done, Gavin left the office first. He was in a hurry to get back to Faith. He'd told her he had a meeting with a potential author. I saw him out and locked the reception room door after him. Then I fixed my hair, washed my face, and left about twenty minutes after him."

"How did you get home? Couldn't he have given you a ride?"

Stephanie looked embarrassed, smiled a sickly smile. "I asked him to, but he said he was in too much of a hurry and your house is out of his way. He gave me the number of a cab company."

Jane nodded. In Shady Hills there was only one: Shady Hills Taxi. At this time of night, Stephanie probably got Erol, who'd been driving for the company for more than thirty years.

"I left the building and waited in back, on the steps. I'd told the taxi dispatcher I wanted to be picked up there. I mean, I couldn't very well be standing out front at this time of night!"

Apparently Stephanie did have some modicum of shame. Jane waited for her to go on.

"I waited a good ten minutes, but the taxi never came." Stephanie looked irritated. "It occurred to me that maybe the dispatcher hadn't told the driver to come around to the back, so I hurried around to the front of the building, thinking the taxi might already be waiting there. To get to the front, as you know, you have to take that narrow drive at the end, and there's no light there, Jane," she said, as if that were Jane's fault. "It was almost completely dark—I could barely see a foot in front of me."

Jane thought of pointing out to Stephanie that in a town like Shady Hills, it's not likely that someone will need lights in an alley beside an office building at midnight. But she didn't point this out.

Stephanie's head dropped, her face screwed up in its rat expression. "Jane, I heard someone behind me. One footstep. I froze. My heart felt like it was going to pound right out of my chest. I've read you're not supposed to run in these situations, so I forced myself to just continue walking, slowly and calmly . . . and he—whoever it was—suddenly grabbed me! It was a man, Jane, a strong man. He grabbed me tight and we struggled. He pulled so hard I heard my mink coat and dress tear." She indicated the torn sleeve. Jane nodded sympathetically. "I screamed. Then I just ran. When I got to the front of the building, the taxi was just turning in at the drive and I waved him down."

"Stephanie, you poor thing, that's *awful*. We'll have to call the police. Did you tell Erol about it?"

Stephanie gave her a baffled look. "Who's Erol?"

"Oh—" Jane laughed. "Sorry. That's the driver you would have had at this time of night. Erol's very level-headed; he would have known what to do. Did he radio in to Trudy to call the police?"

"No," Stephanie said, gazing at Jane as if she were dimwitted, "of course not. Jane, I can't have it known that I've been cavorting around town at midnight. How would I have explained being there? Working late?"

"Certainly not that. Mm, you're quite right."

"Damn straight I'm right. And in this town? It would be headlines in the—the *Shady Hills Gazette* in the morning."

"*Shady Hills Beacon.*"

Stephanie drew an aggravated breath and looked as if she wanted to throttle Jane. Jane had to admit to herself that she was not trying her best to be sympathetic.

Now there was no doubt about it: She definitely did not like this Stephanie—Kenneth's cousin or not—who had embarked on a tawdry affair with the husband of her best friend, her best friend who had given her a job when she needed one.

"Besides," Stephanie went on, rising, "I don't need to call the police. I know who it was."

"You do?"

"Of course." Stephanie's tone implied the word *idiot* at the end of the sentence. "It was that bum person."

"Ivor?"

"Sure. He hangs out there; I've seen him. He'd probably bedded down in that alley for the night, heard me coming, and decided to try to rape me. I smelled the booze on his breath. It was him."

Stephanie reached the door and turned. "Thanks for listening."

"I don't feel I've been much help. Is there anything I can do?"

Stephanie smiled—a nice smile, grateful, sweet. "You've done a lot for me already, Jane, more than you know. I really appreciate it. Good night."

After she'd gone, Jane took out the book again, but no matter how many times she read the same paragraph, it didn't sink in. She was trying to conjure an image of Ivor—tall, rangy, desperate—grabbing Stephanie from behind and struggling with her, trying to subdue her . . . but it was no use.

What did anyone really know about Ivor? Was Rhoda right? Should he be removed from town? Jane shook her head firmly. Stephanie had accused Ivor simply because he was homeless. Her attacker could have been anyone.

At that moment Winky awoke and a lump traveled

up the bed toward Jane until the cat's mottled brown-and-orange face emerged from under the sheet. Jane stroked her soft smooth head and the cat began to purr loudly, like a fluttering motor.

"If Gavin had been a gentleman," Jane said very softly to Winky, whose eyes popped open at the sound of her mistress's voice, "if he'd given Stephanie a ride home, that wouldn't have happened. He may be married to a former princess," she went on, placing the book on her night table and switching off the lamp, "but he is definitely no prince."

Chapter Nineteen

Jane gazed down at the two mailing lists for Carson & Hart's upcoming solicitation for *Classic Dolls*. She was to find and delete any names on list two that were duplicates of those on list one. Bouncing her gaze back and forth, she found one and pounced, drawing a thick black line through *Beecher, Muriel*.

She looked up, aware suddenly of how ludicrous her being here was. Carson & Hart was quirky and idiosyncratic, like any family-owned company, but as far as Jane could see, the only thing out of the ordinary and at all interesting was Stephanie's self-confessed affair with Gavin. But that, of course, was not what Stephanie had wanted Jane to find. Stephanie did not know what it was she wanted Jane to find, had only said something wasn't right.

On that score Stephanie herself could not have been more correct.

Stephanie's door was closed. Jane got up, attracting an interested look from Sam, but ignored him as she crossed the hallway and knocked softly. When Stephanie called to come in, Jane opened the door and peeked inside. "Could I have a word with you?"

Stephanie smiled tightly, which in itself bothered Jane. She entered, closing the door behind her, and sat in Stephanie's visitor's chair. "Stephanie, this is silly."

"What's silly?"

"My being here. *Why* am I here? What is it exactly you want me to find? I'm very busy at my own business. I have an auction going on for a project I'm handling, and in three days I'm supposed to go on vacation and I haven't wrapped up any of the business I'd wanted to wrap up before I left. I'm sorry," Jane said, rising, "but I'm going to have to"—Jane made quotation marks with her fingers—"quit."

Stephanie looked crushed, her eyes bulging out, her black brows knitted together. She leaned forward on her desk. "But you promised to help me. You said you'd have a look around and tell me if things were on the up-and-up. *I* don't know anything about publishing, Jane. *I* don't know what's normal and what isn't. I need someone like you to tell me."

"Of course this place isn't normal. It's nuts. There's a former queen in the office next door, you're having an affair with your boss, one of the assistants is the former crown prince of Ananda—not to mention a pervert with a disturbing fascination with cannibalism . . ."

At this, Stephanie gave Jane a startled look.

"Nuts!" Jane cried. "On the up-and-up? I don't know. Is a vanity press on the up-and-up? Morally wrong? Sometimes. Legally wrong? Usually not. Because that's what Carson and Hart is, you know: a glorified vanity press. So if your question is, is Carson and Hart a viable commercial publisher on the order of the big guys in

New York City, the answer is no. But I think you knew that. So just what is it," Jane said, narrowing her eyes, "you thought I might find?"

Stephanie paused, her mouth slightly open. "I just thought—oh, I don't know. I just thought things were . . . strange here, and I wanted you to tell me if I was right."

"Okay, they're strange. Now what are you going to do with that? What would you have done with anything I came up with?"

"I—"

From the office next door, Faith's office, came a re-sounding thud, as if Faith had fallen. Both women sat up in alarm.

"We'd better go see—" Jane began, but stopped when the thud was followed by a loud and quite ob-scene curse. "Guess she's all right," Jane said with a little laugh.

Now there came more bangs and booms, as if Faith were throwing things around her office. Something glass shattered, and Stephanie jumped. "What on earth . . . ?"

"Sounds like she's mad about something."

Stephanie shrugged. "Faith's always had a violent temper. It'll blow over. Now about you, Jane . . ."

"Right. This is my last day."

"Oh, Jane, please, I beg of you," pleaded Stephanie, who fell across her desk dramatically, then lifted her head to look at Jane, at the same time sweeping a stiff lock of hair away from her face. "Just a little longer. I know you'll come up with something. I . . . just need to know that this is a safe place for me to work." Her eyes welled with tears. "This is all I have, you know."

"What do you mean?"

Two more loud thumps came from next door.

"I'm not what you think, Jane."

Exactly what, Jane wondered, did Stephanie think Jane thought Stephanie was? "In what way?"

She tossed back her head theatrically. "You think I'm this glamorous society woman who tossed off her job because it bored her and came down here on a lark. That's not true. I was fired from my job. They told me to get out within thirty minutes. It was pathetic. I asked about my belongings and was told that anything I left behind would be destroyed. I couldn't find a box, so I took a green plastic garbage bag and filled it with my stuff. Ten minutes later I was out on Boylston Street with the bag over my shoulder like Santa Claus, trying to flag down a cab. I've never been so humiliated in my life.

"But there was more humiliation to come. I had to *beg* Faith for a job here." Stephanie's face twisted in resentment, giving her that rodent look. "As if it would be a hardship for her to give me a job. I practically had to get on my knees."

"I understand the company was struggling," Jane said reasonably, "which was why they had to give up their offices in New York and move out here to Shady Hills . . ."

"Oh, bullshit!" Stephanie cried. "Faith and Gavin are loaded. You'll probably never see the house they bought in Mountain Lakes, but I've seen it, and believe me, Jane, it's not a house you or I would ever be able to afford. Loaded. Faith—my old friend, my *roommate*—took great pleasure in making me grovel to get this job, to find some way to make a living."

"But surely there were other things you could have done. Other jobs in Boston . . ."

"Didn't I tell you that part? I wasn't fired a few weeks ago, Jane. I was fired a year ago. And ever since then

I've been trying to find one of those 'other jobs' in Boston. No one wanted me." Stephanie's gaze implored Jane. "Who *would* want me—a homely middle-aged woman with no discernible talents and a lousy personality."

"Stephanie!" Jane felt compelled to say.

"No illusions, Jane, no illusions. I know what I am. That story I told you about Lowell. A lie. *I* was the one who took him from Audrey, not my sister Caroline. Wasn't that a shitty thing to do, Jane? I'm a shit!"

Jane just sat very still, horrified at this explosion, without a clue as to how to respond.

"And now," Stephanie swept on, "I'm bonking my best friend's husband. Nice, huh?"

"No," Jane said calmly, "not nice at all. And if you know it's not nice, why are you doing it?"

Stephanie's gaze dropped. "Why do you think? To solidify my position here. Because if it turns out that this company is legitimate, a place where I can work and not get put in jail, then I don't want to lose this gig. As I said, it's all I have."

Jane shook her head, impatient with Stephanie's self-pitying rationalizations. "There are other ways to solidify your position within a company. Like working hard and being a good employee."

"But don't you see, Jane! I won't be! I wasn't at any of my other jobs, and I won't be here. I know that about myself. So I exercise a talent I do have—a talent any woman has—to achieve the same effect."

The image of Stephanie stroking her lustrous mink coat flashed into Jane's mind. "Is that . . ." she hazarded, "how you got your mink?" *You have no* idea *what I had to do to get that coat.*

Stephanie threw back her head and laughed bitterly.

"No! That's what you were supposed to think, of course—that some man who was obsessed with me lavished me with outrageously extravagant gifts." She nodded in the direction of the coat in question, hanging on a hanger on the back of her office door. Jane could see the torn shoulder seam. "I bought that coat myself at a secondhand fur store. It's the most valuable thing I own."

Another crash came from Faith's office.

Stephanie seemed to have talked herself out and sat staring into nowhere. Jane rose. "I think we'll just table my leaving for now—though you are aware that I wasn't going to stay past Friday in the first place."

"I know, Jane," Stephanie said, gratitude in her moist dark eyes, "and if you haven't turned anything up either way by then, I'll let the whole thing drop. But please . . . please see what you can find out."

Jane gazed down at Stephanie, then gave a quick nod, turned, and left the office. As she sat down at her desk and took up the subscription lists, she was aware of Sam watching her.

"Getting briefed on an important project?" he asked, his tone amused.

She decided not to answer.

Suddenly the door of Faith's office flew violently open and Faith stormed out, her face a dark red, set in an expression of pure hatred. As if no one else were around, she stomped down the corridor to Gavin's office and, without knocking, burst in, slamming the door behind her. Now from Gavin's office came the sounds of Faith and Gavin screaming at each other, though Jane could not make out their actual words. Sam turned to Jane with a look of absolute glee, then returned his attention to Gavin's closed door. There were more shouts, then the unmistakable sound of a hard slap. A very hard slap, Jane reasoned, if it could be heard through a closed door.

Immediately Gavin's door opened again, and Faith marched out, heading toward her office. But she overshot it, stopping to stare into Stephanie's office. From where Jane sat, she could see Stephanie look up with a blank expression. Jane could also see the look of pure loathing on Faith's face. This look lasted a good five seconds; then Faith returned to her office and slammed the door.

"It appears," Sam observed nonchalantly, returning to whatever it was he'd been doing, "that our queen has been dethroned."

"What do you mean?" Jane asked, though she knew.

Sam swiveled energetically in his chair to face Jane. "Our Gavin is clearly enchanted by Stephanie, and is now *shtupping* her. Bitch," he added in a barely audible voice.

"Why do you call her that?" Jane whispered, checking to make sure Stephanie hadn't heard this exchange. Stephanie was on the phone now, half turned at her desk.

"I tried to make time with Miss Stephanie when she first joined our illustrious ranks."

"*You?*"

"Mm," he said matter-of-factly. "Why does that surprise you?"

"She's a good bit older than you."

"So are you," he said.

"And I'm not interested."

"Yet."

She rolled her eyes. "Do you find her attractive?"

"Yes, in a sixties sort of way. She's got a kind of—I don't know—Leslie Gore look."

"I don't think Stephanie would have wanted—"

"She made it all too clear what she wanted. She told me straight out that she would never go out with a *secretary*."

"Obviously," Jane said drily, "the fact that you are the son of her best friend was not an issue."

"Obviously not, if even her best friend's *husband* is fair game."

If Kenneth had only known what his cousin was really like, Jane thought, then reflected that perhaps he had.

"But it gets better!" Sam said, startling Jane. His mouth was twisted in a bitter grin. "Not only did she reject my advances, but she then told my mother I'd tried to force her to kiss me. A total fabrication. I have no idea why she would have told Mother that, why she would go out of her way to lie. All I did was ask her—a bit suggestively, I admit—if she would have lunch with me. But," he said with a sigh, glancing down at his papers, "a lowly secretary has no chance with Stephanie Townsend, not even if that secretary is a crown prince." He tilted his head in the direction of Gavin's office. "Now, the *president* of the company—well, that's evidently an entirely different story. Bitch," he repeated, and the bitter loathing in his voice surprised Jane.

She returned to her subscription lists as Sam swiveled back to face his desk. Just as she found another duplicate name and was drawing a line through it, she heard Sam mutter under his breath, "She'll be sorry."

* * *

Ten minutes before noon, Jane's phone rang. It was Daniel. "Hello, *Lana*. Two more editors who have *The Blue Palindrome* have said they'll be bidding but have questions for you."

"That's just fine, Mother," Jane said, casting a glance at Sam, who was doing a terrible job of pretending not to listen. "Who are they?"

Daniel gave her the editors' names.

"All right, Mother, I'll talk to you later." She hung up.

"Mom okay?" Sam asked.

"Fine." Jane gave a little giggle. "Two of her favorite stars are on TV this afternoon. She wanted me to know."

"Ah. And who are they?"

"George Clooney and Benjamin Bratt," she said, naming two of her own favorites.

"My, Mom's a horny old thing, isn't she?"

"Excuse me," she said, offended, though her mother had of course been dead for years, "this is my *mother* we're talking about."

But he just chuckled, shaking his head.

She rose.

"Going to lunch?" he asked.

"No, it's a bit early for lunch. I need some fresh air. I'm feeling a little queasy. Maybe it's the heating system; I'm not sure if it's working properly yet."

"Or maybe it's me."

"Maybe," she said, taking her bag from her bottom drawer. She got her coat from the closet and went out through the reception area.

Outside, in the parking lot behind the building, she called the two editors in turn on her cell phone, answering their questions about Nathaniel Barre and confirming her closing date of December 5. As she was finishing with the second editor, she saw Kate coming toward her from the alley on the right. The young woman's face was troubled, preoccupied. She walked with her hands shoved deep in her pockets, her shoulders hunched.

Jane hurriedly concluded her conversation and stepped into Kate's path.

"Oh!" Kate said, startled, and smiled. It crossed Jane's mind that she really wasn't such a bad-looking girl. "I didn't see you there."

"I needed some air. It was a little stuffy upstairs. Has the heating system been fixed yet?"

"Yes, days ago," Kate said, looking puzzled. Then her gaze went to the cell phone in Jane's hand.

Jane looked down and realized she hadn't slipped the phone back into her bag. *Damn.* "I remembered I had to call someone."

But Kate seemed not to have heard her, or to have lost interest in the cell phone. She looked preoccupied again, and peered intensely into Jane's face. "Lana . . ."

"Yes?"

"Have you noticed anything odd going on in the office lately?"

Have I! "Why, no, Kate. I'm not sure what you mean?"

"I guess I'm not sure, either." Kate shrugged, shook her head. "You going up?"

Jane nodded and they went into the building together. On the elevator, Jane thought of something to say to break the awkward silence. "Did you have a nice lunch?"

"To be honest, no," Kate replied. "I hurried back because Gavin wants to see me in his office at twelve-thirty."

Jane frowned. "That's an odd time. You'd think he'd have allowed you more time for your lunch."

She laughed ruefully. "You don't know Gavin. He does that on purpose. It's a control thing."

"I see. And I don't suppose you could have told him that was an inconvenient time for you."

"No," Kate said firmly. "You'd think I could, my mother being a partner in the company and all, but the truth is that Gavin runs the shop, and even my mother does everything he says. If I ever complained about Gavin to her—which I haven't done and won't do— she'd only take his side."

They arrived at the second floor and went through the reception area into the suite. As Jane hung up her coat, she watched Kate walk to Gavin's office at the other end of the corridor, look into the open doorway, and shrug. Apparently Gavin hadn't honored his own appointment. Kate went into her office, at the end of the corridor on the left.

Sam looked up as Jane settled herself at her desk. "Feel better?"

"Much."

"You and my sister getting chummy, are you?"

She gave him a disapproving look. He really was extremely impertinent. "We were chatting on the elevator. She's very nice."

He shook his head in wonder and returned to his work. A few minutes later, Gavin came in from the reception area. After hanging up his coat, he went to Stephanie's doorway and asked to see her in his office. She followed him there. A moment later Kate reappeared in the corridor and knocked on Gavin's door. He asked her to come in; then Jane saw him close the door.

"Wonder what that's all about," Sam said, twiddling a pen between two fingers, and gazed thoughtfully at Gavin's closed door. "Stranger and stranger."

Jane wondered, too. It was very quiet in Gavin's office. Suddenly the door banged open and Kate appeared. She was biting her lower lip hard between her teeth, as if to keep from crying, but a tear ran down her cheek as she ran down the corridor to her mother's office. Faith looked up in surprise. "What is it?"

Kate blurted out something, of which Jane could only make out "Gavin" and "Stephanie."

"I'll speak to him," Faith told her calmly, and Kate, her face now streaked with tears, ran back down the corridor and rushed into her office.

At almost the exact same moment, Stephanie appeared in Gavin's doorway. Unlike Kate, she looked thoroughly pleased; the word *preening* came to Jane's mind.

To Jane's surprise, Stephanie made her way down the hall and stopped at Jane's desk, her face gleeful. "Guess what."

"What?" Out of the corner of her eye, Jane saw Sam watching Stephanie with an expression of disgust.

"Gavin's made me managing editor."

Sam broke in, "But that's Kate's job."

Stephanie turned to him, her expression suddenly icy cold. "Not anymore. She's an editor now—and of course she'll continue with her photography." She spoke the last word with disdain.

Gavin appeared in his doorway. For a moment he just stood there, looking around, as if he were uncomfortable but making an effort to maintain some dignity. He strained his neck upward in his shirt collar, as if it were too tight.

Sam gave a low chuckle. "Our genital manager," he said softly.

"Congratulations, Stephanie," Florence said, handing her a plate containing roast beef, mashed potatoes, and peas. "Mrs. Stuart told me about your promotion."

"Why, thank you, Florence," Stephanie said, sounding surprised, as if she would never have expected congratulations from the nanny/housekeeper.

"Yes," Jane said brightly, though the image of Kate's tear-streaked face was vivid in her mind, "isn't that wonderful? Talk about moving up fast!"

Nick stuffed an entire roll into his mouth and said something unintelligible.

"Nicholas!" Jane said, unable to keep a trace of a smile from her face. "Please do not speak with your mouth full. And how did I teach you to eat a roll?"

Nick chewed hard and seemed to swallow the whole mass at once. "Yeah, yeah, break off little bits." He turned back to Stephanie. "Are you pulling six figures?"

They all burst out laughing.

"What'd I say?" Nick asked.

Stephanie gave him a sweet smile. "No, Nick, I'm afraid I'm not yet, but maybe someday. You never know!"

"The great thing about it," Jane said, amazing even herself at her bubbly insincerity, "is that Stephanie will now have more responsibility, more things to do, and that makes her job more interesting."

"Absolutely," Stephanie said with gusto, and speared a piece of meat. "Florence, this is heavenly."

"Thank you." Florence looked both surprised and pleased.

"It's nice to see you in such a good mood, Steph-

anie," Jane said. "Do you still think there may be . . ."
Jane cast a quick glance at Nick, "things going on at
Carson & Hart?"

Stephanie looked at him, too, frowning a little at
Jane's having brought this up. Turning to Jane, she
gave a tiny shake of her head that said she didn't want
to discuss this now. But she said, "I feel better about
things, but I still feel something's going on. But I may
be on the verge of uncovering it myself."

"Uncovering what?" Nick asked.

"Never mind," Jane said, reproaching herself for her
indiscretion.

Stephanie said to Jane, "Just a little longer . . ." and
Jane knew she was reiterating her plea for Jane to continue working undercover.

"All right," she said, though she'd had about as
much of Carson & Hart as she could stand.

With a silent leap, Winky appeared in the center of
the table.

"Hey, Wink!" Nick cried in delight, and tossed her a
piece of roast beef from his plate. Winky tore into it
with gusto.

Florence, Jane, and Stephanie watched in horror.

"Nicholas!" Jane cried, standing, and shooed Winky
off the table.

Stephanie threw back her head and laughed. "You
know, seeing Twinky eating like that reminds me of
something awful I saw today. I was in the alley beside
our building, and I noticed something moving at the
foot of the Dumpster. I thought it was a possum, but
when I got closer, I saw that it was a big rat! Isn't that
awful?"

"A rat—in Shady Hills?" Jane said.

"Sure was. When I realized what it was, I jumped

back, and who should I bump into but that horrible bum, Ivar."

"Ivor," Jane corrected.

"And my cat's name is Winky," Nick said, "not Twinky."

Stephanie ignored both of them. "*Well,* after my little episode the other night, bumping into this creature nearly gave me a heart attack. I mean, I didn't know which was worse—the rat or this despicably filthy man. He smelled like a brewery, not to mention his body odor. I'm certain he would have reached for my hand-bag if I hadn't run away."

"Stephanie," Nick said, now leaning forward in an obvious attempt not to be ignored again. She looked at him, her face blank. "Hasn't anyone ever taught you that it's wrong to judge people by how they look or how they smell?"

Stephanie's jaw dropped slightly. She continued to stare at him.

He went on, "Those things are *surface* things. They have nothing to do with what a person is like inside. Do you really think that because he drinks and smells, he would have stolen your pocketbook?"

Stephanie drew a deep breath, her expression earn-est as if framing a response during a serious interview. "He did come up behind me."

"How do you know you didn't just back into him?"

Jane, looking at Nick as he waited for a response, fairly burst with pride. So would Kenneth have done, if he were only there.

But Nick never got a reply. Stephanie glared at him a moment longer, impatiently puffed air out her nostrils, and returned her attention to her meal.

Nick wouldn't let it go, however. "And I don't appreciate your calling my cat a rat."

"I didn't call him a rat," Stephanie protested.

"*Her.* Winky is a girl. You said she reminded you of a rat." He suddenly pointed the tines of his fork at her. "You are a very rude person."

"Nicholas!" Jane and Florence said in unison.

He shrugged uncaringly and put down his fork. "I'm done. May I please be excused?"

"Yes," Jane said softly, and looked down, unable to meet Stephanie's gaze. But she realized she must, and turned to her. She was surprised to see that there were tears in Stephanie's eyes. "I'm sorry, Stephanie. He's only ten, of course, and sometimes he gets this way. I often wonder if it's because he has no father, whether I ought to get him some counseling. I'll speak to him, get him to apologize to you."

"That's not necessary." Stephanie pushed a pea around her plate, her face tilted down and a little to the side. "He's right. It was rude of me. I do and say things like that a lot; I know I do. Like what I said about Daniel in the car after I first got to town. I don't *mean* them the way they come out, but I can't help it. I . . . I don't know what's wrong with me. I sometimes think I'm just not a very nice person, but I don't know what to do about it."

She could start, Jane thought, by not having affairs with the husbands of her best friends. But of course she didn't say this. She just smiled sympathetically.

"I'll start clearing," Florence said briskly, rising, and with a polite smile she reached for Stephanie's plate. "And I'll get us some coffee."

"Not for me, thanks, Florence," Stephanie said, also rising, and walked quickly out of the dining room.

"Ditto," Jane said, and went to find Nick.

He was in his room, cross-legged on his bed, reading a video-game magazine. He didn't look up as she entered the room and closed the door behind her.

"I know what you're going to say," he said in a weary voice. "I shouldn't say things like that to people."

She sat down on the edge of the bed. "If you know," she said gently, "why did you?"

He met her gaze, his eyes fierce with outrage. "Mom, I was starting to like Stephanie, but now I see she's a terrible person. Can't you see that? Why is she here? Why doesn't she leave?"

"It's not for us to judge her," Jane said, feeling a complete hypocrite, because she found herself judging Stephanie constantly. "All that's important is that she's Daddy's cousin. She's part of our family, and she needs our help. Family helps family."

He just shrugged, looked down at his magazine.

"I want you to apologize to her."

"I knew you were going to say that," he grumbled. "Let's get it over with."

To her surprise, he put down his magazine and got right up from the bed, leading the way out of the room and down the hall to the guest room. Halfway down he turned to Jane. "Is she in there?"

"Probably."

Jane knocked on the guest room door. "Come in," Stephanie called.

Jane looked in. Stephanie sat at the small vanity that stood against the wall opposite the bed. There was nothing on the vanity's surface. Had she been staring at herself in the mirror? She gave Jane a wan smile.

"Stephanie, Nicholas has something to say to you."

"All right."

Jane ushered Nick into the room. He stood just inside the doorway like a soldier and said, "I'm sorry I said those rude things to you."

She gave him a sweet smile and nodded. "Thank you, Nick. And I'm sorry for what I said."

He looked surprised at this, as if he might reconsider what he'd said about her. He looked up at Jane for permission to leave.

"Thank you, Nick," she said, and pulled open the door. He walked out, still strangely stiff.

Jane closed the door again. "I'm sorry, too, Stephanie. I don't know what came over him."

"No, it's okay, Jane, really." Stephanie indicated the bed. "Sit for a minute." When Jane had sat, Stephanie went on, "It's something I needed to hear, because he's right. What is it they say? From the mouths of babes?" She looked at Jane searchingly. "What do *you* think, Jane?"

"About what?"

"About me. Am I such an awful person?"

Despite the invitation, Jane just couldn't be as honest as Nick. "Of course not," she scoffed.

Stephanie looked at her shrewdly, the corners of her mouth curving upward. "Tell me what you really think."

Jane paused, considering. "All right," she said at last, and keeping her voice reasonable, unaccusing, went on, "I do think it's wrong to have an affair with your friend's husband."

Stephanie grabbed her lower lip between her teeth and nodded. "I knew it. It would look awful."

Jane frowned. *"Look* awful?"

Stephanie turned in her chair to completely face Jane. "Faith doesn't love him, Jane. She hasn't for a very long time."

"She's told you that?"

"No . . . Gavin has."

"Does he love her?"

"He says he did, once. That was a long time ago—long before they were married, actually."

Jane's eyes widened.

"It's true," Stephanie said. "I know from Faith that he started flirting with her almost immediately after he starting working for Ravi. And I know from Gav that he was absolutely enchanted with her the moment he set eyes on her. She was beautiful, forceful, glamorous . . ."

"And what was he to her?"

"Interested. Ravi had already lost interest in Faith by this time. Remember, when Gavin arrived at the palace, Faith was near the end of her pregnancy with Surya—Sam. Ravi had no interest in a pregnant wife. Besides, Faith had lost respect for him a long time before. He was a lazy, self-indulgent child. Faith was also fairly certain he was having an affair, maybe several. After Sam was born, relations between Faith and Ravi only got worse. He showed no interest in the baby."

"Neither did she, apparently. In her own book she says she entrusted him to the care of nannies."

"She *had* to. She had responsibilities, things she had to do for Ananda because Ravi the playboy wasn't doing them. But even so, she did find time to spend with the baby. Ravi, on the other hand, went for weeks at a time without seeing him.

"Once, when Ravi flew to Calcutta on what he said was state business—Faith was pretty sure he was going to see one of his women—Gavin asked to be excused from going with him, saying he was ill. Since hiring Gavin, Ravi had never gone anywhere without him, but he said he understood, told Gavin to rest, and flew off by himself. But Gavin wasn't sick. He wanted to be with Faith. And she welcomed his attention.

"They finally surrendered to their attraction," Stephanie said dramatically, stars in her eyes. "Faith told me it was the deepest of passions. Of course, they continued seeing each other, taking elaborate precautions not to be discovered.

"Once in a while, when Ravi remembered she existed, he slept with her, and soon Faith was pregnant again with Ravi's child.

"It was a girl. Faith called her Ketaki, the Hindi name for a cream-colored flower.

"Only a few weeks after the baby was born, three off-duty palace guards went down to the village, which wasn't far from the palace. Several men appeared in the middle of the street and shot the guards dead. The killers were members of a new pro-Chinese rebel group. They disappeared and were never caught.

"Faith wrote to me that she was terrified. The political climate in Ananda had changed completely; it was volatile, dangerous. She pleaded with me to come to Ananda and stay with her at the palace for a few weeks."

"Did you go?"

"Of course! I was thrilled to be able to see her again, see the children. When I got there, I was immediately struck by how much Faith had changed. She'd always been so carefree and fun-loving. Now she was serious, guarded. I could tell she was terribly troubled—by what was going on in her marriage, in the country. She told me her only comfort was Gavin, and of course the children. Only when she was with her babies did the warm, happy Faith I'd always known show herself.

"But her life was a misery. One day at breakfast she

touched my hand and asked if I would stay on indefinitely. She said she needed a friend with her. I told her I had a job back in Boston, that I couldn't just throw it away. But she pleaded with me. She told me I could always get another job, but that if I ever did have trouble getting one, she would help me, either by giving me money or by using her connections to get me a job. She truly was desperate. Of course I said I would stay.

"Then a horrible thing happened. In the palace there was an elderly servant, a shriveled old man named Satyajit who'd been there since before Ravi was born. He hated Faith, and as we later learned, he'd been watching her carefully. He caught on to her affair with Gavin—actually saw them . . . together—and told Ravi.

"I know what happened next because Ravi told it to Faith later. Ravi, by his own account, was shattered to learn about Faith's infidelity. He adored Faith and said that despite his reputation as a playboy, he'd never been unfaithful to her."

Stephanie rolled her eyes. "Yeah. Right. Anyway, he decided to wait before taking any action. In the meantime, he asked Satyajit to keep watching Faith and Gavin and to report to Ravi. Over the next few weeks, Satyajit told Ravi he'd seen Faith slip out of the palace, presumably to some unknown meeting place, but Ravi still did nothing. He didn't know what to do; as he told Faith later, his heart was broken.

"But finally he couldn't stand it anymore. One day he lied to Faith and Gavin that he had to leave on business in Agra, a city in India not far from Ananda. In reality, he was waiting for a signal from Satyajit that Faith was leaving the palace. When he got it, he secretly followed her to a tiny abandoned temple on a mountainside near the palace. He waited; then he burst in on Faith and Gavin.

"They were making love—quite savagely, Faith told me later. Faith wore the necklace that bore the Star of Ananda, that magnificent jewel. And that was all she wore."

Chapter Twenty

Jane leaned forward, fascinated.

Stephanie continued, "There was a hideous scene. Ravi went into an insane rage and screamed to them that they had brought shame to him and his country. He told Gavin he'd thought they were friends and that Gavin had committed the ultimate betrayal. He ordered Gavin to leave Ananda immediately and never return, or he would reveal Gavin's treason and have him executed—now that Faith had made executions fashionable in Ananda again.

"He screamed to Faith that he would divorce her, said he should never have married a spoiled American debutante in the first place. He said he was ashamed and angry at himself for letting her coerce him into treating his own people as abominably as he had. He shrieked at her to remove the necklace. Frantically pulling on her clothes, Faith took off the necklace and dropped it in her pocket. Then she ran back to the palace in tears. When she got to her rooms, she placed the necklace in a small safe in which she kept all of her jewelry." Stephanie raised one eyebrow. "You'll see in a minute why I'm telling you these details.

"In her overwrought state, Faith apparently closed the safe but forgot to lock it.

"She gathered up her courage and went to see Ravi. She told him he was right and that she was ashamed of her behavior. She said she and the children would leave immediately. But Ravi forbade this. *She* could leave, but *his* children would remain in Ananda. Faith was terrified. She said she couldn't accept that; then she burst into tears. She told Ravi they would discuss the matter again and ran out.

"When she returned to her rooms, she realized she'd forgotten to lock the safe. When she went to do it, she discovered that the Star of Ananda, that fabulous necklace, was gone. She heard a sound and saw one of the doors to her room closing. She ran to the door, looked out, and saw the back of a servant, a woman draped in robes, running. Faith ran after her, but she lost her in the maze of corridors. And she had no idea which servant it had been."

"Satyajit?" Jane said.

"That was my first thought. But if Ravi had wanted the necklace back—which he would have—he would simply have demanded it back. And Satyajit would never have done that on his own. He was as loyal to Ravi and the royal family as anyone could have been.

"Faith went to Ravi immediately and told him what had happened. Ravi called in the police, and all the servants were searched and questioned—but no necklace. The entire palace was searched minutely, but the Star of Ananda was nowhere to be found.

"That night Faith paced in her rooms, mad with fear

that she'd lose the children. Suddenly Gavin was standing on her veranda. He told her he'd only pretended to leave. He had to see Faith. He had to tell her that if she left in disgrace, she would get nothing. She had rights, he said. She was the Queen of Ananda; she was married to the king, was the mother of his children. Ravi couldn't just throw her out like some peasant who'd been caught stealing a loaf of bread.

"Faith told him it was only what she deserved for what she'd done—what they'd done—but that she couldn't bear to lose the children. If she could just get them away, she said, she and Gavin could have a life together—a freer life, without secrets—in Paris, London, Rome, New York . . . wherever he wanted. She was sure Ravi would give her *some* money; that wouldn't be a problem. Besides, she had some money of her own, from her family; not a lot, not as much as everyone thought, but enough. It was the children she was worried about. She couldn't leave them. She needed them. They needed her. She told Gavin they would work something out. What mattered was that they loved each other and would be together.

"She asked him jokingly if he would still love her when she wasn't the queen and had gone back to being just plain old Faith Carson. She said maybe moving back to America would be best; they'd fit in best there, be nearer to her family. But first she had to resolve the matter of the children.

"Gavin tried to calm her down. He said of course what mattered most was that they'd be together—*where* didn't matter—but surely Faith must see that Ravi would never let her take the children. *He* was the one with the power, especially after discovering Faith's infidelity. Surely Faith must see that Ravi would manipulate the situation so that he kept the children—one of whom was, after all, the crown prince."

"Did Faith agree with this?" Jane asked.

"She told Gavin she thought Ravi was more reasonable than Gavin was giving him credit for. She was sure she could get Ravi to agree to a joint-custody arrangement. After all, this was the twentieth century. Ravi was enlightened enough to see that children needed their mother. Gavin said he would be back; then he slipped back out onto the veranda and off into the shadows of the palace grounds.

"The very next morning, Faith and Ravi discussed the future. I happened to be in a nearby room, having my breakfast, and I heard them yelling at each other. Faith told me afterward that to her horror, Ravi flatly refused to even consider joint custody of Surya and Ketaki. He wanted her to simply leave the country as soon as possible. If she fought him, he would tell the world what she and Gavin had done, shame her. Faith told him she didn't care about herself, but that that would be terribly unfair to the children. Ravi said that in that case, she had better leave immediately. Faith burst into tears and ran out."

"Did Gavin come back?" Jane asked.

"Yes, later that morning. Faith told him what Ravi had said. Gavin told her to speak to a lawyer—perhaps her family's lawyer, back in Boston. Gavin said he was sure things could still be worked out. Faith agreed to call the lawyer.

"Gavin came back about a week later. She told him she'd spoken to the lawyer, who was working on the case and would be flying to Ananda within the next couple of weeks. Ravi had agreed to speak with the lawyer. Gavin urged her not to leave the palace until she had an agreement, signed by Ravi, that she was satisfied with.

"Faith agreed that this made sense and said that in the meantime, she and Ravi had agreed to keep up appearances. In a few days they would ride together through the village on festival day."

Stephanie's face darkened. "That day came. Faith and Ravi, though they weren't even speaking to each other, rode together in the back of a white Mercedes from the palace down to the village, where people waved and cheered. I was riding with Satyajit two cars behind them.

"Suddenly a gunshot rang out. Time seemed to stand still." Tears welled in Stephanie's eyes. "Faith told me later that Ravi's head whipped back sharply and masses of bloody matter burst out of the back of his head. Faith went into a kind of shocked hysteria and climbed up the back of the seat to get this matter . . . Ravi's brains. Then when she realized what she'd done, she pressed against the car's closed window and raised her bloody hands—that famous photograph everyone has seen, that would be published and broadcast all over the world.

"Women in the crowd screamed. There was another shot. I told our driver to stop and got out. At the side of the road I saw a man lying dead. Then there were police all over him. The police had killed Ravi's assassin. Later, the man was found to have been a member of the pro-Chinese rebels, the same group that had killed the palace guards. They were rabidly in favor of China's annexing the kingdom and hated the decadent, apathetic royal family. The assassin may even have been a spy for China; they never found out for sure."

"How horrible," Jane whispered.

"Yes . . . That's when I flew home. Faith was now the king's widow, the queen mother. Fortunately, Ravi hadn't yet told anyone of his and Faith's troubles. Faith immediately dismissed Satyajit, warning him that if he ever spoke about the royal family, she would have him arrested for treason. Now there was no longer any reason for Faith to leave Ananda. She attended Ravi's lavish funeral and made her plan. Gavin would continue in his position as assistant—Faith's assistant—handling top-level affairs of the palace, and their secret affair would go on.

"The night of the funeral, he came to her again in her chambers and they made love. They were elated. They could enjoy the privileges of the palace without ending their affair."

Jane said, "But it didn't happen that way."

"No, it didn't. Less than a month after Ravi was assassinated, a large band of rebels stormed the palace gate and brutally murdered the guards. Faith, Surya, and Ketaki barely escaped with their lives, smuggled out by dark of night just as the rebels descended on the palace itself. On the outskirts of the village Gavin met them, and together the four of them fled Ananda into India, taking advantage of the general confusion in the country and of special arrangements Gavin had made with the guards at the Ananda police checkpoint.

"From India they flew to London, and from there they watched televised reports of Ananda's bloody overthrow. The palace was ransacked. All the symbols of the Anandese royal family—priceless objects, centuries old—were destroyed. The rebels turned the palace into their headquarters. Ananda was put under military rule. Within a matter of weeks, China annexed the country.

"Faith wanted the comfort of her family in the States, so she and Gavin and the children flew to Boston and set up household in the Carson compound in Cambridge. They maintained strict privacy from the prying eyes of the press and the public. Of course, Faith and I saw each other often.

"Gavin and Faith married and lived a lavish lifestyle in a house they bought in Cambridge. Surya and Ketaki—Sam and Kate—attended the best private schools. But it wasn't long before Gavin and Faith's money had nearly run out, including Faith's own family money. She and Gavin needed a source of income.

"Faith had the idea of trading on her grandfather's famous name and starting a publishing company. She and Gavin and the kids moved to New York, and she and Gavin founded Carson & Hart. Faith was excited about this venture. She went after the same big projects the major publishers were going after. She even got some of them. But she quickly saw that if she continued this way, Carson & Hart would soon be out of business.

"Faith and Gavin decided it had been a mistake to try to compete with publishing's big players. Instead they decided to use their connections to find society figures who wanted to publish their autobiographies, novels, photo collections, that sort of thing. These books would be published on what amounted to a vanity-press basis, with the wealthy authors themselves subsidizing publication."

"Which is what they're doing now," Jane said.

"Mostly, yes. And it worked, but they still found themselves struggling financially, barely keeping their heads above water. For one thing, they needed to move to cheaper office space.

"One day Puffy went to New York to have lunch with

Faith, and Faith mentioned that she and Gavin were looking for new space. Puffy told her about the building she and Oren own. A doctor had moved out of one of the suites, and Puffy still hadn't found a replacement. She said Faith and Gavin were welcome to use the space rent-free, if they were willing to move to New Jersey.

"I don't think Puffy ever thought Faith and Gavin would live in New Jersey, but they were very interested. A few days later they drove out here, looked at the suite, and liked it. They told Puffy they would accept her offer. Then they started looking for a place to live out here, not wanting to do a reverse commute from New York City every day. They ended up buying the house in Mountain Lakes."

"Hardly an inexpensive community," Jane said.

"True, but still more affordable than the place where they were living in the city. They're going to sell that— it's a co-op. When I lost my job at Skidder & Phelps, I called Faith and said I wanted to come here for a visit. I rented a car and drove down. I told Faith I'd lost my job and begged her for a job at Carson & Hart. Without even consulting with Gavin, she said I could be an editor."

"Do you think Gavin resented her doing that?" Jane asked.

"Faith told me he did, that he even told her to tell me it was off, but Faith refused.

"As I've told you, I was thrilled. I'd never worked in publishing, and to be working with my old friend would be priceless. That night, after dinner with Faith and Gavin, Faith showed me around the house. It's a massive old place; Faith says it's a Hapgood—he was some famous developer. Most of their stuff was still in boxes, but on the wall above the fireplace in the living room, Faith showed me her royal portrait. She looked so serene and beautiful, and around her neck was the Star of Ananda, that magnificent star sapphire among diamonds." Stephanie closed her eyes. "I've never seen anything so magnificent.

"I told Faith I was surprised she'd been able to smuggle the portrait out of Ananda, even though the whole painting couldn't be more than two and a half feet square. Faith looked at it sadly and said if she couldn't have the Star, if she couldn't be a queen anymore, she would at least have this portrait, to remember."

For a moment Jane regarded Stephanie, seemingly lost in her own memories of her role in the fairy-tale phase of Faith's life. Then she looked at her watch and realized she'd been here in the guest room with Stephanie for nearly an hour. She rose. "I had no idea it was so late."

Stephanie snapped from her reverie as if she'd been awakened from hypnosis. "Yes," she said, shaking herself a little, "I guess it is. How did I end up telling you that whole story?"

"We were discussing whether it's nice to have an affair with your friend's husband."

Stephanie looked uncomfortable. "I suppose that to many people, like you, it wouldn't look very nice at all. But as I've told you, Jane, Gavin doesn't love Faith anymore, and she doesn't love him. Their marriage is simply a business arrangement. So, you see, I'm not really doing anything wrong. I'm not taking anything away from her that she wants." She smiled serenely. "I'm still her best friend, her oldest friend."

Jane rose from the bed and crossed to the door. Reaching for the knob, she cast a glance back at Stephanie, who sat facing the mirror above the vanity, staring intently into her own dark eyes.

Chapter Twenty-one

Jane reached greedily for one of Florence's fresh-baked banana muffins.

"Uh-uh-uh!"

Jane spun around as if caught doing something naughty. Florence stood a few feet away, her arms folded grandly. "I do not think my banana muffins are on Dr. Stillkin's program . . ." she said, her tone smug and singsong.

"You're right."

Florence chuckled. "I was only joking with you, missus. If you want a muffin, have it!"

"No, I shouldn't. I'll never look good in my new swimsuits at this rate." Jane grabbed a fresh banana from the counter, peeled it, and mashed it in a bowl with a fork. Then she got a jar of bran from the cupboard and sprinkled it liberally on the mashed banana. She grabbed a spoon from the drawer and took a mouthful. She couldn't help grimacing.

Florence bent over laughing. "Oh, missus, you should see your face!"

"*You* try this and we'll see what kind of a face you make!"

"No, thank you. I don't claim to be skinny, but if I want to take off some pounds, I won't go on any cockamamy diet—if you'll excuse me."

Jane waved away her concern and had to laugh herself. "In all fairness to Dr. Stillkin, I haven't given his diet much of a chance. It doesn't help that I keep forgetting I'm on it. Or else I remember but don't care!"

"You've had a lot on your mind." Florence gazed sadly at the plate of muffins. "I just remembered where I got the recipe for those. From Una. She told me her little brothers always loved them the way she made them." A tear ran down Florence's smooth dark cheek. "Poor Una."

"Yes," Jane agreed quietly.

"Have they found out anything, missus? The police, I mean?"

"No, but they're still working on it." Jane shook her head regretfully. "If only I'd told Detective Greenberg what you told me Una saw, she might not have been killed."

"Don't do that to yourself, missus. Una swore me to secrecy, and I swore you. You couldn't betray that confidence."

"No, but if I'd known that by doing so I might have saved Una's life, I would have."

"Would have, should have. Let's leave it alone. Poor Una's gone and we can't bring her back."

"True . . . Stephanie loves your banana muffins, too, Florence. Don't forget to save her some."

Florence gave her a funny look. "She's already had two of them. She was down here at six-thirty, had her breakfast, and left. She said she had some errands to run before work—the drugstore, dry cleaner, I forget what else she said."

"How unlike her," Jane said thoughtfully. "Usually she has trouble leaving the house at the same time I do."

"Who?" Nick asked, appearing in the doorway, his wet hair sticking out in wild brown spikes.

"None of your beeswax. Don't eavesdrop. Here, have one of Florence's muffins and a nice glass of milk. Then we'd better get you to school."

Jane stopped in at Whipped Cream to see Ginny. Unlike Florence, Ginny had completely forgotten about Jane's diet and brought Jane a large mug of coffee and an especially delicious-looking apple-raisin muffin, Jane's favorite.

Longingly Jane eyed the muffin's crumbly crusted top glistening with sugar. With a great effort, she pushed the plate away. "Sorry, Ginny, can't have it. Not on Stillkin."

"Ooh, right, sorry." Ginny snatched the plate away. "What can I bring you instead?"

"This coffee's fine. I'll have it black."

Ginny grabbed the cream pitcher from the table and put it on the counter. Then she sat down opposite Jane. "I'll take a break while it's quiet." The only other customer in the shop was a young man Jane recognized, though she didn't know him by name. He was one of the train commuters to New York who stopped in at Whipped Cream for breakfast.

"So," Ginny said, "how's Operation Stephanie going?"

Jane laughed. "It's not going anywhere, I'm afraid. Despite Stephanie's conviction that something nefarious is going on at Carson & Hart, all I've seen so far is the usual sort of office hanky-panky, and that all seems to center on Stephanie herself!"

Ginny's eyes widened and she leaned forward avidly. "Really?" she breathed.

"Mm-hmm," Jane said with gusto. "The woman is—"

At that moment Stanley Greenberg entered the shop. Jane looked up and smiled, genuinely pleased to see him; then she remembered that the last time they'd spoken, he'd been angry at her, and she made her face serious.

But he seemed to have forgotten all about that. He walked over and kissed her on the cheek, greeted Ginny warmly, and took a seat at their table. "Knew I'd find you here at this time of the morning," he said to Jane. "I keep meaning to ask you how your vacation plans are coming."

"Very well. I'm going to Antigua day after tomorrow."

"Really? When did you make this decision?"

"Saturday."

"Now that you've had more time to consider your vacation plans, perhaps you've changed your mind about taking me with you." His eyes sparkled devilishly.

The thought appealed to Jane, she had to admit, but she wasn't ready for that yet. "I'm afraid not," she said with a gentle smile. "Maybe next time."

"I'm going to hold you to that."

They all laughed. Then Jane looked at him earnestly. "Stanley, have you got any leads on who killed poor Una?"

His face grew troubled. "We don't exactly have a theory, but there's been a bit of disturbing news that may be related. A dangerous character we thought left Shady Hills some time ago was just spotted in town, prowling around some of the more affluent homes. The man's known to be dangerous. In fact, he's suspected to have killed a man, though it's never been proved. We're looking for him." Suddenly something occurred to him and he looked at Jane. "You've met this guy. It's Gil Dapero."

"Gil Dapero!" Jane exclaimed. A chill ran through her at this news. She remembered all too well this thug who had been the boyfriend of her former nanny. Shivering at the thought that he was back, she rose. "I'd better run," she said, and headed for the door, promising to speak to them both soon.

She stopped in at her office and found that Daniel hadn't arrived yet. She sorted some mail he'd left on her desk, wrote out a few notes for him, and hurried out.

When she entered Carson & Hart, she found Sam at his desk, a smirk on his face. As Jane sat down at her desk, the sounds of Gavin and Faith screaming at each other came from behind Gavin's closed door.

"Morning fireworks," Sam said without looking up.

The fireworks lasted a good five minutes longer. Then Gavin's door opened and Faith emerged, her face as white as powder. She'd obviously been crying. She marched resolutely to her own office and slammed the door.

Sam looked up. "I guess Mumsy isn't willing to put up with Gavin's philandering any longer. What a day!"

Jane had to smile. "What a day? It's ten past nine."

"A lot has already happened, though. I got here earlier than usual, and when I came in, I realized someone was already here. I looked around and found Miss Stephanie in the mail room."

Jane looked across the hall and saw that Stephanie's office was empty.

"The mail room?" she asked softly. "What was she doing in there?"

Sam shrugged. "I went up behind her and said good morning, and she jumped as if I'd stuck her with a cattle prod. Which isn't a bad idea, come to think of it," he said thoughtfully. "She said I'd startled her terribly—scared the shit out of her, was actually how she put it—and to stop sneaking around. Then she went back to what she was doing."

"Which was what?"

"It looked like she was packing up a manuscript to mail."

Jane nodded pensively and started leafing through some papers on her desk.

"But there's more," Sam said. "I came back to my desk, and after a little while Stephanie came out of the mail room and went to her office. Not long after that, Gavin arrived. He went straight into Stephanie's office and shut the door. I couldn't hear a thing, damn it. After a few minutes, the door opened and Stephanie came out. She was *extremely* upset; she was crying. Ignoring me completely—as always—she grabbed her coat from the closet and hurried out.

"I think Gavin broke up with her. Whatever he did, he must have been upset, too, because he went straight to his own office, closed the door, and hasn't come out since."

So Gavin and Stephanie, it seemed, had ended their brief affair. That was a relief to Jane. Gavin must have wanted to see Stephanie first thing this morning to tell her it was over. Then he and Faith must have argued again about the affair, even after Gavin told Faith he'd ended it. It occurred to Jane that it would be just like Faith to hurl a few last recriminations at him, even after he'd just told her his transgression was over.

Jane busied herself with her work. As the morning passed, she looked up every so often, expecting to see Stephanie come in. But when noon arrived, Stephanie still had not returned.

Chapter Twenty-two

Jane waited until Sam had left for lunch; then she went to the closet for her coat. She'd sneak over to the agency and see what was going on.

"Oh, Lana . . ."

Jane turned. Gavin had come out of his office for the first time today and was striding down the corridor toward her.

She smiled pleasantly and met him halfway. Looking at him now, she realized he really was quite an attractive man, and that he must have been even more so years ago. The image of him and Faith making "savage" love in the abandoned temple flashed into her mind, and she just as quickly forced it out.

"Lana," he said, his face serious, "I want to talk to you about your cat, Slinky."

"Winky."

"Right. Winky. Stephanie said he—"

"She. Winky is a female."

"Mm. Stephanie said Winky would be just right for

the jacket of *Mew's Who's Who*. She said you and she discussed it. Would you be willing to have her pose for it?"

She threw back her head and laughed airily. "My
celebricat! Certainly."

"Marvelous."

"When would you like her here?"

"Midafternoon would be about right, I think. Say,
three?"

"She'll be here." She shrugged on her coat.

"I'll walk out with you," Gavin said, grabbing his
charcoal-gray overcoat from the closet, and they went
out together through the reception room, down the
corridor, and onto the elevator.

"And how are you liking our little publishing house?"
he asked as the doors opened on the lobby and they
started toward the building's rear entrance.

"It's . . . charming. I never realized publishing was so
interesting."

He held the door for her. Outside, it was bright
and cold, with a biting wind. The bare branches of the
trees that rose at the edge of the parking lot rattled,
as if trying to rid themselves of the last of their brown
leaves.

"I'm off," Gavin said, stopping at a white BMW and
fishing in his pocket for his keys. Jane remembered that
this was the car she'd seen when Gavin and Faith drove
Stephanie home after Puffy's party. "Have a nice
lunch."

"Thanks. You, too." Just as she was turning, she noticed a small slip of paper tucked under one of Gavin's
windshield wipers. Gavin appeared to notice it at the
same time. He frowned in puzzlement and pulled it
out. Reading it, he lowered his brow in a frown.

"Palm reader or car wash?" she called to him with a laugh.

He jerked, as if he'd been unaware she was watching him. He smiled, glanced down at the slip of paper, and laughed a decidedly artificial laugh.

"I'm always finding those on my car when I go to the supermarket," she said. "Must be a suburban thing."

"Right," he said, and crumpled the paper and stuffed it into his coat pocket. "See you later."

He got in and drove away. Jane started toward the alley leading to Packer Road, then stopped and glanced back at where Gavin's car had been. Not three feet away, at the edge of the asphalt, stood a trash can. Yet Gavin had put the slip of paper in his pocket. Perhaps he hadn't seen the trash can. She shrugged and walked on.

Daniel was happy to see her. He hurried to his desk, where he had arranged little piles relating to various projects on which he needed her input. After they'd discussed these, they went through her mail and phone messages. Then he brought her up to date on the Nat Barre auction.

"This is going to be lively, Jane."

"Of course it is. It's a wonderful book."

"All but two of the editors have said they're definitely in."

"Fabulous. That'll really drive up the price. We'll get this man out of the pharmacy and in front of his computer full-time, writing."

She thanked Daniel once again for taking care of things while she was away, then drove home and, under Florence's bemused gaze, put Winky in her carrier and grabbed her food and water bowls, a bag of dry food, a small bag of litter, and a large clean plastic garbage bag. She took an apple to eat in the car.

Driving back down into the village, Winky protesting loudly from the backseat, Jane considered parking behind Carson & Hart's building in order to shorten her walk with the heavy carrier. But she immediately nixed this idea. She couldn't afford to be seen pulling in there. Instead she parked in the municipal lot, which was closer to Carson & Hart's building than the lot behind her own building, and hurried with the carrier toward the office building, keeping her head down.

Walking down the alley, she spotted Ivor asleep near the Dumpster and shook her head sadly. Slowly she approached him. He lay on his back, parallel to the edge of the pavement, his arms limp at his sides. His mouth hung slightly open.

She remembered her vow to try to help him and was suddenly filled with new resolve. Gently setting down Winky's carrier and the supplies, she approached Ivor, knelt down, and spoke his name. He didn't respond. "Ivor," she said again, louder. Still no response. Lightly she touched his shoulder, gave him a tiny shake. Nothing. He was out cold. With a shrug she stood, taking up the carrier and supplies. At that moment a woman who must also have worked in the building started down the alley toward her, and Jane quickly moved on.

When she got upstairs, Sam was at his desk. As Jane placed the carrier on the floor beside her desk, he looked over and his eyes widened curiously. "Is this Take Your Pet to Work Day?"

"For me it is," she replied in a bored tone.

"Meaning?"

She rolled her eyes. "Gavin wants to use Winky on the jacket of *Mew's Who's Who*."

He squinted at her. "Winky?" he repeated distastefully.

"Yes, that's her name."

"Do you know what a winky is in my family?"

"I think I can guess," she replied, and turned away.

"Gavin is one cheap son of a bitch," Sam grumbled. "He won't even spring for a stock photo of a damn cat."

"That's okay," Jane said lightly. "My son will be thrilled."

Sam shrugged and returned his attention to his work. Jane looked over and saw that he was playing tic-tac-toe again. She decided to do some filing.

For twenty minutes or so, Winky lay curled up in the carrier, apparently content. Then she began to pace, occasionally mewing at Jane through the carrier's wire door.

"Let her out," Sam said in an exasperated tone, not even looking up from his *X*'s and *O*'s.

"Do you think it would be all right?"

He swiveled to face her. "This isn't exactly Random House, Lana. I'll make sure everyone keeps the door to the suite closed so she doesn't get out."

Jane thanked him and opened the door of the carrier. Winky stepped out gingerly, casting wide-eyed glances around this alien environment. She let out an especially loud cry that sounded like "Mrowlll!"

"Ah, freedom's cry!" Sam said, watching the cat walk toward Stephanie's empty office. "Sally forth and explore, Stinky!"

"Winky!"

He seemed not to have heard her, engrossed again in his game.

Jane watched Winky prowl down the corridor, stepping cautiously, as if the floor might explode at any moment, jumping at the slightest sound. It occurred to Jane that the cat would be back at her desk soon, and she filled Winky's bowl with the dry food and set it on the floor beside her. She carried the other bowl to the ladies' room, filled it with water, and set it beside the food. Finally, she got a cardboard box from Mel in the mail room, borrowed a packing knife from him, and cut down the box's sides. She carried it to her desk and, placing it against the wall behind her, lined it with the plastic bag. Then she poured in a generous amount of litter.

"Home away from home," Sam said dryly, and rolled his eyes.

Jane ignored him.

Winky did return several times to nibble at her food, but appeared to grow increasingly comfortable with the atmosphere of Carson & Hart, and ventured off to explore farther after each snack.

At two o'clock, Sam rose and announced that he was going out for a cigarette.

"You smoke?" Jane asked.

"Just started."

She opened her mouth to comment, then thought better of it. Twenty minutes later he was back. "Have you seen Stephanie?" he asked.

"No, why?"

"She's been gone since she ran out of here early this morning. Don't you find that odd?"

Jane wouldn't have been surprised by anything

Stephanie did, but kept this thought to herself, too. Perhaps whatever Gavin had said to Stephanie had upset her so much that she had quit. Whatever had happened, Jane would no doubt hear about it from Stephanie herself at the end of the day. Jane just smiled mildly at Sam and shrugged.

"And Mother's been holed up in her office all day," he murmured, half to himself. Jane regarded Faith's closed door, then returned to her work.

Around three, a haggard-looking Kate emerged from her office and approached Jane's desk.

"Lana, Gavin says you brought your cat for the *Mew's Who's Who* jacket shot?"

"Yes, I'll get her."

"Here she is," Kate said, looking down at Winky at her feet, and she knelt to pick up the cat. "What a beautiful kitty you are," she crooned into Winky's fur. "Aren't you? Yes, yes." Winky, immediately at home in Kate's arms, began to purr softly. "We're going to make you a star." She turned to Jane. "I've got everything set up for the shoot. Do you want to help, or can I just take her?"

"She seems right at home with you. Just call me if you need me."

Kate carried Winky down the hall and into her room, and Jane returned to her desk. Fifteen minutes later, Kate returned with Winky in her arms.

Kate was smiling. "Thanks, Lana. She's a real sweetheart. You didn't tell me about her condition."

At this, Jane and Sam both looked up with curious frowns. "Condition?" Jane said.

"Didn't you know?" Kate hugged Winky tighter. "This little lady's going to have kittens!"

Jane's jaw dropped. "Winky!"

Sam made a *tsk*ing sound. "Ooh, you little tramp."

Jane got up and took Winky from Kate's arms. "We *have* been letting her go outside lately. How can you tell?"

Kate gently turned Winky over, exposing her soft white underside. "A rounded belly, for one thing. But I could feel it when I picked her up."

Jane stroked Winky's belly. Winky mewed in protest.

"She won't want anybody feeling her stomach," Kate said, gently placing Winky on the floor.

"Any idea when we can expect this blessed event?" Jane asked.

"A cat's pregnancy only lasts two months, a little more. I'd say this lady is about three or four weeks along. You'll want to speak to your vet about what to do when the time nears."

"Unbelievable," Jane said. "My son will be ecstatic."

"You'll have to figure out what to do with the kittens," Kate pointed out. "I can help you there. And you'll probably want to have her spayed as soon after she gives birth as possible—unless you want more kittens."

"No—at least, I don't think so." Jane sat down at her desk. "I'm just so amazed by this news."

"It *is* earth-shattering," Sam said, looking utterly bored. He turned to his sister. "Since when are you such a cat expert?"

Kate shook her head in wonder. "I've always loved cats. I can't believe you don't know that about me. Or maybe I can. Mother won't let me have a cat in the new house; she's never let me have one. But when I'm in a place of my own, I plan to have several."

"How cozy," Sam said in a falsely sweet tone, and swiveled back to his work.

Kate shrugged, winked at Jane, and headed back down the corridor.

Winky spent the afternoon continuing her exploration of Carson & Hart, appearing at Jane's desk several times, once for a sip of water, once for a snack, and once to use her litter box. Hearing her scratching in the litter, Sam turned in his chair and saw what she was up to. "Oh, for Pete's sake!" he cried, his face contorted in disgust.

But neither Winky nor Jane paid any attention to him, Winky finishing her business and wandering off again, Jane starting some new filing.

At a quarter to four, Winky reappeared at Jane's desk. This time she began mewing insistently, standing near Jane's feet and staring directly up at her.

"What's up, Wink?" Jane asked in puzzlement. "You've got everything you need—food, water, litter box."

Winky's mewing grew even more spirited.

Jane gazed down at her shrewdly. "Is something wrong? Do you want me to come with you?"

At this, Winky let out a loud yowl.

"Lassie!" Sam cried mockingly. "What are you trying to tell us, girl?"

"Be quiet," Jane said. She got up to follow Winky, who turned and led the way calmly down the corridor, stopped at the door to the mail room, which stood ajar, and looked up at Jane.

"In here?" Jane asked, and in response, Winky pushed the door farther open with her nose and scooted inside. Jane followed.

Mel stood at the large table in the center of the room, filling boxes with books and Styrofoam peanuts. He looked up and scowled at Jane. "I need my knife back."

"I gave it to you right after I used it." She scanned the table. "There it is, where I left it."

Mel glanced at the knife and returned to his packing.

Winky let out another cry and now led Jane to the back left corner of the room, where there stood a steel utility table on which sat a postal meter and scale. The table was a good six inches from the wall, and Winky walked around to the table's side and peered intently into this space. Then she stepped back.

"What's in there, Wink? A mouse?" Jane peered into the dim space. Something dark and rounded appeared to have fallen behind the table and sat suspended between it and the wall. Reaching in, Jane was just able to grab its edge and pull it out.

Looking down at the object in her hands, she felt a mild chill run through her. It was Stephanie's black leather Coach handbag. She turned. "Mel?" When he glanced up and grunted, she held up the bag. "This was back here behind the mailing table. Any idea how it got there?"

He looked at her as if she were insane. "How the hell should I know?"

Again she regarded the bag, and was suddenly overcome by a vague sense of dread.

Winky was wandering around the mail room.

"Get him out of here," Mel grumbled.

"Come on, Winky," Jane said absently, Stephanie's bag clutched at her side. Winky fell into step at Jane's feet.

When Jane had nearly reached the door to the hallway, she noticed a door open on her right and heard the sound of running water. Looking in, she saw Norma, the cleaning lady, in what appeared to be a large utility closet. She stood hunched over the sink, rinsing out the head of a mop.

Something caught Jane's eye. Just inside the closet, on a small shelf, lay a copy of the *Romantic Times* that contained Jane's photo from the Romance Authors Together convention. Instantly Jane grabbed it, tucked it firmly under her arm, and returned with Winky to her desk.

"What was it?" Sam asked.

"A mouse." Jane laughed. "Her weakness."

"Great, the offices are infested." He shook his head. "Thank you, Puffy Chapin."

Jane stuffed the magazine and Stephanie's handbag into her bottom drawer with her own bag.

"Sam, when Stephanie ran out this morning, did she have her purse?"

He scowled at her. "How should I know?"

"You saw her."

He thought for a moment. "Yeah, she had it. She was in that awful mink coat and she had her bag. I remember because as she was leaving, she opened it and pulled out some tissues, because she was crying."

Down the hall, the mail room door opened and Norma emerged, pulling a large wheeled bucket of soapy water with the mop standing in it. She made her way down the corridor and stopped suddenly at Sam's desk.

"Sam," she said in a heavily accented voice, pronouncing his name *Sahm*, "you seen my magazine book?"

"Garbo speaks!" Sam cried.

Norma glared at him, his joke lost on her, waiting. "You seen?" she asked again, her tone impatient. "Loving magazine."

"A loving magazine, eh, Norma?" Sam's eyes danced with mischief. "Have you been smuggling those copies of *Playgirl* into the office again, you naughty little girl?"

Understanding that she was getting nowhere, Norma gave an aggravated shrug, took up her bucket, and continued down the hall.

"Animal!" Sam cried after her.

Jane's phone rang. It was Daniel. "Jane, I'm sorry to bother you, but Patsy Frank at St. Martin's wants to put a floor on *The Blue Palindrome* and needs to speak with you. Can you go somewhere and call her back?"

"Sure, Mother, that's fine. No problem," Jane said, and hung up.

She opened her bottom drawer, took out her bag, and went to the ladies' room. Locking herself in a stall, she rummaged in her bag for her cell phone and called Patsy. The floor she offered was far too low to consider. When Jane told her this, she laughed in embarrassment and said she guessed she'd wait for the auction, then.

When Jane returned to her desk, Sam was gone. He appeared a few minutes later. "Had to take some letters to the mail room," he told her. She nodded, idly wondering why he'd volunteered this information.

A moment later Winky was back, and this time the mew she let out was one Jane recognized clearly as a cry of hunger. Jane peered over the edge of her desk at the food bowl. It was empty. Jane had filled it with all the food she'd brought. Then she remembered some kitty treats she always carried with her. Her bag was still on top of her desk, and she opened it and gave Winky three of the treats. Then she opened her bottom drawer to put away her bag.

She blinked. Stephanie's bag and the copy of *Romantic Times* were gone. In their place was a sheet of lined white paper, folded in half. She opened it. A message was scrawled slantingly across it in ballpoint:

Lana—I need your help. I have to talk to you. I'll come up to the office after everyone has left tonight.
                        Stephanie

Chapter Twenty-three

A violent chill shook Jane. Something had happened to Stephanie—there could be no doubt about that now—and this note had obviously been written by whoever had done whatever had been done to her . . . by someone in this office, someone who thought Jane's name really was Lana. But if the person who had written the note was the same person who had taken the *Romantic Times*, wouldn't he or she have seen Jane's photo and therefore known Jane's real name? Maybe the thief hadn't looked at the magazine yet when he wrote the note. Then again, even if he had, he would have had no way of knowing that Stephanie knew Jane's real name. It was all quite bizarre.

"Love note?"

Jane jumped, frantically folding up the note.

Sam sat gazing at her, grinning. When he saw her face, his grin vanished. "You look *awful.* Are you okay?"

"Feeling queasy," she said, rising. "Maybe what I had for lunch. Excuse me."

Taking up her bag, she returned to the ladies' room

and called Stanley Greenberg on her cell phone. In a low voice she told him what had happened—Stephanie's bag stuffed behind the mailing table, the bag and the magazine disappearing, the strange note.

"Of course you're not going to meet whoever wrote that," Greenberg said. "That's the kind of thing stupid heroines do in the Gothic romances you sell." He laughed, much amused by his own remark.

"Funny. I haven't sold a Gothic in decades. Stanley, I have to do this. Whoever wrote that note has done something to Stephanie. The only way to find out who it is and what he's done is to play along. You know that."

"Jane, you're crazy to play with fire like this. I know you too well to think I can talk you out of doing something you've set your mind on, but you've got to let me be present as well, for your protection."

"No way," she scoffed. "That would ruin the whole thing. I will, however, let you stand by."

" 'Stand by'?"

"Yes, hide nearby in case I need you. That should satisfy you."

He laughed ruefully. "And keep you alive. All right. How should we do this?"

"Meet me in the parking lot behind this building at five o'clock. It will be pretty dark by then, but you should still keep out of sight. At the end of the parking lot—the end closer to Grange Road—there's a little clump of woods. Wait for me in there."

"Yes, ma'am."

"Stanley," she said in a fierce whisper, "this isn't funny! I think something awful has happened."

"All right, all right," he said placatingly. "Sorry. I'll be in the tree clump at five."

"Good. Thank you. And don't come in your patrol car."

"You must think I'm pretty stupid. Besides, the police station is across the street. I'll walk over."

"Just making sure."

She switched off her phone and returned to her desk.

"Feeling better?" Sam asked, eyeing her suspiciously.

"Much, thanks."

Distracted by her thoughts, a sickening tingle of fear in her stomach, Jane returned her attention to her work, trying to maintain a semblance of normalcy. At one point Faith's door opened a crack, Faith peered out, and the door shut again.

Jane's phone rang. She jumped, then glanced over at Sam and was glad to see he hadn't been looking. It was Daniel again. "Jane, Patsy called again about a floor. She's changed her mind. She'll go higher, but she wants to talk to you."

"I can't talk to her," Jane mumbled into the phone. "Call her back and tell her to stop dicking around. I want her best floor offer, and she has to relay it through you. I'll let you know if we'll accept it or not—after I run it past Nat Barre."

"All right," Daniel said slowly. "Is something wrong? You sound funny."

"No, I'm fine. This is a strange place, that's all." Why should she worry him, too?

"Okay. I'll get back to you."

She hung up and shot a glance at Sam. He was staring at her, holding his right elbow in his left hand, chewing pensively on the end of his thumb. "My, my, you *are* a fast learner."

"What do you mean?"

"Who were you talking to?"

"None of your business."

He leaned closer to her. "But that's just it. This *is* my business. My mother's business. Same thing . . . all in the family. So what's up? Something about a 'floor offer'? Sounds like a book auction to me."

"It's still none of your business, but if you must know, I'm advising an agent friend of mine. Jane Stuart, the agent here in town I used to work for. It's from her that I know as much as I do about publishing. We're quite close."

"I see . . . Mumsy says she doesn't know this Stuart woman. Apparently, she was at the little party Puffy gave for Mumsy and Gavin, but we didn't meet her—or at least I don't recall meeting her. Was she there?"

"I don't know," Jane said matter-of-factly. "I didn't see her there. But there were so many people."

"Mumsy says she's supposed to be a bitch on wheels."

She should talk, Jane thought, and just smiled. She checked her watch: 4:40. "I'm going to take Winky home. I think she needs some rest."

"In her condition."

"Right. I'll be back, though. I'm going to stay late and get that filing done."

She found Winky, placed her in the carrier, and gathered up the rest of her things.

Sam was still watching her as she took her coat from the closet and left the office.

By the time she had dropped Winky and all her paraphernalia at home, driven back down into the village, parked in the municipal lot, and hurried along Packer to the alley beside the office building, it was only a couple of minutes to five.

Reaching the back of the building, she walked the length of the parking lot, already half emptied of cars, to the clump of trees at the far end.

"Stanley?" she whispered hoarsely into the darkness.

He stepped from the shadows. "Who else?"

"Good," she said briskly. "Come with me."

After checking first to make sure there was no one in the building's rear lobby, she led him inside. "We need a place to hide you," she mused, looking around. To the right a narrow passage led off the lobby, and in this passage was one door. Jane opened it. Inside, stairs led upward. "This will work."

"The utility stairs?"

"It doesn't matter, as long as you're out of sight."

"How can I possibly help you from down here?"

"Where's your cell phone?"

"Right here in my pocket." He took it out and looked at her strangely.

"Good. All you have to do is keep it switched on. If I need you, I'll call."

"But—" he began, but she closed the door on him.

She took the elevator upstairs and found Sam getting into his coat. "Care to join me for dinner before you burn that midnight oil?"

"Thanks, Sam." She smiled, shook her head. "Maybe another night."

"Happy filing!" he said, and left.

She busied herself at her desk. There actually was some filing to do, so she worked on that for a while, and during this time Mel, Norma, and Kate left the office, wishing her a good night. At 5:15 Faith came out of her office, ignoring Jane, and left. Gavin left shortly thereafter, wishing Jane a pleasant evening. It occurred to Jane that no one except Sam seemed to have noticed that Stephanie had never come back.

Once everyone was gone, Jane sat at her desk, tidying, her heart beginning to thud. *Now what?* she asked herself. Perhaps the note had been simply a hoax, a practical joke.

Her cell phone rang and she let out a cry of surprise, her heart pounding even harder, faster. She grabbed the phone from her bag.

"So what's up?" Greenberg asked.

"Nothing yet," she whispered. "Everybody's left."

Then she heard it. The dry squeak of a door slowly opening. A shiver of fear crept up her spine. "It seems *someone's* still here," she told Greenberg.

"But who—"

She severed the connection and put the phone back in her bag.

Then all the lights in the office went out.

Chapter Twenty-four

She sat in pitch-blackness, her gaze darting about but discerning nothing. She held her hands before her face and couldn't see them, it was that dark.

A giddy thrill of hysteria rose in her chest and she wanted to scream but didn't dare. Nor did she dare grope for her bag to call Greenberg back, because whoever had turned off the lights could be anywhere—Jane had no idea where the switches were—and if he didn't know where Jane was, she wasn't about to let him know. She sat absolutely still.

She heard a footstep, soft, careful; then another, and another. The darkness was disorienting, but the footsteps seemed to be coming closer . . . coming down the corridor toward her. Whoever it was couldn't have been more than a few yards away.

Barely able to keep from screaming, she rose slowly from her chair, felt her way around her desk, and walked slowly toward the door to the reception area. For all she knew, she was crossing inches in front of whoever was coming down the hall, but she made it safely through the open doorway and continued walking across the reception area toward the door to the outer corridor.

She heard a single footstep, another. They were turning; whoever was stalking her in this darkness knew she had moved. She reached the door of the reception room and madly turned the knob. It held fast, as if someone was pulling it from the other side. With all her strength she yanked it open, screamed "Stanley!" and ran straight into a man's hard chest.

She shrieked.

"Jane, it's me, Stanley!"

"Oh, Stanley," she gasped, "there's someone in there. He turned off all the lights . . . He was coming after me."

Greenberg flipped a switch just inside the door and the office's fluorescent lights burst brightly to life. The reception room was empty.

"He must be inside," she said.

"Stay behind me."

She followed him closely as he moved through the suite, checking every room.

"Nobody," he said.

"But there was."

He gave her a pitying look. "Jane, everybody left except you."

"Someone could have come through the reception room," she pointed out. "The door wasn't locked."

"Don't think so. The elevator hasn't moved, and no one used the stairs—except me."

At that moment, from somewhere outside the building, came the sound of a woman's hoarse screams.

"What on earth—" Greenberg said, heading back toward the reception room.

They hurried out and down the utility stairs.

Emerging from the building, they realized the screams were coming from the left, in the vicinity of the drive where Jane had seen Ivor. She and Greenberg ran in that direction. Turning, they saw a figure huddled in front of the Dumpster. Approaching, Jane realized it was Norma, the cleaning lady. She was crying, nearly hysterical.

"Norma—" She put her arm around the old woman, who shook in her gray cloth raincoat. Her face was twisted in horror. "Norma, what's the matter?"

The old woman stuck her hands into her teased hair. Then she pointed at the Dumpster, and Jane now saw that the door in its front, a square metal trap that allowed easier access, stood open. Greenberg gently pushed Jane aside and looked in. "Oh God . . ." he groaned. He withdrew himself from the hatch. "Jane, don't look."

"What . . . ?" she said, searching his eyes. "What is it?"

"Don't look at it, Jane. It's—it's Stephanie."

She couldn't help herself. Before he could stop her, she peered into the hole.

The smell was overpowering, a smell of rot and decay. She clamped her hand over her mouth and nose but continued to scan the contents of the Dumpster— mostly green garbage bags, one on top of another, in the ghostly glow of one of the parking lot's sparse lights.

Then she saw it. An arm, the palest white, poking from a dark mink sleeve. Stephanie lay facedown across the garbage bags, as if she'd opened the Dumpster's front door and dived in. From the center of her back protruded the large hilt of what appeared to be a kitchen knife.

Jane began to shake. "Oh my God," she said in a whisper, drawing back from the horrible sight. "Stanley . . ." She leaned toward him and he put his arms around her, but she couldn't stop shaking. "Who would do this?"

As if not hearing her, he addressed Norma. "What were you doing in there?"

Jane turned to look at the old woman.

"Doing?" she repeated, not understanding.

"Why were you in the Dumpster?" he asked, pointing.

"Looking!" she said. "Looking my loving magazine. Maybe throw away!"

Greenberg looked thoroughly baffled.

"I know what she's saying," Jane said. "In the office, I took—she lost her copy of *Romantic Times*. She thought it might have been thrown out by mistake."

He nodded, though his expression made it clear he thought this quite strange.

"I am police," he told Norma, enunciating clearly. "Po-*lice*. I need you to come with me." He turned to Jane. "I'll take her across the street. You should go home, Jane. There's nothing you can do here. Do you want a ride?"

"No," she said, as if in a daze. "My car is just over there, in the municipal lot."

"All right." He was watching her, concern on his face. He took out his cell phone and called the station, told Buzzi what he'd found and to send the appropriate people over.

Jane started along the alley toward Packer Road.

Then Norma began to scream again, and Jane jumped, spinning around. Now the elderly woman was pointing to something under the bushes not far from the Dumpster. Jane and Greenberg hurried over to look.

It was Ivor, lying on his side, his face twisted as if in pain.

"Another!" Norma screamed. "Dead! This is crazy place!"

Greenberg knelt and checked his vital signs. Then he rose, shaking his head. "He's been dead for some time. Looks like he finally drank himself to death."

Jane gazed down at the pathetic sight. The poor old man. Though she felt dizzy, as if she might faint, a thought registered: For the first time since she'd met Ivor, there wasn't a bottle in sight.

Somehow she got to her car and drove home through the dark hills like a zombie.

When she entered the bright kitchen through the door from the garage and saw Florence's bright smile, she burst into tears.

"Missus!" Florence rushed up to her and took her in her arms. "What is it, missus?"

She told Florence about Stephanie.

Florence's hands flew to her mouth. "Murdered . . ."

Then Jane told her about the coincidence of finding Ivor dead not six feet from Stephanie.

"So sad," Florence said. "Poor man. But murder! First Una, now Stephanie. Who would do this?"

Jane shook her head. What had Stephanie found out, and about whom? Who had chased Jane through the office? The same person who had killed Una and Stephanie? Had the same person killed both women? It was a nightmare.

"What is going on in this town?" Florence wondered aloud, as if reading Jane's thoughts.

"Mom," came Nick's voice from the family room. Quickly Jane wiped her eyes. She shook her head quickly, signaling they mustn't tell him what had happened to Stephanie. Florence nodded her understanding, and Jane put on a cheerful smile as she turned to greet her son.

Chapter Twenty-five

E arly the next day, Saturday, Greenberg called.
"I need all the information you can give me about
Stephanie—family, et cetera."

"I'll tell you what I know, which isn't much. She was
Kenneth's cousin."

"Okay, I'll get it all from you later."

"Have you . . . learned anything?"

"About her? She'd been dead all day, was most likely
killed yesterday morning."

When she'd run out of the office . . .

"From what we can tell, the killer surprised her,
stabbed her in the back. The knife is a large kitchen
knife, the kind you could buy anywhere. It looks as if—
well, it looks as if she was still alive when whoever stabbed
her opened the front door of the Dumpster and threw
in her body."

"Poor Stephanie," Jane said softly, and tears came to
her eyes. "A horrible end." To a sad life.

"Never knew what—or who—hit her."

Jane wondered who she would need to tell. Stephanie's sister, Caroline.

"There's other news," Greenberg said, breaking into her thoughts. "About Ivor."

"Ivor?"

"Mm. Turns out he didn't die naturally. I mean he didn't die from drinking too much, or from exposure to the elements."

"No?"

"He was poisoned."

"Poisoned!"

"Mm. Easy to do, really. Just give the old man a bottle of booze with the stuff added."

"What stuff?"

"Insecticide, it looks like."

"Insecticide!"

"Yet we haven't found any bottle near him—"

"Of course you haven't," she said impatiently. "Whoever poisoned him gave him the bottle, let him drink from it, came back later, and took the bottle away."

"If you'd let me finish, I'd have told you we've come to the same conclusion. Of course, we'll know more after the autopsy. We'll know exactly what liquor he'd been drinking. Then we can canvas liquor stores in the area, though the chances of coming up with anything that way are slim. The bottle could have been one the killer had had around a while."

Jane shook her head, baffled. "Why would anyone have done that to him?"

"Why would someone light a vagrant on fire in a park? Why does anyone do something cruel and unthinkable to another human being?"

"Stanley, Ivor's murder couldn't have anything to do with Stephanie's, could it?"

"Doubtful, but we don't know. For now, I want you to pretend none of this has happened. Just behave normally. We're keeping a lid on these murders for the time being."

Jane had no sooner hung up than the phone rang again. It was Kate, calling from home in Mountain Lakes. Jane was shocked at first, wondering how on earth she'd gotten Jane's number. Then she remembered she'd put it down on her job application.

"I really hate to bother you on a Saturday, Lana, but I'm kind of in a bind."

"What is it?"

"I need you to bring Winky back to the office today if at all possible."

"Didn't the photos come out well?"

Kate laughed. "Quite the opposite. When I showed the proofs to my mother, she loved them so much she decided to use additional shots of Winky for a special direct-mail piece we're doing for *Mew's Who's Who*. But we have virtually no time. The book itself is already overdue to go into production. So everybody's coming in today—Mother, Gavin, Sam and I, Stephanie . . . if she's coming back." She sounded uncomfortable, as if she hoped Stephanie didn't come back.

This was the last thing Jane needed. Now that Stephanie was gone, there was no longer any reason for her to be at Carson & Hart, to continue this charade. But she had become part of the little company in a small way, and now she was being asked a favor by someone who cared about her work.

"All right, Kate, but it will have to be soon, and we can't stay long. I'm going on vacation and my flight is late this afternoon." Jane realized at this moment that in all the commotion, she'd forgotten to "quit." She'd do that today.

"I understand. The sooner the better, and it won't take long. I'm driving over there now."

"Okay, I'll see you at the office in about half an hour."

"Great. Thanks, Lana, I really appreciate it."

Before leaving, Jane called Greenberg to let him know she'd be going into the office today. She got his machine and left a message.

Arriving at Carson & Hart on a Saturday and pretending that two murders had not just occurred had a surreal quality. So did the fact that no one seemed to have noticed Stephanie was still missing—or if they had noticed, they didn't care.

Sam greeted Jane, then Winky in her carrier, with a sullen wave. "Welcome to the Saturday salt mines."

"Come on," she chided him. "A little overtime won't kill you."

"Easy for you to say. *I* have a life."

"Oh, bite me," Jane said, and out of the corner of her eye she saw him whip around in surprise. "By the way," she went on innocently, "do you know if Stephanie is coming in today?"

"Beats me. I don't know if she's *ever* coming back. I bet Gavin and Mumsy do, though."

"Mm," Jane murmured thoughtfully.

At that moment Faith emerged from her office, all smiles. "Lana, darling, your Dinky is a total star!"

"Winky."

"So photogenic. Thank you so much for coming

back in like this." Faith bent down in front of the carrier. "And thank you, too, Dinky."

Jane just sighed. "Have you heard from Stephanie?" she asked Faith, watching her closely.

Faith's grin faded and she shook her head. "I'll let you know when Kate and I are ready for the shoot."

Jane watched her walk away, then let Winky out of the carrier. She seemed happy to be back, and trotted happily down the corridor. Jane noticed a slight swing to Winky's belly that hadn't been there before, and realized that in all the commotion, she'd forgotten to tell Nick and Florence the news of the impending blessed event. She smiled, deciding she'd spring it at dinner tonight.

She glanced down the hall again, in time to see Winky approach the door to Gavin's office, which stood slightly ajar. The cat sniffed at the door, then slipped into the room.

A moment later from Gavin's office came the sound of his voice, loud with annoyance. "Shoo! Shoo! Get out of here!"

Jane hurried down the hall to retrieve Winky. When she reached Gavin's doorway, Winky was standing on Gavin's desk next to a mammoth stack of paper that Jane recognized as the page proofs of *Mew's Who's Who*. Winky brushed up against it, and Gavin, standing a few feet away, made a move to stop her from knocking the loose pages off his desk.

Jane reached out, too, trying to stop Winky, but in an instant it occurred to Jane that Winky was actually *trying* to knock over the proofs. Before either she or Gavin could reach the cat, she succeeded in pushing the top half of the proofs off the desk; as if in slow motion, the pages separated and flew everywhere. Gavin let out a string of obscenities.

"I'm so sorry," Jane said, reaching for Winky, but the cat evaded Jane and, quite deliberately, walked over to the far wall of the office and sat down in front of it. Under the cat, Jane noticed, was one of the fallen proof sheets.

Looking at Winky, Jane frowned, puzzled. Something wasn't right, didn't look right. She moved closer for a better look and saw what it was.

The sheet of paper on which Winky sat was half hidden under the wall.

Jane stared, open-mouthed.

It all came clear to her now.

As Gavin watched, she reached over to the wall and pushed on it. It moved a little and she pushed harder. A door-sized portion of the wall swung outward.

She nodded. It was a door, perfectly camouflaged in the wall. Beyond it was the second-floor corridor. Suddenly Winky ran out.

Moving quietly, Gavin walked around his desk to the camouflaged door and pulled it closed.

"So this is why you wanted this office so badly," Jane said. "Not because it's got a big window or because it's larger, but because of that door. This office belonged to a psychiatrist before you moved in. He had an elite clientele and installed this door to protect his patients' privacy. A patient would arrive through the front reception area, but when his session was over, he would leave by this back door so as not to encounter the next patient waiting in the reception room. It's a common feature among more exclusive psychiatrists and psychologists."

Gavin just stared at her, a calculating expression on his face.

"Using this door, you were able to slip in and out at will without anyone knowing you'd even left the office. That's how you were able to come back in last night after I thought you'd left the office. It's how you were able to go after Stephanie and stab her in the alley yesterday, while appearing not to have gone out."

Jane thought for a moment, putting the pieces together. "Ivor saw you, though," she said slowly. "He saw you from under the bushes, where he sometimes slept. He saw you murder Stephanie. He tried to blackmail you by leaving that note on your windshield. So the poor man had to die, too. That would have been easy— a bottle of booze laced with insecticide."

Gavin nodded. "I congratulate you—and Blinky—on your skills of detection."

"But *why* did you kill Stephanie?"

"I can tell you that. But then I'll have to kill you." He laughed easily. "I had to kill her because she'd found the Star of Ananda in Faith's office, put two and two together, and figured out I'd killed that stupid maid, Una. Stephanie told me what she knew and asked what I would give her to keep her quiet. Then she even took the Star," he said, a pained expression passing across his face, "and I still don't know what she did with it."

"You took her purse after you killed her," Jane said.

"That's right. But it wasn't there."

"Why did you put the purse behind the table in the mail room?"

He looked surprised, narrowed his gaze. "You *have* been busy. I couldn't keep it in my office, could I? What if someone had found it? I waited for Mel to leave the mail room and stuffed the purse behind the table until I could get rid of it later."

"That's what I thought," Jane said. "Why did you kill Una?"

"Una had to die because she, too, saw more than she should have. She saw Lynch, the thief Faith hired to steal the Star from Lillian Strohman. Then she saw Faith paying Lynch for the Star. Worse yet, just like pathetic Ivan, or whatever the old drunk's name was, she tried to blackmail Faith with what she'd seen. Faith told me and didn't know what to do about it. I did."

"And Lynch himself?"

He looked at her as if she were simple. "He had to die because of his knowledge of what he'd done and whom he'd done it for."

Jane frowned, shaking her head. "But how did Lillian Strohman get the Star of Ananda?"

"Years ago I sold it to a broker in New York City. Obviously, he sold it to Lillian. When Faith went to breakfast at Lillian's to discuss Lillian's doing a book for us, Lillian took Faith to her bedroom and showed her her jewelry collection, including the Star. Needless to say, the foolish old woman had no idea what it really was, that it had once *belonged* to Faith.

"Faith got the broker's name from Lillian and went to see him. Man named Wachtel. He betrayed me. He told Faith I'd sold him the Star all those years ago."

"So he had to die, too."

Gavin sighed. "Yes. When I think of all I've had to do to protect Faith . . ."

At that moment they heard a sound at the doorway and turned. Faith had come silently through the door, which had been slightly ajar. Her beautiful face was set in an expression of cold determination.

This is the end for me, Jane thought.

Gavin gave Faith an indulgent smile, then turned back to Jane. "It was all for her," he declared simply. "It was Faith—forgive me, darling—who had a weakness . . . a weakness for the Star of Ananda. When she saw it at Lillian Strohman's, she just had to have it."

Faith spoke. "Had to have it *back.*" Her eyes narrowed to slits. "It was you who took the Star from the safe in my room at the palace that night . . . you who dressed in servant's robes and let yourself be seen running away." She moved closer to him. "You, I know now," she said in a tone of wonder mixed with horror, "who paid one of the rebels in the village to murder Ravi."

Gavin stared at her in shock. Then his eyes grew pleading. "I had no choice—don't you see that? After Ravi found us together, you had no hope of getting what was rightfully yours. The only way was for Ravi to die."

"But I loved him," Faith said hollowly.

"You loved *me.*"

"No. I had *an affair* with you. I *loved* Ravi." Her eyes grew distant. "Poor, sweet, hapless Ravi. You killed him."

Another sound came from the doorway. Jane turned. Sam and Kate stood behind Faith. It was clear from the expressions on their faces, eyes wide, mouths slightly open, that they had heard everything.

"*You* killed our father," Sam spat out.

Abruptly Faith disappeared from the doorway. A moment later she reappeared. Her gaze fixed on Gavin, she slowly raised her right arm. In her hand was a revolver. Using her left hand to steady her right, she took careful aim at his head.

"Mother!" Kate gasped. "What are you doing? Where did you get that gun?"

"I've had this since the trouble started in Ananda," she answered in a monotone, unmoving. "It was your grandfather who taught me to shoot it. Looks as if that may have been the only useful thing he ever did."

"Don't you see!" Gavin screamed, his eyes wild. "I did it all for you! Because of me, you got to keep your children! From the money we got when I sold the Star, we were able to build a whole new life for ourselves. *You're* the one who ruined everything. *You're* the one who had to have the Star back. If only you'd left it alone. Don't you see, you stupid woman—everything I've done has been *for you!*"

Faith kept the gun trained on him. "I let you corrupt me," she said in a dazed monotone. "I let you turn us into a couple of common thieves, stealing from our 'authors.' But a murderer I'm not . . . and I never asked you or anyone else to kill for me."

The room was silent, no one moving or speaking. Finally Faith, still keeping the revolver aimed at Gavin, turned to Jane. "Lana, please call the police."

"Her name isn't Lana!" Gavin cried, clearly desperate now. "Her real name is Jane Stuart—she's a *literary agent,*" he said with a sneer, as if describing earth's lowest life form.

Faith, Sam, and Kate turned to her inquiringly.

"It's true," she said. "Stephanie was my late husband's cousin. She said she thought something was wrong in this company and asked me to help her figure out what it was. I realize now that she was using me to try to dig up dirt to use as blackmail material—anything to solidify her position here." She glanced at Gavin. "But through her own snooping she found all the dirt she needed, and the best prize of all—the Star."

She turned and went out to the corridor to call Greenberg. Halfway out, she stopped and turned to Faith. "You're sure you're okay?"

"I'll be fine," Faith replied, and moved the gun a little closer to Gavin, aiming it now at the middle of his face. "Just fine. Besides, this really is a family affair."

Chapter Twenty-six

An hour and a half later, Jane descended the stairs to the foyer, a suitcase in each hand. Fortunately, she'd packed them the day before.

Florence appeared from the family room. "I do hope you have a wonderful time, missus."

"Thanks," Jane said sadly. "I'm not in much of a vacationing mood."

"You will be. And remember, your not going can't bring anyone back."

"True."

"By the way, the mail has come. Would you like to see it before you go?"

"Sure, why not?" Jane set down the suitcases and followed Florence into the kitchen. On the counter was a stack of envelopes on top of a box.

"Who's that from?" Jane asked, pointing to the box.

Florence drew it out, glanced at the label, and shrugged. "No return address."

Could it be a manuscript? Were writers now going to start sending their books to her at home? She went to the counter, took a knife from the drawer, and slit open the box. She frowned. Instead of pages, the box was filled with Styrofoam peanuts. Baffled, Jane felt around inside. Her fingers touched paper wrapping; she pulled this out, laid it on the counter, and peeled back the layers.

Both women gasped.

A magically luminous creamy blue stone the size of an egg floated in a sea of diamonds.

"The Star of Ananda," Florence whispered, and put her hand to her mouth. "What is it doing here?"

Jane had told Florence everything she'd learned in Gavin's office. "This was at the heart of it all. Stephanie mailed it to herself here." She had a thought and reached for the box, glanced at its label. "This isn't addressed to me; it's addressed to Stephanie. She had to get it out of the office. What smarter way than to disguise it as one of the many manuscripts constantly being returned to writers?"

"How did Gavin know Stephanie had found it?" Florence asked.

"I've been thinking about that. I believe that in addition to the camouflaged door, Gavin's office was equipped with a one-way mirror that looked into the next office. Remember, Dr. Kruger treated children as well as adults. He would have used this one-way window to observe children playing in the therapy room— now Faith's office. Gavin, of course, used it as a means of spying on his wife. He must have hung a picture over the window to hide it when he wasn't using it. To Faith, it was a mirror left behind by the previous tenant.

"In order not to be seen on the observing side of a one-way window, the lights must be out. Through this window Gavin must have seen Stephanie searching Faith's office, must have seen her find the Star where Faith had hidden it. While he was watching her, he must have moved in such a way that light from the window behind him shone through. Stephanie, who was sharp if nothing else, noticed this light change but couldn't figure out what had happened. Faith's office, after all, had no windows. That's why Stephanie told Nick that riddle about light changing in a room without windows."

Reverently, Jane lifted the heavy necklace, walked behind Florence, and fastened it around her neck. It shone like blue and crystal fire against her smooth brown skin.

"Oh, missus," Florence said in a low voice, raising her hands to touch it but apparently afraid. Then the Star's beauty seemed to overcome her, and she felt its perfect surface as if she couldn't resist its attraction.

From a drawer Jane removed a hand mirror she sometimes used to put on makeup. She held it out to Florence, whose eyes sparkled almost as brightly as the jewels as she moved slightly from side to side.

Jane gave her a warm smile. "I don't know if this will go into a museum, or if Faith will get it back. But for a few moments," she said wistfully, "we can have a little piece of the fairy tale."

Half an hour later, on Jane's front steps, she hugged and kissed Nick and Florence good-bye, then picked up Winky and kissed her on her mottled nose. "Now don't you have those kittens before I get back," she warned the cat playfully, and gently set her down.

Stanley Greenberg pulled into the driveway, hopped

out, and put Jane's bags in the trunk. Then they both got in, waved to Florence and Nick, and headed down Lilac Way and, ultimately, to Newark Airport.

They rode in silence until they reached Route 280. Then Greenberg shook his head. "I still can't believe what happened. Poor Stephanie. And pathetic Ivor, who'd have been better off staying in New York."

"Yes. It's all very sad." Jane gazed out the window at the passing trees. "It all started, really, when a young girl from Boston thought she could really live a fairy tale." She shook her head. "It never works."

When they got to the airport, Jane insisted that Greenberg just drop her at the curb. "It's easier this way, anyway; I'll use the curbside check-in. Besides, you need to get back to work. I appreciate the ride."

"If I were coming with you," he said mischievously, "I wouldn't have to leave you at all."

She smiled, kissed him on the lips. "Oh, Stanley. Just give me a little more time."

"All right," he said understandingly. "But hey . . ."

"Hey what?"

"When you get back, I'll be waiting for you. And that's no fairy tale."

Jane's smile widened. For now, that was good enough for her. She gave him a decisive nod.

A skycap approached the car. "Morning, ma'am. And where are we flying to this morning?"

"St. John's, Antigua," she told him, gave Stanley another kiss, and got out.

The skycap took her bags from the backseat and led the way toward the terminal. "You're on your way," he said over his shoulder.

Jane looked back one last time at Greenberg and

waved fondly. He waved back, his smile sweet; then he was distracted by having to pull the car back into traffic.

"Ma'am?"

Jane turned. The skycap was waiting for her at the counter.

Quickly he checked her ticket and passport and handed them back to her. "You're there!" he said, and he, too, smiled kindly, as if somehow he knew how badly she needed this vacation. She tipped him generously and, free of her luggage, strolled lightly into the terminal.

Yes, I'm there.

She could already feel the tropical sun hot on her skin, smell coconut-scented tanning oil, hear the breeze whispering through the fronds of the palms.

She got on the escalator, thinking of fairy tales.

Please turn the page for

an exciting sneak peek at

Evan Marshall's newest

Jane Stuart and Winky mystery

ICING IVY

Coming in hardcover in November 2002!

At dinner, Jane, sitting between Daniel and William Ives, glanced around the room, wondering where Ivy was. As if reading her thoughts, Daniel whispered, "Isn't Ivy coming to dinner?"

"I don't know," Jane replied, and at that moment Ivy appeared in the doorway.

She looked like hell, as if she hadn't bathed or changed her clothes since yesterday. She made her way over to Jane, Daniel, and William and took a seat next to William. Watching Ivy sit down a little too carefully, Jane wondered if she'd been drinking.

The atmosphere was subdued—Adam, Rhoda, and Ginny serving, everyone quietly eating. Adam, crossing the room with a tray, gave Jane an imploring look. She nodded.

"Well!" she said brightly. "How are everyone's stories coming along?"

They all looked at her, wary expressions on their faces.

Finally William looked up and smiled at Jane. "I

think mine's a real humdinger! Maybe I'll get myself one of those movie deals. But I've got to executive produce!"

Everyone laughed, the atmosphere loosening up.

"I've got a hell of a story," Ivy suddenly blurted out. The room grew silent again. Everyone watched her, waiting.

"Mm-hm," she said matter-of-factly, spearing a piece of broccoli and putting it in her mouth. "It's going to put someone in jail for years."

Again the uneasy silence. Jane didn't blame Ivy for feeling bitter toward Johnny, and was happy that her friend was rid of him, but she didn't like the way this conversation was going.

"What about you, Carla?" Jane asked.

Carla looked up and scowled at Jane, who refused to be intimidated.

"How is your novel coming along?"

"Fine," Carla said brusquely, and looked away. "Pass the butter, please."

Jane gave up. The remainder of the meal was eaten in virtual silence.

The atmosphere of that evening's group session made Jane nervous, as if the atmosphere was charged.

Tamara read from her novel, about a woman dying of breast cancer. Red Pearson ripped it to shreds, calling it maudlin and melodramatic.

When he read from his novel based on the Boriken Social Club tragedy, Tamara got him back by loudly scoffing at least three times.

William Ives, in his thin, shaky voice, read a passage

from his novel about a lost woodsman. To Jane's surprise, it was extremely well written. She noticed Arliss, William's instructor, nodding approvingly at the other end of the room. Jane wondered, perhaps uncharitably, if Arliss had rewritten William's material. Brad Franklin, as if reading Jane's thoughts, called out, "Sounds like your teacher helped you with your homework!"

"What is that supposed to mean?" William asked.

Brad laughed, his shoulders rising and falling once. "It's obvious. Arliss rewrote your stuff. Or maybe she just wrote it, saved you the trouble of doing anything at all."

A hush descended on the room. Arliss was watching Brad with a shocked, hateful look in her eyes. "That remark was totally uncalled for, Brad," she said, "and I resent it immensely."

Brad laughed again. "Sorry, sorry—I was just joking!"

"You know," Ivy said, and everyone turned to her, "I think Brad is the last person who should object to someone's writing being 'ghosted,' since that's what he does for a living."

Brad's face grew serious. "I just told you, I was joking."

Ivy appeared to ignore this. "Damn cushy setup," she muttered. "Cushier than people think."

Brad gave her a surprised, murderous look.

Paul Kavanagh read more of his coming-of-age novel, a passage in which the protagonist experienced his first homosexual encounter. In the middle of it, Red yelled out that he hadn't come to this retreat to hear porno. This time Paul, who seemed to have girded himself for blows such as this, simply finished reading and took his seat.

Ellyn Bass read lovingly from her romance, dwelling on the heavy Scottish accents. Tamara rolled her eyes. To Jane's surprise, Jennifer criticized the passage, saying that dialect would make her book difficult to read. Bertha rushed to disagree, saying she thought the dialect was marvelously authentic. Listening to this exchange, Ellyn looked as if she would burst into tears at any moment. When Bertha reminded the group that her last Scottish historical, *Highland Rapture,* had been number 31 on the *New York Times* extended best-seller list and that she should know whereof she spoke, Jennifer rose a little in her chair and narrowed her eyes. Eager to avoid another battle, Jane stood up and asked Larry if he would like to read. He gave her a puzzled look and reminded her that he hadn't written anything new. She apologized, moving on to Carla. She had succeeded in preventing another scene. Taking her seat, she glanced at Ivy, who was watching Larry closely.

When the session was over, Adam came in and reminded everyone of the reception he and Rhoda were hosting in the dining room. Ivy said softly to Jane that that was one party she'd pass on. Jane had no desire to attend either, though she knew she should. She decided to take a few minutes' break in her room first.

She took the back stairs to the second floor and made her way down the corridor. Passing Arliss's room, she heard Arliss speaking harshly to someone.

"If you want to keep this working," she was saying in a tone of exasperation, "you've at least got to *read* them. Just how lazy are you? You should have just told her you're not allowed to talk about them."

What was she talking about, Jane wondered, and to whom was she speaking?

Entering her room, Jane threw herself onto the bed and stared up at the ceiling. Her thoughts wandered to Ivy and Johnny, and she grew angry as she thought about how they had used and manipulated her.

She was also certain that Ivy knew more about the gunman incident than she had let on. Ivy hadn't gone to Adam and Rhoda's reception and must be in her room. Impulsively, Jane decided to speak to her, to confront her friend about what she'd done.

She crossed the hall and knocked on Ivy's door. There was no answer. Either Ivy had already gone to bed or she was still downstairs, in which latter case Jane wouldn't want to speak with her now anyway. The things Jane wanted to say could only be said in private. Besides, Jane had decided not to attend the reception at all, and didn't want to be spotted and buttonholed.

Deciding to speak to Ivy in the morning, she went to bed.

She was awakened by a knock on her door. Morning light shone between the curtains. "Who is it?"

"Jane, it's me, Stanley."

She jumped out of bed, made sure her hair looked all right, and threw open the door. He seemed surprised when she put her arms around him and kissed him. Then she noticed a man in uniform standing behind Stanley, who cleared his throat uncomfortably. "Jane, you remember Officer Raymond."

"Yes, of course," Jane said, serious now. "How are you?"

"Fine, ma'am, thank you."

Stanley said, "The road's finally clear, obviously. Now,

can you tell me everything you saw relating to this gunman incident?"

"Yes, of course. Just let me throw on some clothes."

She closed the door and quickly brushed her teeth and dressed. Then she asked both men to come in and told them what happened.

"I'd like to speak to Ivy," Stanley said.

"Her room's just across the hall," Jane told him, and led the way. Stanley knocked on the door. No answer.

"That's odd," Jane said, a shiver of fear running through her. "Where could she be?"

"In another room?" Stanley ventured.

"No . . ." she said thoughtfully, "there's nowhere else she would have spent the night. Stanley," she said suddenly, "I want Adam to let us into her room. What if she's done something—something to herself."

Stanley's eyes widened. "All right." He turned to Officer Raymond. "Pete, would you please go get Adam?"

Raymond nodded and ran down the stairs. A few moments later he and Adam appeared.

"What's going on?" Adam asked Jane.

"I want you to open Ivy's door. She wasn't in her room last night and she doesn't answer the door now."

"All right," Adam said, and taking a ring of keys from his pocket, unlocked the door and led the way in.

The bed was neatly made, the room empty.

Stanley sighed ominously. "It's clear no one spent the night here."

"Where could she have gone?" Jane asked, though not expecting an answer.

"Jane, I want you to show me where Johnny and the man with the gun ran."

She nodded and led them along the corridor, down the stairs, and out the door. It was still quite cold, a moistness in the air, the sky overcast and foreboding. Jane showed Stanley and Raymond the footprints leading into the woods. "But they peter out pretty quickly," she told them.

Stanley was moving slowly among the trees, deeper into the woods. "No, they don't," he said thoughtfully, taking one careful step after another, and Raymond, Jane, and Adam followed him. Soon Stanley had led them onto a wide trail.

"Where does this lead?" Stanley asked Adam.

"To the pond."

"See here," Stanley said, pointing to the ground. "The prints come out of the woods and onto the trail. And here," he said, pointing along the trail in the direction of the lodge, are two more sets of prints. They all merge here."

"But what does that mean?" Jane asked.

Stanley didn't answer, but followed the merged prints, the others close behind. "Ah," he said suddenly, pointing. "Two sets of prints veer off the trail again into the woods."

"Could Johnny and the other man have come this way?" Jane wondered aloud.

"It's possible," Adam said. "Eventually they would have come to another trail. There are so many of them in these woods, and many of them lead all the way down the mountain."

The remaining two sets of footprints continued along the trail, and Stanley, Raymond, Jane, and Adam followed them to the edge of the pond, which was larger than Jane had expected, its surface completely covered with snow.

Stanley was standing at the pond's edge, his hands on his hips. He seemed to be staring at something. Jane came up beside him.

"What?" she asked.

Stanley pointed to an odd mound of snow about a foot from the shore.

"What is it?" she asked, wondering why it was so interesting to him. "A rock?"

Wordlessly, Stanley approached the shape, knelt down, and brushed away some of the snow. To Jane's surprise, a bit of bright red was revealed. She frowned, puzzled, and went closer.

Stanley, intent on what he was doing, brushed away more snow.

Suddenly Ivy's face was looking out at them, her blue eyes open, staring, her cheeks bright red.

"Oh my God," Jane gasped, and grabbed Stanley. "It's Ivy. Is she . . ."

"Dead." Stanley nodded.

Jane felt her face contorting and she began to cry. "This is horrible. Poor Ivy."

Stanley was brushing away more snow. He stood, turned, and took Jane in his arms.

"She must have come down the trail for some reason," Jane said through her tears, "and not realized she'd reached the pond and fallen. She must have hit her head on the ice."

Gently, Stanley took Jane by the shoulders and looked into her eyes. "Jane, Ivy's death was no accident. I'm sorry, I don't want to have to tell you this, but you might as well know now. She's been stabbed."

Jane drew in her breath. "Stabbed?"

He nodded. "With a small, sharp instrument. If I'm not mistaken, an ice pick."

An ice pick . . . The world began to spin. "Like Trotsky . . ." she said, and suddenly Adam was reaching out to her and Stanley had his arms around her, trying to hold her up, and everything went black.

ABOUT THE AUTHOR

Like his sleuth Jane Stuart, Evan Marshall heads his own literary agency. A former book editor and packager, he has contributed articles on writing and publishing to numerous magazines and is the author of *Eye Language* and *The Marshall Plan for Novel Writing*. He lives and works in Pine Brook, New Jersey, where he is at work on the next Jane Stuart and Winky mystery. You can e-mail Evan at evanmarshall@thenovelist.com.

Grab These
Kensington Mysteries

Your Favorite Mystery Authors
Are Now Just A Phone Call Away

___Buried Lies   1-57566-168-3 $5.50US/$7.00CAN
   by Conor Daly

___Skin Deep, Blood Red   1-57566-254-X $5.99US/$7.50CAN
   by Robert Skinner

___The Murder Game   1-57566-321-X $5.99US/$7.50CAN
   by Steve Allen

___Twister   1-57566-062-8 $4.99US/$5.99CAN
   by Barbara Block

___Dead Men Don't Dance   1-57566-318-X $5.99US/$7.99CAN
   by Margaret Chittenden

___Country Comes To Town 1-57566-244-2 $5.99US/$7.99CAN
   by Toni L. P. Kelner

___Just Desserts   0-7860-0061-7 $5.99US/$7.99CAN
   by G. A. McKevett

Call toll free **1-888-345-BOOK** to order by phone or use this
coupon to order by mail.
Name_____
Address _____
City_____ State _____ Zip _____
Please send me the books I have checked above.
I am enclosing $_____
Plus postage and handling* $_____
Sales tax (in NY and TN only) $_____
Total amount enclosed $_____
*Add $2.50 for the first book and $.50 for each additional book.
Send check or money order (no cash or CODs) to:
Kensington Publishing Corp., 850 Third Avenue, New York, NY 10022
Prices and numbers subject to change without notice.
All orders subject to availability.
Check out our website at **www.kensingtonbooks.com**